COWBOYS'S CUPID

LOVE'S MAGIC SERIES- BOOK 1

NIKI MITCHELL

Printed in the United States of America

❀ Created with Vellum

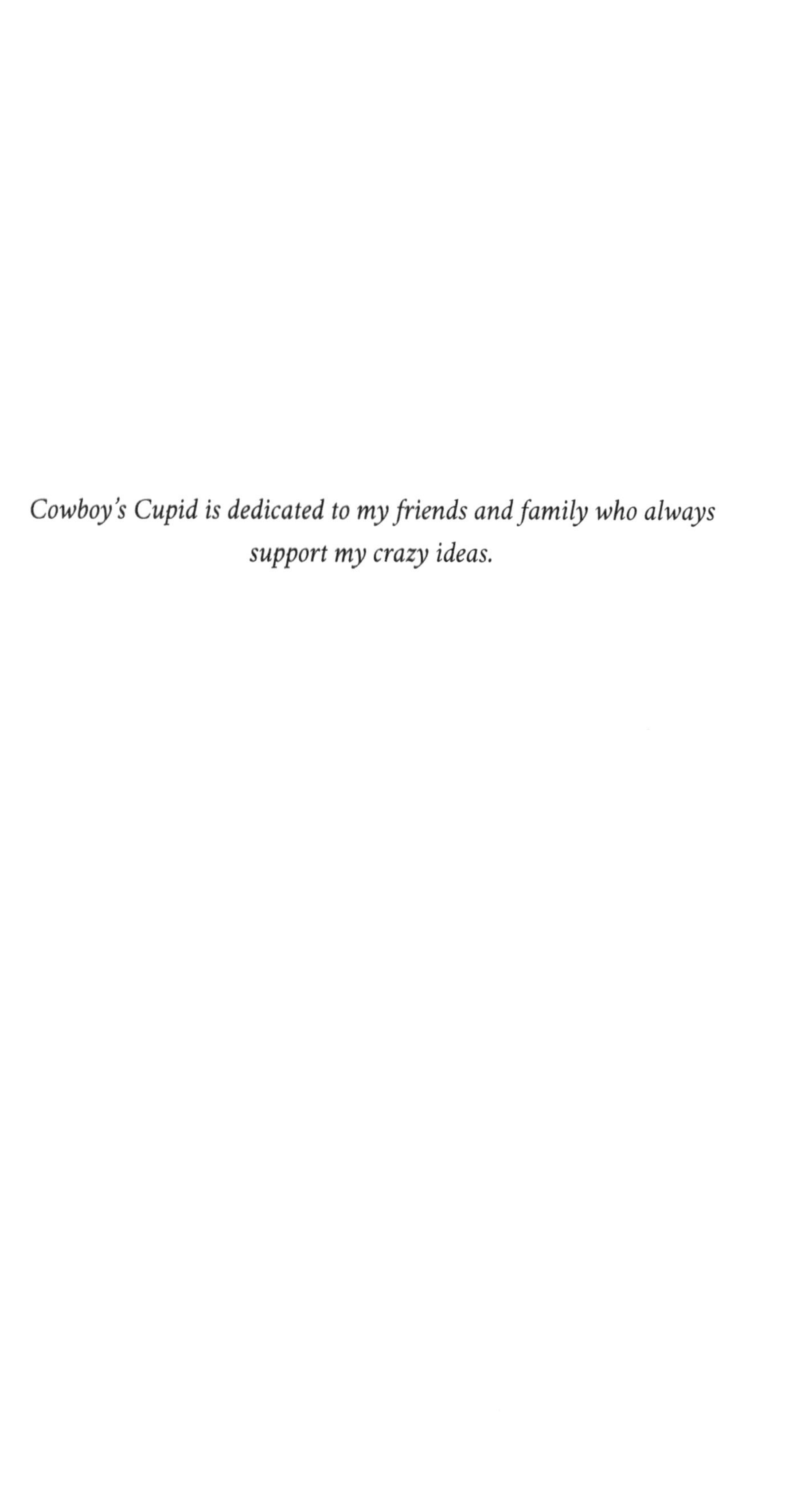

Cowboy's Cupid is dedicated to my friends and family who always support my crazy ideas.

Cowboy's Cupid

A Forbidden Love

When Cupid's arrow accidentally strikes the wrong cowboy, she's supposed to fix her mistake—not fall for the alluring mortal.

Cami Calypso receives her first assignment just in time for the Valentine season. As a newbie Cupid Archer, her life is perfect until her arrow accidentally strikes the wrong man. She has sixty days to secure a job as his housekeeper on a ranch and find the cowboy his soul mate—not keep him for herself.

Rhett Holloway needs a housekeeper and cook.

He doesn't need an adorable blonde to distract him.

He doesn't need her to fix his love life.

But here she is, and he finds her irresistible.

CHAPTER 1

The Realm of Cupid's Corner

Ever since the pint-size Cupid, Cami Calypso, held a bow, she dreamed of becoming an elite archer like her father. She used to sit on his lap while he told her about his adventures on Earth. He'd been all over the world, promoting love with a special love-potion arrow.

With her town suspended above puffy cumulous clouds, Cami longed for her own chance to slide down a sunbeam and experience Earth for herself. Today, if she wins the Golden Arrow Challenge and secures a spot at the Archery Academy, her wish might come true. Since it was the beginning of January, she'd receive her initial assignment in time for the Valentine's season. The best season of all.

She had to win.

A soft breeze from Lake Aphrodite cooled her face as she furled her wings with shimmering pink hearts. She sucked in a breath of determination. Selected as the first shooter, she had her pick of the four traditional style targets lining the field.

Each target sat on tripod stands precisely three inches from the regulation neon pink line. She knew the ring colors on the target by heart. Golden yellow in the center surrounded by rings of red, blue, and black. Two was her lucky number, so she chose the second target from the right.

As she flew to her spot on the cushy cloud-topped field and stood behind the plum colored waiting line in the center of Cupid's Stadium, she wiggled her toes inside her satin slippers, stretched her fingers, eyed the yellow center of her target, and silently psyched herself up for a victory.

The championship is mine.

Out of habit, she flipped her braid behind her and glanced sideways at the grandstands. Pink and blue pennants waved. Every family in Cupid's Corner must be out there.

She squared her shoulders and checked out the competition. The teenage girl on her left bounced on her toes. Definitely anxious.

At almost twenty-two, Cami had maturity on her side, but she also knew better than to be overconfident and let down her guard.

Her eyes strayed to her main opponent on her right. Zander Eros. They'd grown up as neighbors. Friends. Since she and Zander were toddlers making fairy dust castles, their families had nudged them together. As they grew older, they frolicked in the lush, grassy meadows where he'd make her bouquets resplendent with poppies, lupines, pansies, lavender, and pink lady slippers. Lately, Zander had been pushing for a romantic relationship. She'd balked, blaming her hesitancy on wanting to secure her career. Both of their mothers hinted about marriage and grandcherubs. Right now. Cami desired neither a husband nor babies.

She reminded herself this wasn't the time to allow her mind to wander, not if she wanted to win. Jitters threatened to undo her tightly controlled resolve.

"Cami Calypso is up first," the announcer called. "She's the daughter of Clark Calypso. I'm sure you're all aware of his three consecutive Golden Arrow wins before the age of eighteen. Let's see if Cami has inherited her father's accuracy."

The announcer might as well say she would never compare to her dad.

With her back to the audience, she took her archer's stance and nocked the arrow. Breathing in divine oxygen calmed her nervousness. *I've got this.*

Drawing her bowstring, she aimed and released. Her arrow swooshed into the bullseye.

Yes! One down.

Applause followed. Excitement buzzed as she looked toward the stands. Pink flags waved.

Cami gazed up at the majestic snowcapped mountains to the north and thanked the gods for the ideal mid-sixties temperature, not bitter cold like last month.

Her powdered-pink long-sleeved silk gown grazed her knees. The knit stockings kept her legs cozy warm.

"Go Cami! Go Cami!" someone in the audience chanted. Another Cupid in the top bleacher did a flip in the air.

"Nice shot, Cams," Zander said, wearing a metallic gold suit that reminded her of a foil wrapped candy bar. He gave her a confident I've-got-this-bagged smile and released his arrow. No surprise, seconds later Zander's arrow zipped into the golden center. He rarely missed. He wasn't her only competition, but it suddenly seemed that way.

A male Cupid, two targets over from her, hit an inch above the mark and groaned.

The other female contestant's tip struck the middle.

It was Cami's turn again. She shut out the noise and concentrated. Her second arrow sailed dead center into the bullseye.

The crowd cheered.

Zander took his shot.

She silently said, "Please miss." He didn't need this victory. Two years ago, he attended the Archery Academy. She deserved this chance.

Naturally, Zander made his mark. Cocky, he blew a kiss to the crowd.

The other female archer shifted back and forth on her feet. The skittish Cupid's arrow missed center, the second red ring, and stuck into the edge of the third. Her error took her out of the final round. The poor girl's eyes misted with tears.

After making a similar error, an error that cost Cami a win in last year's finals, she sympathized with the girl. It had been a devastating blow to Cami's ego, and her father barely spoke to her for a full month. When he did, he had never called her a disappointment, but she could see it in his eyes.

This time things would be different. She hoped anyway.

The next guy missed the center by a good two inches, and shouted, "Cursed Cyclops!"

Cami laughed on the inside. She had been taught to watch her language in public, but she could totally relate.

"Tied for first, Zander Eros and Cami Calypso," the announcer called. "Now for our favorite part of this exhibition. These young folks move on to the final round with virtual human targets." He pushed a lever, and the standing targets disappeared.

A grassy park, complete with sidewalks and trees, replaced the cloudy ground. Six animatronic humans appeared where the targets had been. The moving people shone with a translucent quality. They walked in clusters, their hearts twinkling, their heads bobbing, their steps unpredictable.

She couldn't lose to Zander again.

Okay, I can beat him like I did last fall. I just have to shut out everything around me.

"Cami you're up first," the announcer called. "Remember, all three shots must be done while you are in the air, or you're disqualified."

Breathe. Think about the hours of practice. Hundreds of perfect shots. Breathe. Tune out the audience. Breathe.

She knew the drill and shot up in the air several yards, slowing her wings to a rhythmic flutter.

A woman strolled on the sidewalk next to a man holding her hand. With most humans, their aura appeared with heightened emotions. His pale-yellow aura meant he was the target.

She stopped and faced the man.

Perfect, they had eye contact.

Holding her bow, Cami aimed and released.

A brilliant heart flickered on the front of the man's shirt.

One down, two to go.

Somebody shouted from the stadium bleachers, "Go, Cami!" Her young and carefree sister in the second row gave her a thumbs up. Unlike Cami who normally braided her hair, her sister, Affinity, preferred her blonde tresses loose and blowing in the wind.

With a renewed sense of determination, Cami spotted her next target, a couple glaring at one another. The scenario seemed almost too easy. They faced each other, the woman with her hands on her hips. Cami circled above them three times, cognizant they could change course in an instant. Just like she'd figured, the girl turned away. Her boyfriend with the yellow aura grabbed her arm and forced her to look at him. Three-sixtying around the couple, she notched the arrow, drew, aimed, and released. Swoosh. The tip embedded into the heart on the human's shirt and it flashed a red light.

The applause made her confidence soar. She might actually win the competition. In the stands, her mother waited on the edge of her seat with her fingers crossed.

She centered in on the last couple walking a virtual dog. The woman kneeled to pet the animal. Cami's shot was tricky. If the woman stood, Cami might hit the animal.

Patience had never been her strong point, but to win this contest she must show restraint. The man grabbed the leash from the woman. "Give Duke back!" the woman yelled facing her boyfriend. Cami aimed carefully, checked that everything lined up, and released. A heart glowed on the woman's shirt.

Cami had made all three shots. Spectators cheered as she gracefully floated down to the ground. She wasn't sure who yelled louder, her mother or her best friends, Belle and Serenity.

Zander stood next to her. "Way to go, Cams."

His one-syllable nickname, Cams, made her feel mundane and boring. She shook off the negative sentiment, and said, "Thanks."

It was his turn. The first two arrows hit their mark. Zander released his third arrow. Magical dust scattered from the feathers as the arrow whooshed across the field. A glittery line of gold added pizzazz.

"Show off," Cami muttered under her breath, not at all appreciative of his stunt.

His arrow hit the man's shoulder. Crazy, weird, uncharacteristic.

No sparkling heart.

He missed.

She'd won, she'd really won. Adrenaline hummed through her veins like Poseidon racing across the ocean. She'd won the coveted Aphrodite's Golden Arrow, wresting the championship from Zander.

Her mother hurried up to her, happiness filling her shimmering eyes. "Sweetie, I'm proud of you."

Her sister gave her a high-heaven hand slap. "Knew you'd win."

"Too bad your father's judging the ten-year-olds' meet and

missed your stellar performance," Mom said. "He did promise to watch the live video feed on his Cupitron watch."

Mother tended to cover for her dad, trying to keep peace in their family. The truth was her father's absence proved he still hadn't gotten over last year's loss in the finals.

Her roommate, Belle, hugged her. "You were spectacular."

"Awesome shooting." Serenity made a three-way embrace.

Attending the Academy, she'd fulfill her dreams, dreams she'd had since she first held a bow.

Zander stepped in front of her, donning a weird grin. "Good match. Can't believe you beat me."

"Me neither."

He winked, the kind of wink that felt too personal. "You're gonna love the Academy. Once you graduate, I'm sure we'll do assignments together."

Wait a minute! "Did you intentionally lose? You know I'd never accept a win that wasn't true." The idea had her fuming. She was an excellent marksman. after countless hours practicing for this event, she deserved the victory. It didn't set right with her that he may have rigged his shot. This made her wonder about his motives. Did he figure once she had two or three Earthly travels out of the way, she'd be ready for a serious relationship?

"I can't believe you're asking me that, Cams." He looked her in the eye. "I wouldn't do that for you or anyone else."

Since his eye didn't twitch. His eye tended to twitch when he lied, so she took his words at face value and felt bad. "Sorry."

"You've worked hard. Revel in your success."

"I will." She stared at Zander. He seemed to be her best

choice as far as suitors were concerned. Handsome, talented, and quite a catch. Why did she feel like something was missing?

The group fluttered toward the square administration building; its style was similar to the Parthenon in Greece. Two young assistants flew between the outer columns of the porch and trumpeted with golden horns.

The captain's wings flickered with red and white lights as he floated down to center stage. "Would all the archery contestants please come forward?"

The heart emblem on Cami's wrist sparkled in a rainbow prism. Unfurling her wings to stretch out on each side, she flew up the stairs and took her spot with Zander and the other archer.

"We've had a thrilling contest today," the captain said with an infectious grin. "Now for our winners."

Cami found herself smiling.

"The Bronze Arrow goes to Vanessa Venus."

A cute blonde fluttered, accepted her arrow, and waved to the audience. Cheers abounded.

"The Silver Arrow goes to Alexander Eros."

Zander accepted his arrow and added it to the two golden ones already in his quiver.

"Miss Calypso, please step forward."

Excited, she held the sides of her flowing silver gown, lifted her chin, and curtsied.

"On behalf of our council, I award Cami Calypso with Aphrodite's Golden Arrow. Please kneel." The captain anointed her, touching the top of her head with ambrosia from the arrow's tip.

Her heart filled with jubilation.

"I'd like to congratulate all the contestants for their excellent marksmanship." The captain shook each of the archers' hands and excused everyone, while motioning for Cami to stay.

A young student gave the captain a scroll, and he unrolled the glittery parchment.

She'd waited so long to be sent to the Academy.

"In recognition for your archery accomplishment, the council hereby invites Cami Calypso to attend the Academy of Archers."

Yes! She restrained herself, holding in the urge to shout at the top of her lungs. Instead, she waved to the crowd.

"Classes shall begin two days hence."

"Thank you, captain. I am pleased and honored to be selected."

He nodded. "Once again, let's give a round of applause for Miss Calypso."

Unbelievable. These cheers were for her.

The captain pivoted on the heels of his white leather boots and exited the ceremonial stage.

Amazing. Her first Earthly assignment would be in the Valentine's season. Breathless, she dashed down the steps.

She couldn't wait for new adventures far from this community.

~

CEDAR SPRINGS, California

. . .

THANKS TO A COUPLE of hours attempting to break a cantankerous stallion, Rhett Holloway needed a good stiff drink. His back spasmed, his shoulders throbbed, and nearly every muscle in his twenty-nine-year-old body ached.

He limped into the rundown Last Call Saloon. A scratchy song drifted from the jukebox as old as the building. "Can't Help Falling in Love" crooned, sung by Elvis. A love song. Ugh! How could someone pay to hear this miserable drivel?

Three or four yards across the room, he spotted his friend's blond hair at the bar and walked toward Ace. Something pink lay on the scuffed floor, and he picked up a woman's Stetson. Pink. His ex wore a pink hat similar to this one that painful Valentine's night two years ago.

He threw the lame hat on top of the long mahogany bar and slid into the barstool next to his high school buddy.

"Trying to change your image?" Ace taunted as he motioned to the hat.

"Actually, I brought it for you."

The Stetson's heart-shaped centerpiece sparkled with rhinestones. Hearts reminded him that his family's Valentine's Day party would be in two weeks. To avoid dealing with well-intended meddling, he'd hang out with the cute brunette working at his neighbor's ranch.

The bearded bartender wiped down the counter. "Want a draft?"

"You bet. Make it lager." From a side room, pool balls clacked. Somebody groaned, another person broke out in laughter.

Handed a mug, Rhett took a swig of the dark brew. He overheard a lady's distressed voice at a table behind him. "You can't work on Valentine's Day."

"I have no choice," a man answered.

Rhett considered Valentine's Day another way for florists and jewelry stores to make a buck.

"Rough day?" Ace said. "You get that horse broke yet?"

"Not sure who's breaking who." Rhett laughed. "Think it might be time to change professions. Must be nice to stay home and get paid to play video games."

"Hey, I'm a programmer." His stocky friend punched Rhett's sore shoulder.

Rhett winced and held back a moan. Asshole stallion.

"You okay?"

"I'll live."

Ace motioned the bartender for another beer. "Want one? I'm buying."

"Sure." Rhett removed his hat, set it next to the ridiculous pink one, and asked the bartender, "Any idea who might've lost this?"

"My guess it's one of the out-of-towners playing pool."

"I noticed those chicks when I walked in. They're hot." Ace put on his white Stetson. "You up for a game of pool?"

Rhett shifted so he could watch a leggy redhead. She leaned over the pool table, her long hair fell forward as she positioned the shot. She must've sensed his eyes on her because she glanced over her shoulder and smiled in his direction. He raised his glass. The motion made his shoulder twinge.

"You comin'?"

"Not this time." Rhett took another drink.

Ace shrugged. "Mind if I try 'n' find the owner?" He snatched the pink hat and twirled it on his finger.

"Go right ahead." He watched his friend chat with the ladies. Usually, Rhett would have joined him, flirted with the women, and let the night develop, but his aching muscles kept him rooted to his seat.

The redhead donned the pink hat, reminding him of that fateful Valentine's Day, and ruined any attraction he had for her.

CHAPTER 2

The Academy's chariot skidded to a stop in front of Cami's apartment where she waited on the sidewalk with family and friends. Ecstatic to be fulfilling her dream, she tapped her fingers against the side of her leg.

"Wish I'd seen you win in person." Her father gave her a friendly I'm-proud-of-you smile, the smile he usually reserved for public officials. "Show the professors what *we* already know, you're a top-notch archer."

"Oh, Dad." Her eyes teared at his approval.

"I love you, sweetie." Her mother dabbed a lacy handkerchief to her dripping eyes and dragged Cami into a tight embrace. Would she ever quit thinking of Cami as a child?

"Wow, a true Pegasus." Her younger sister, Affinity, stroked the wing of one of the horses. The driver tipped his white beret.

"Cams." Zander leaned down, gave her a quick peck on the

lips, and grinned. His eyes glimmered as he gazed at her with more than admiration.

Why didn't she feel the least little spark for him? He had electric blue eyes that should make her swoon. Chivalrous, he picked up her two bags—one with her bow and arrows, the other with her wardrobe, and handed the luggage to the driver. Zander took her hand and assisted her inside the chariot, and said, "See you soon."

"You ready, miss?" the driver asked.

"More than ever." She held onto the chariot's front bar anxious for her adventure to begin.

The man flicked the reins, and the horses soared. Her family and friends became tiny dots below. Her own apartment shrank.

"Hold on tight, miss. I'm picking up our speed."

Faster than she had ever gone, they flew over Aphrodite's Castle. The frosted heart-shaped windows glistened. She counted ten pink spires on top. Her village became minuscule and disappeared.

"The Academy," he commanded the horses.

The animals neighed and flew through thick cumulous and stratocumulus layers. The white fog made it hard to see her own hands.

Above their destination, he called to the winged steeds, "Descend."

A medieval style guard tower wedged between the castle's three-story buildings. Trails mazed around the residence. Shrubs and trees created a picturesque scene. The horses landed in the clearing in front of the main building.

A woman in a stark white uniform approached with confident strides. "Welcome, Miss Calypso."

"It's a pleasure to be at such a fine institution." Soon, she hoped to have her name on the wall next to the prestigious archers who'd attended here.

"I'll show you to your room."

"Thank you." Cami followed the woman to Cottage Three.

"You'll be rooming with Aurora. She arrived an hour ago and is already on the range."

Cami knew Aurora, the mayor's daughter, a year younger than she. Aurora had already spread her things onto the bed on the right side of the room. Cami dropped her luggage on the left side near the wall. "Am I the last one to report in?"

"You are."

She opened her archery bag, looped her bow and quiver over her shoulder, and headed for the door.

"Take the north trail. It'll lead you to the archery course."

"Okay." Breathless excitement filled Cami as she flew. In minutes, she'd be with the other award-winning Cupids. Above the cobblestone pathway, she flittered forward around the curve until she heard voices. She spotted two dozen traditional circular targets nestled between the thickets. At least twenty archers took shots. She landed on the soft ground several yards behind the archers and furled her wings.

The male instructor drifted to the ground and greeted her. "I'm Sarge. Saw your performance the other day at Aphrodite's Contest. Quite impressive."

"Thank you."

Sarge played a five-note melody on his piccolo. "I need everyone to stop shooting and find a seat under the gazebo."

Archers fluttered to a structure at the back of the field and took their seats in one of the three rows. Cami sat in the front on the far right.

The gray-haired instructor took the podium and addressed the group. "I'm Sargent Quicksilver. Everyone calls me Sarge. I'll be your morning instructor for the next five days. We'll concentrate mainly on marksmanship outside in this marvelous fresh air. In the afternoon, my colleague, Celeste, will train you on the more technical aspects inside the main building. She'll be going over your responsibilities as archers and teaching you how to read relationship cases. With both sessions you will be given ample opportunities to refine your skills."

Cami couldn't wait to try the top-notch simulations she'd heard about.

"As you are well-aware, the intensive training is to prepare you for this year's Valentine season. Successfully pass your mastery demonstration, and you will become eligible for your first terrestrial assignment."

The mention of Earth enhanced Cami's euphoric state.

"You wouldn't be at the Academy if you hadn't already proved you have phenomenal skills. Aurora won the Grand Goddess Match. Zeke, the Heracles Contest. Lelanie, the Sagittarian Archer Award. Cami, Aphrodite's Golden Arrow."

Cami had practiced with most of these archers, except for a handful of Cupids from Lover's Landing or the Providence of Dione. While the instructor droned on with other Cupid's accomplishments, she imagined her first mission.

"Think of Celeste and I as guides to assist you in perfecting your talents." Sarge said, "Still, I can't stress to you enough: never, never, never forget our motto, patience and precision."

The class automatically repeated the line they'd heard since grammar school, "Patience and precision."

"It is imperative that you always use restraint. Make a mental plan of action. Humans are unpredictable, so be ready to change course. Never rush your shot. Every shot must be perfect and exact with no room for error. Precision occurs when all the elements line up."

Precision Cami could do. Patience, well, not really her forte, but she had matured.

"That's all I have for now. You have forty-five minutes to practice before lunch."

The archers spread out. Cami took the target to the left of Zeke, a friend from school.

"Congrats on the victory." Zeke high-heavened her.

"Thanks." She nocked her arrow, aimed, released and hit the bullseye.

Life was good. Birds chirped. A slight breeze cooled her cheeks. She checked the other targets. Everyone hit their mark.

TWO HOURS LATER, the training moved inside to a simulated American restaurant.

An older Cupid flitted inside and stood on a pedestal. She said, "Welcome to the Academy. Please find a seat at one of the tables."

The Cupids shuffled in. Cami sat next to Zeke. To her left, six empty booths had pink and red leather benches.

"We've got a lot to cover over the next few days, so we'd better get busy. We'll begin with your basic knowledge of the location of the human heart." Celeste flicked her fingertips and formed glittery, shimmering dust. A transparent image of a 3-D human floated in the center of the room. She used her arrow as a pointer. "The heart is located just behind and slightly left of the breastbone. We all know it can be tricky to hit. Since this is your first human assignment, you will be eager. That eagerness is one of the reasons we start you with the less potent love boost assignment. Once you prove yourself, you will move on to the powerful love potion arrow."

Cami understood their rationale; still she couldn't wait to assist a couple to fall in love. The power of the love potion would be strong.

"Mentally tell yourself, patience and precision." Celeste said, her mouth pressed in a serious line. "Aim carefully. Practice control. Never rush your shot, and you'll be fine."

Cami squirmed recalling a recent meet she'd lost by being impatient.

"On to practical applications." Celeste snapped her fingers.

Cami's wrist emblem darkened from pink to fuchsia as did the other females. Every male's emblem displayed ruby red. "Each of you are now gifted with full Cupid powers."

The class cheered.

"Set your heart emblems to individual sound and pull up the demo file."

Cami used her mental thoughts to call up the information. A virtual page floated in front of her.

"Focus on the turquoise heart entitled restaurant. I'll give you a few minutes to digest the information. Remember every detail, no matter how minor."

A holographic professor appeared on the page. His voice played in her ear. "A human's love-light is an unreliable marker because it can be masked. Thus, you need to look at auras. Unlike Cupids whose auras are non-existent, the human's aura often intensifies with heightened emotions." He pointed to a chart. "Let's take a quick refresher on how to interpret the colors." Cami knew these auras like the back of her arrow.

The professor talked about a couple who lost their young child. Both grieving, the man tried to reach out to the woman. She pushed him away. Recently, she had moved in with her sister. This was their first meeting a month later.

Celeste snapped her fingers and their virtual pages disappeared. She waved her arrow. Glittery particles swirled and formed into four transparent humans in the middle booth. A couple materialized at the farthest booth on the left. "We'll begin with something simple." She flicked her dust in a straight line. "See if you can find the distressed human."

Cami scanned the room. Not the man with the orange-red aura full of confidence or the lavender color of the daydreaming woman.

Celeste pointed to Cami. "Do you know?"

"The man on the far right with a burnt yellow aura mixed with dark green."

"That's correct."

"Finding a distressed person is easy, but how can I be certain I'm choosing the correct lover?" Aurora asked.

"Watch the eyes. A human's eyes express emotions. By the end of this training, you should have this down." Even though Celeste was such a tiny thing, she had a loud voice.

"To recap, we've determined the woman seated next to the distressed man is our target." Celeste clutched her bow in her right hand. "But I always remember to practice control. I check for the best angle. Make sure I have a clear shot of the heart. For our purposes today, I made this one easy." She nocked her arrow and released. Success showed with the glowing woman's heart. Everyone applauded.

"You're all excellent archers but need to refine your skills. Each of you will have five assignments today in various rooms. Call up your Day One file and open Case A. You'll find a room number in the upper right corner."

"When you're ready, go to your denoted room," Celeste said. "This is practice. Learn from your mistakes. I'll be available to answer questions and assist you if necessary."

Cami was assigned to Room Sixteen.

Don't rush. Remain composed and collected.

She read over her case four times. It seemed fairly straightforward. A couple had been arguing because the man worked long hours. Their last fight had the man ready to end their marriage. He needed a renewal of love.

She headed for the room and found the couple in the kitchen. With only two people, there was no question who needed assistance. Leaning against the counter drinking coffee, the man faced his wife. Flitting above them, Cami told herself *patience and precision,* and flew around the couple to analyze her best strategy for delivery. Concentrating, she held her bow, nocked her arrow, and checked her angle. She waited another few seconds to evaluate the situation. Everything worked, so she released the arrow.

A heart glowed in the center of the man's shirt.

Patience and precision paid off.

How could I have thought Zander threw the last archery match? I belong at the academy.

THE NEXT FOUR weeks went by in a blur. Before heading back home, Cami earned the coveted Precision Arrow. Only five of these prestigious arrows had been given out to the hundreds of elite marksmen in the last decade. This arrow had special properties, said to reach into the heart of even the most stubborn recipient. Her possession of the Precision Arrow came with big responsibilities because it had the power to change the heart of even the most resistant man. Cami had never been happier.

SATURDAY AFTERNOON, Cami rocked back and forth on her heels at the bottom of the headquarters stairs. Excited, euphoric, and a bit shocked, she still couldn't believe her last week.

"The ceremony should begin any minute," her mother said from beside her. "Relax and stand straight."

Her dad wore a huge grin. She'd finally gained his respect. "It's such an amazing feeling to be up on that stage."

Someone behind her put strong hands on her shoulders. Surprised, she twisted out of the hold.

"Hey," Zander said. Tall and muscular for a Cupid, he just wasn't her fantasy. Maybe that's why she tried to keep their relationship casual.

"Bet you're psyched." Zander inched closer to her.

"I am." She kept her tone cool and backed up a couple of steps.

French horns broadcasted the council members' arrival. Five older Cupids landed on stage and stood in a line.

The captain approached the podium. "I'm pleased to announce our newest Academy inductees. Council members, join me in presenting diplomas to nineteen of the finest archers in Cupid County."

The sky looked bluer. The air seemed fresher. The chatter surrounding her—gleeful.

"Please come to the stage when I call your name. Aurora Arrow." The Mayor's daughter fluttered up the stairs, accepted her diploma, shook the hand of each council member and moved onto the top riser.

"Bryan Baxter." He followed Aurora.

"Cami Calypso."

She hurried toward the captain. It seemed surreal to be on the stage again so soon.

He handed her a diploma. "Folks, can you believe Miss Calypso is the first academy student to hit every single simulated target?"

Cami smiled. For once, she'd done better than her father.

Thunderous applause followed.

She shook hands with each member. The last council member, Zander's uncle, Andre Eros, said, "Outstanding results."

"Thank you." She flitted up the riser to take her place on the top and tuned out the names of other archers collecting their certificates. Her thoughts were on Earth. Would it be as wonderful as everyone said? The graduates filled in the top row and flowed into the bottom riser.

"Let's give a round of applause to our graduates," the captain called. "We're counting on successful missions. We all know how love fills our galaxy with vitality and happiness."

He turned to the group. "You shall receive word of your assignments within the hour. Again, congratulations to all of you."

Elation soared through Cami as she dashed down the stairs. Her hard work had finally paid off.

Zander was the first to greet her. "You did it, Cams."

A white message flashed on her wrist emblem. "I'm going to Cedar Springs, California." Tomorrow she'd land in a new world.

"I'll be working in California, too. Treasure Park. I wonder if your town's close." Zander used his magical dust to form a 3-D map. "Look at this. My assignment's a few towns over. Maybe we can meet up after you're done and fly home together."

"Maybe," Cami said, but she'd rather fly back by herself.

THE NEXT AFTERNOON, Cami stood with her family in front of the sunbeam.

Her father embraced her. "It seems like only yesterday I showed you how to hold your first bow."

"I barely remember." She lied, recalling how her father became gruffer once her archery instructions began.

"Can't wait till it's my turn." Her younger sister sighed.

"It'll be here soon."

Her mother's fast blinking showed nervousness. "Please be cautious. Whatever you do, never underestimate a human."

"I know, Mom." Cami kissed her cheek. "See you in a few days." She sprinkled dust from her fingertips to make her body transparent, opened her wings, and glided to the sunbeam's edge. Her spirit soared. Wrapping her arms around the radiant column, she slid down to Earth toward her destination, the Last Call Saloon. A few seconds later, she landed with an umph on top of a pool table.

A sweaty man wearing a leather jacket shot a ball with a long stick. The white ball hit her in the ankle and bounced to the right.

Uh-oh! She'd interfered with the game.

He walked over to where she'd landed and gazed in her direction.

Did he see her translucent form? His hand moved toward the felt table, and she flew upward avoiding contact.

"What's wrong with this table? I had that," the biker barked.

"Sure you did." The friend chuckled. None of these humans seemed aware of her presence.

She floated near the ceiling, moved toward the long counter, hovered and searched for a glowing aura.

A man in a dark cowboy hat laughed with friends at the bar. He had a wonderful laugh, full and hearty. The man, taller than his friends, captivated her. She guessed his height to be at least six feet.

His stature and coloring made him different from the fair Cupid males in her town. She dropped down to examine the human closely, lingering inches from his face. His complexion tanned by the sun had a healthy glow. Coppery brown hair touched the top of his collared shirt. His spicy, masculine cologne filled her senses.

Her heart began to quadruple its thumping.

He turned, appearing to gaze directly at her. His eyes followed her as if he detected her presence. Impossible. Her fluttering wings should distort her visual image completely. As if in a trance, she slowed. Their eyes met, his whiskey colored, intense and wide with bewilderment.

Unnerved, she flew forward and looked in front of her. *Oh no!* A wall loomed less than a foot away, and she veered right to keep from colliding. What was she supposed to be doing?

Focus on the assignment. Do not get distracted. Find the couple needing a love infusement.

She flittered over several round tables on the bar's left. A muddy-yellow aura surrounded the man seated with his back to the bar. A woman's lips pinched together, as she glared at the man across from her.

Mr. and Mrs. Smith. According to the couple's record, a year ago their marriage had been blissful. Lately, Mr. Smith withdrew. He barely spoke to his wife. The couple led separate lives. Presuming her husband no longer desired her, she'd contemplated divorcing him. This outing had been set to bring them closer. At the moment, their hearts' love-light glowed faintly, close to becoming extinguished.

"I can't do this anymore," Mrs. Smith groaned, her aura filled with gray sadness. The file said she wanted her loving husband back.

Mr. Smith looked away, oblivious to the hurt in her eyes. "Figured this would be coming." He winced. A memo said he'd failed to make a decent salary. He believed his wife deserved more, and she'd be better off without him.

Sensing Mrs. Smith was about to leave, Cami floated next to a wagon wheel chandelier and tried to find the best angle. The husband folded his arms across his chest, blocking a clear shot at his heart. Over his shoulder, she had a distinct view of the guy at the bar.

Cami floated close to the husband. Even if she moved in, she wouldn't be able to hit his heart.

"I'll never please you." Mr. Smith picked up his beer, took a sip and moved his arm.

Cami had to hurry. She lowered down to the table's level, nocked her arrow, aimed and drew the bowstring.

The wife stood. "Figured you'd say that. Always quick to blame me for your own inadequacies."

As Cami's fingers released the arrow, the husband groaned and leaned over to grab his wife's hand. The arrow passed over his shoulders and hit the bar guy.

Holy Zeus! What just happened?

The bar guy stared at Cami again. If she didn't know better, she'd swear he saw her. A spark of attraction sizzled through her veins.

Ignore him. Concentrate. Think.

What should she do now?

Her heart thwacked hard and fast as dread filled her chest.

She'd blown it, big time.

CHAPTER 3

Rhett's head pounded like a sledgehammer hit his temples. He should've stuck with beer last night at the bar. He never should've downed a single whisky shooter much less four or five.

The rooster cock-a-doodled and cock-a-doodled and cock-a-doodled.

"I oughta butcher you for tonight's supper!" he shouted to the damn bird.

Throwing the covers off, he rubbed his eyes and headed for the bathroom. He picked up a T-shirt he'd left on the floor. It passed the sniff test, so he yanked it over his head and went into the dining room.

His brother, Michael, leaned his chair back at the table, stopped scrolling on his phone and glanced up. "You look like hell."

"Aren't you full of compliments?" Rhett pushed through the swinging doors to the kitchen. Every dish in the house was piled into the double-sinks. He washed a bowl, added Corn Flakes, snatched the milk container from the fridge, and found the carton exceptionally light. He poured. Less than a tablespoon of milk dribbled onto his breakfast.

This is going to be a long day.

He snagged a cup of coffee and joined his brother. "Don't forget we're interviewing housekeepers at three."

"Hope we find somebody who cooks. I'm tired of Top Ramen and canned soup." Michael's phone chirped with a text. "Gotta run. Promised Mom I'd help with the Valentine's Party."

"Already? It's not for over a week." For as long as Rhett could remember, his parents hosted a Valentine's Day party in their barn. If Rhett had his way, Valentine's Day celebrations would be cancelled permanently. He dreaded another matchmaking scheme. Last year, his mother tried to set him up with a whiny neighbor whose hair reminded him of a scarecrow. At twenty-eight, he planned to stay single and avoid heartbreak again. Love meant spending money on useless doodads and sappy talk and losing beer night with your friends. As far as he was concerned, relationships weren't worth the hassle.

Three cups of coffee and too many aspirins later, Rhett fired up the hay truck and let it idle. A fleeting image of a female with pretty eyes like a blue sky tinted with dark thunderclouds came to mind. Had he really seen her? He recalled a pint-sized translucent woman had materialized as she slowed her fluttering wings and moved inches from his face, only to vanish a moment later. A ruler-sized flying female? He definitely needed to cut down on the booze.

He drove past the stables his great-grandfather built, across the metal bridge to the south field and turned at the fork. On the ground, patches of snow interspersed with brown grass and pine trees. Close to a hundred cattle grazed. He stopped his truck. On cue, the Herefords mooed and ran close to the fencing. He jumped out and threw about a dozen hay bales over the barbed wire.

In less than twenty minutes, he parked outside the stables and headed inside. His horse whinnied as he approached his stall. "You're a good boy." Reaching into his pocket, he held a carrot flat in his hand, and the horse chomped.

Rhett mucked out the stall, piled the road apples into a wheelbarrow and hauled the smelly stuff outside to the manure pile. Based on his shadow, it was quarter to two. Because he smelled like cow dung, he'd better take a quick shower before the applicants arrived.

HOLY ZEUS! Cami hit the wrong human. As her body propelled upward, her pulse ticked fast. She landed inside Cupid's Corner Council Chambers with a thump. Bright lights shone in her eyes. She blinked to adjust her vision and stared up at a V-shaped marble table set on top of a three-foot tall pedestal. Five members glowered at her from their white leather chairs. Their elevated position had her knees knocking underneath her flowing gown.

A virtual world map floated to the left side filled with pink connection dots. Pink for love. Except for the black dot, the flashing black dot that displayed her name in red. A thunderbolt of fear filled her veins. She was in trouble. Big trouble. Scandalously big trouble.

The chief council member, Andre Eros glared at her. She'd known Zander's uncle since she was little, but that didn't make him any less intimidating.

He pressed a red button on the table, and the screen disappeared. "Miss Calypso, why did you hit Mr. Holloway instead of Mr. Smith?"

"Um, it was an accident." The arrow Cami released connected her directly to the human she hit—making her the mortal's guardian. She sucked in a deep breath and told her stomach to quit twisting.

"An accident? More like a major blunder—one that you are responsible for correcting." Andre's stare sent heartbumps shivering up and down her arms. "What exactly happened?"

"You see, I had a clear shot of Mr. Smith and didn't expect him to lean over and grab his wife's hand. My arrow went over his shoulder and ... um ... hit the man behind him." Darn it. Her impatience may end up ruining the couple and the other man's love life.

Andre's eyes bored into hers. "Miss Calypso, at the Academy I believe you were given implicit instructions to show restraint."

"Yes, sir." She tried not to shudder.

His raised brows unnerved her. "When this arrow hit Mr. Holloway, did he make eye-contact with a female?"

"Um … I'm pretty sure he gazed at a brunette walking by." She glanced at her silver slippers and curled her toes.

"Did this man happened to look in your direction?"

"I do not believe so, sir." She shouldn't have lied, but the words seemed to spill out on their own accord. The human's whiskey-colored eyes danced with flecks of gold as he gazed right at her, but she doubted her arrow would bind their love. At least, she hoped it wouldn't.

"You hit the wrong human with a love boost. A boost intended for fixing fading relationships."

"Yes, sir." She exhaled. Her situation might not be so bad. If she'd shot a powerful love potion arrow, she might have caused him to fall for the wrong woman.

"Is it your opinion that Mr. Holloway required a relationship booster?"

"Not that I noticed. He sat with a group of friends and … um … I don't recall a fading love-light, but I didn't really see him for long." Another lie spilled out. Cami had fluttered close enough to notice his bronzed complexion and dark hair caressing the top of his collared shirt. She'd got an enticing whiff of his masculine scent. If she had mentioned that, she'd not only embarrass herself but might end up marring her family's impeccable reputation.

"Miss Calypso," Andre said, "please wait outside in the foyer while the council discusses our next move."

"Yes, sir." She hustled out of the chamber, and the cloud door sealed closed.

Not desiring to anger the council any further, she sat at a marble bench and folded her hands.

What would they do to her? No doubt, she'd be reprimanded. They might suspend her magic, restrict her to her apartment for a month, or even clip her wings. There was always the threat of banishment, but she had never heard of anyone actually being kicked out of Cupid's Corner. Don't become hysterical. Just breathe.

While she continued to wait, she imagined a bluebird perched on her shoulder and whispering in her ear, saying, "Everything will be fine." Her illusion failed to settle the knots tightening in her stomach.

"Miss Calypso, the council is ready," a young attendant said.

Stepping inside, her feet dragged as if they were made of granite.

"Approach." Andre gave her a stern nod. "First off, your academy professor, Celeste, is attending to your intended recipient, Mr. Smith."

"Thank you, sir." Whew! One problem was resolved.

"As you are aware, your own magical dust was incorporated into the arrow that hit Mr. Holloway. Your arrow links you to the human. For the rest of his life, you connect with him as his liaison of love." Andre gawked at her.

She was well-aware of this link. Still, she stared back and tried not to flinch.

Andre cracked his knuckles. "However, we believe an antidote may work to reverse your arrow's effect."

"Okay. So, what do I need to do?"

"We'll be giving you two arrows, one as a backup. Our sorceress, Yuphenia, formulated the first part of the concoction.

She's used rose oil and laurel leaves to restore harmony and balance. Your own magical dust will bind this potion."

"This will cure him?" She crossed her fingers, but Andre's sour expression implied there'd be more.

"Not without an added love potion," Andre said. "Because the male didn't have a soulmate when you hit him with your love booster, he must find his soulmate and soon. It is your job to mediate and set him up with a proper match? Your task will not be easy. The antidote stipulates when the arrow connects, the couple must kiss for it to work." The captain's expression became solemn. "If their lips do not touch, their love will not be sealed."

"I will do my best." Cami fought to keep her voice steady.

"Do better than your best." Andre cast the words at her without a hint of empathy. "If you fail, not only will that mortal lose the ability to love but his melancholy will affect our very community. Cupid's Corner flourishes on the vitality of successful relationships. The last time an error of this magnitude occurred, the divorce rate rose on Earth. Do you understand your mission's severity?"

She gulped. "I do, sir."

Andre stretched his hands above his head. "While you waited outside, we investigated Mr. Holloway. According to his online advertisement, he is in need of a housekeeper."

"The human's interviewing candidates this very afternoon." The only woman council member took off her glitzy purple spectacles and twirled them.

"I'm to be his employee?" *Holy Aphrodite.* A housekeeper's

position entailed cleaning and cooking. *Relax. With my magical dust, it won't be that hard.*

Andre gave a gruff, "Yes. We've already sent in your application to ensure your name is on the list. But you must secure the position by yourself."

She'd get the job.

"It won't be easy. For some unknown reason, all access to his past records are locked. You will have to go by instinct to find Mr. Holloway the right mate. This task must occur within a sixty-day window of time." Andre and the other council members nodded.

Cami had heard hushed conversations about a Cupid being sent to the chilly world high up in the cirrus cloud formations, but she doubted those rumors were true. The council might be strict, but they weren't heartless.

"Do you have any further questions?"

"No, sir."

The attendant walked in. "Serenity Sands has arrived."

Serenity was Cami's friend who lived in the same apartment building.

"Very well." He turned to Cami. "Serenity will prepare you for your mission and provide you with the proper mortal attire. You have one hour until you are expected at the interview on Earth."

Humiliated and remorseful, Cami refused to cry. She blamed herself. If only she could turn back time, she'd do things differently.

"Miss Calypso, please follow me?" Serenity pressed her lips

together in a stern line, as she led Cami to a room a few doors down. Dozens of garments spread on a table.

"Oh, sweet ambrosia, do I have to dress like a human?" This ordeal was becoming too much to handle.

"Sorry," Serenity said quietly. "I know what you did wasn't intentional."

"I totally botched up my assignment."

"We all make mistakes." Serenity hugged her.

"It means a lot to have you on my side."

"Always. You up for some more bad news."

"Worse than needing to rectify my error?"

"Much. By living in human form, you know that the magic in your wrist emblem won't last long."

"But I will be able to return to Cupid's Corner and replenish my magic, right?"

Serenity shook her head.

It was as if someone stuck a hand in her chest and ripped out her heart. She struggled to remain standing. "If I can't use magic, I'm doomed."

"You're strong, much stronger than you realize." Serenity placed her hand on her shoulders and led her to a chair at the side.

"You're sweet. Wrong, but sweet."

"I didn't say you couldn't use magic, just you'll have to use it sparingly. If you're conservative, the magic in your wrist emblem will last a few days, maybe a week. Once the heart turns white, all power will be depleted."

"Makes everything much better," Cami snapped.

"At least you'll get to see how mortals live." Serenity

straightened her stance. "Pretend you're acting in one of those movies we pirate up here to watch."

"Did someone give you wacky pills?" Joking didn't pick up her spirit.

"Nope. Tried to steal yours but the bottle's empty." Serenity sighed. "Back to business. Here are your arrows. Add your dust to them and this will bind the potion. Cami flicked her fingertips and fuchsia particles swirled and dissolved into the arrows.

"You might as well fill these four vials with your dust now. I was only supposed to give you three but figured you might need an extra in case of an emergency. Use half the vial to change into a Cupid before you shoot your arrow and the other half to change back."

Cami flicked her fingers, watching her shimmering dust swirl inside the vials. "Thank you." She hugged Serenity.

"That's what friends are for."

A tear slipped down Cami's cheek. Would she and Serenity ever hang out again?

"I suggest you change into your human shape while your magic is in full force before you take the sunbeam to leave this realm. Anything you're holding will adjust to your new shape. You'll need luggage." She waved her hand and formed a pink polka-dot suitcase. "The lacy white dress should do for your interview. Wanna try it on?"

"All right."

Serenity's magic swirled the dress around Cami.

It wasn't bad, but she preferred glittery gowns.

"Hmm ... you need shoes." Serenity picked up a pair of white high heels from the middle table and used her dust to changed Cami shoes.

Cami wobbled as she took a few steps. "How do you walk in these things?"

Serenity shrugged. "Practice, I suppose. We'd better get busy packing the essentials. In less than an hour you leave. Anyway, it's cold where you're going. Pick out at least six pairs of pants. Find a good pair of boots. I'll grab you some tops and underwear."

Serenity got busy folding sweaters, blouses, and T-shirts, and placing them into Cami's bag. Cami quickly positioned four pairs of dark blue jeans, and a pair each of pink, red, and white pants inside her luggage. Serenity zipped the pink polka dot suitcase and set it to the side.

"Here's your communicator—your only lifeline to the Cupid's Corner."

"What does that mean?"

"Innovation Production used the concept of a smart watch as their design. Millions of humans wear these devices, so you'll blend right in."

Blend in. Cami figured she'd fit in like an albatross did with the bird family.

Serenity strapped the band on her left wrist. "It's made of plastic, but don't let that fool you into thinking this is a toy. The communicator is sensitive. It's supposedly water resistant. Given its importance to you, I'd avoid getting it wet."

She despised the rigid and annoying device.

"The digital time shows near the top. The green button allows you to place and receive phone calls with humans."

"What about calling other Cupids like you or my family?" She tried not to panic.

"You'll pretty much be on your own. Interference from the electromagnetic waves and solar flares prevent calls between Cupid's Corner and Earth."

"I'll be alone with no support?" The idea made her body shiver.

"Not exactly. The Cupid's Council will be able to contact you by text." Serenity pointed to a red icon near the bottom with the bow and arrow and used her magic to make it flash. "I put the devise in mock mode. Tap it, and you can read the message."

Cami did. A photo of the captain came on the screen. The message in the box read, "Testing."

"Use texts to contact the captain. See that gold button. When it lights up, push it and you will be propelled directly to the council's chamber."

Cami's body quaked. After her recent visit to the council, the chambers terrified her. "What about using it to visit Cupid's Corner on my own?"

Serenity placed her hand on top of Cami's. "You're kinda ostracized. You may see an occasional Cupid on an Earthly assignment, but I doubt it."

An outcast. Her father would be livid. But she'd fix her mistake and gain back his respect. Inside, she worried. What if she failed the human? Whoever he was, he deserved his own happily ever after.

"I know this is a lot to handle, but there's a few more things to cover," Serenity sighed. "Press the white button on the right side to do a voice-controlled search. Not only can you use Earth's internet, but you can watch videos about cooking and cleaning and any job-related task. You should be able to call up a virtual professor similar to the ones we use here." Serenity talked fast. "If you get confused, open up the instructions I left in a folder with my picture."

Conjuring catastrophes. Cami's life was changing.

CHAPTER 4

"Wonder what kinda person will arrive next?" Rhett asked. He and his brother had interviewed a frumpy middle-age woman with a strong inflexible personality, a young brunette with no experience, and they had three no shows. Their chance of finding a housekeeper might not happen today.

The doorbell rang.

"Have a little faith," Michael said as he opened the door. A petite woman sauntered inside. Her high heels accentuated her shapely legs. Her knee-length lacy dress flared and swirled as she swayed closer. Not the right outfit for winter on a ranch, but sexy—very sexy.

His brother gazed at her as if she were a rodeo queen. "You must be Cathy."

"Close, it's Cami." Her voice had a sing-song quality.

Rhett stared at her face. Something about her seemed familiar. Maybe her eyes, but she glanced away. Her long blonde hair danced past her shoulders to her waist. He thought about running his fingers through her soft locks. Wrong thoughts for an interview.

"I'm Michael. This is my brother, Rhett. Please have a seat."

"Nice to meet you both." She eased into the overstuffed chair and crossed her legs.

Michael picked up his phone and scrolled. "So, Miss Calypso, your application says you were last employed in Heavenly Valley. What brings you to our ranch?"

She blinked fast. "Your want ad."

Michael gave her a slow and relaxed smile. "Well, as you know, we are in need of a housekeeper. Tell us about your last job. What were your responsibilities?"

"Um, I had to clean the house." She paused. "Do the dishes." A longer pause. "And of course cook."

Rhett watched her face. Based on her hesitations, she wasn't being honest. "Tell us your specialty dish."

She fiddled with the edging on her skirt. "Crepes filled with cream cheese and drizzled with a light caramel sauce."

"Not exactly filling. Anything else?" Michael wore a goofy-I'm-infatuated-grin.

"Vegetable stew and biscuits, light and flakey biscuits."

"Throw beef into the stew and it sounds perfect," Rhett added. "You worked for a family in Heavenly Valley for two years. Was it full-time?"

For several seconds, there was silence. "Only when they were staying at their cottage."

"Cottage?" That sounded weird.

"Well, they had … a vacation home on the lake. I worked when they were in town.

"Oh." Rhett could sense plenty of holes in her story. "What aren't you telling us?"

"I've never worked for two bachelors."

"Okay." Nervousness *might* explain her actions.

"You're a good cook, right?" Michael cut in.

"Yes." She bit her bottom lip.

"Why do you want this job?" Rhett was curious.

"Because I've always longed to live on a ranch."

Michael frowned at Rhett and turned to the woman. "You have any questions for us?"

"When you hire me, what hours will I work?"

Rhett shook his head. Assuming she'd get the job showed gumption. "If we hire you, you'll work from six to five with most Sundays and Mondays off."

"Me and my brother need to have a discussion in private." Michael smiled at her.

"Of course. Go right ahead," she said.

In the kitchen, Michael leaned against the counter. "She's the best we've interviewed so far."

"Can't argue with that but besides looking pretty, do you really think she can do the job?"

"This place is a mess. We should've hired someone months ago. Let's just give her a try," Michael pleaded.

"Okay, I'm in, but only if her references check out." Rhett hoped they did.

~

Cami leaned back on the couch, and her feet didn't touch the floor. The massive brick fireplace reminded her of the equally massive change in her life. Well, she intended to fix her problem fast. That is, after she got this job.

Her interview had been dismal. With no experience, her answers to their questions had been vague. Plus, the way Rhett kept eyeing her, she was pretty sure he could tell she wasn't being forthright.

She gazed at an enchanting three-foot landscape on the wall across from her. The lush pasture reminded her of the grassy knoll near her home. Framed photographs lined the mantel. A family shot with a mother, father, two boys, and a girl, ranging in ages from toddler to about ten. A graduation photo showed Rhett with a serious expression. Some things never change.

Michael charged into the room wearing an enormous grin. "You're hired."

If she had wings, she do a triple flip in the air. Instead, she scooted forward and planted her feet on the carpet.

"Only because we're desperate we'll let you start, but there are two stipulations. First, your references must check out. Second, you have two weeks to prove yourself." Rhett's guarded gray aura meant he didn't trust her.

"I have no doubt you'll be pleased with my work." She could fix her mistake now.

"Salary's two hundred a week. Includes room and board."

The money didn't matter. "Wait, you don't expect me to live right here in this house." She needed privacy.

Michael shook his head. "We've got a fully furnished studio apartment above the garage. That okay?"

"Yes." She sighed, relieved to have her own place.

"If you'd like, you can move in tonight and start the job in the morning." The sides of Rhett's mouth quirked up for a second.

"Perfect. I left my suitcase on the porch, just in case." She'd be living by herself. Another first.

"You brought your suitcase?" Rhett asked. "That's pretty bold."

"I like to be prepared."

"Good to know. Speaking of prepared, for breakfast scrambled eggs and bacon will be fine," Michael said.

Cook? She could poach eggs, design a platter with pomegranates and plums, and create delicious ambrosia nectar. She knew how to make biscuits and muffins using sunbeam heat, but when she messed up, she had magic to fall back on if necessary. On Earth, her magic wouldn't last more than a day or two. The council made it clear she was on her own. She'd visit Cupid's Corner only by direct summons.

Hoping for inspiration, she asked, "May I see the kitchen?"

"Wouldn't recommend it." Michael frowned.

"Can't be that bad."

"It's a mess." Rhett's eyes gleamed with what? Apprehension? Mischief? "If we show you, will you promise not to run?"

As if she had another choice. "I'm no quitter." She followed them through swinging double doors to a sink filled with cups, plates, bowls, and pots and pans. Washing them would ruin her manicured nails.

"We'll do the dishes tonight, right?" Michael eyed Rhett.

"Yes." Rhett's voice tickled her ears. Deeper than the males from her world, his tone made her body tingle.

Don't get distracted by the good-looking cowboy. Remember my goal. I have sixty days to match Rhett with his true love.

"We'll show you to your apartment," Michael said matter-of-factly.

Outside, she reached for the handle of her huge pink polka-dot suitcase.

"I'll get that." Rhett's fingers brushed hers.

Her stomach got fluttery.

"You have a car?" Michael asked.

"No, um." *I flew in.* "I took an Uber." She walked beside the men. Used to floating along cushy clouds, she found maneuvering stairs in high heels challenging. Near the top, she miscalculated a wooden step and fell backwards.

Rhett put his hand on her waist from behind to steady her. "Careful."

Hot tingles skipped up and down her spine. She needed to be *careful*. Careful to remain on course and fix her error.

Rhett inserted a key into the lock on the weathered door. Locks weren't used in her world. Sheets covered the furniture. The men removed them, filling the air with dust.

She sneezed.

"Sorry. No one's lived here for a while. Good thing you're a housekeeper, or we'd have to hire somebody else to tidy up." Michael's laid-back attitude failed to mask his avocado aura of hurt. Probably experienced a recent break up.

"We'll leave you be." Rhett handed her a rectangular card. "Call if you need anything."

I need things to go back to normal.

Once the men left, she sunk into the couch's cushion. *How will I ever survive here?*

If only she could call her friends and tell them about her situation. They'd drink ambrosia and laugh and figure things out in the process. A tear flowed down her cheek, and she swiped it away. Here on this isolated ranch she had no one. Melancholy hit her hard.

Fate set her hand.

She checked out her studio apartment. A bed nestled in the corner by a dresser. Next to the sink, on the counter sat a boxy black microwave. The bathroom door opened to the left of the kitchen. A brick fireplace filled an entire wall with a leather sofa facing it.

Hollowness filled her chest. This wasn't home.

Her feet hurt. She took off her high heels and hurled them against a wall. Now the muscles in her shoulders burned. Her back throbbed. Her whole body ached.

Conjuring chaos. Becoming a five-foot-two human must've stressed her body.

CHAPTER 5

Beep. Beep. Beep.

What in the heck was that? Cami stretched her arms on sheets that weren't silky soft and opened her eyes to a drab brown and blue comforter. Where was she? Slowly, she lifted the sheet and scrutinized her body. Her five-foot-two human-sized body.

Patience and perfection echoed in her head. She'd said the words in the Last Call Saloon and still ended up hitting the wrong human with her arrow.

She dropped her feet with fuzzy pink socks to the floor. Brrrr. Serenity mentioned that Earth got cold—not frigid.

What time was it?

The nightstand read five-eleven. An obnoxiously early time to be up, and she had less than an hour to get ready for work.

She hefted her suitcase on top of the bed and pulled out human clothing. Removing her nightgown and setting it under her pillow, she stared at her naked body. Her legs were long and slender. Her torso proportionately oversized. Her enhanced stature gave her a sense of empowerment.

Until she remembered her mistake and the urgency to fix it.

She poured the contents of her suitcase on the bed. The course material of her blue jeans lacked the smoothness of her hand-spun silken gown. The soft pink sweater went over her head, but fitting each sleeve was a chore.

In between socks and underwear, she noticed a pearly scroll on her bed. Her stomach knotted as she unrolled it.

Miss Calypso,

You have until the seventh of April to find Rhett Holloway a soulmate.

Failure is not an option.

Sincerely,

The Cupid Council

It was bad enough she was stuck here. Did the council have to remind her of her duty?

She stared at her wrist emblem. Dratted dragons. The magic had faded to rose pink meaning her powers waned. In a day or two, she'd be without any magical crutch. Since she was the new housekeeper, magic would make things easier for today. What about the following days?

She stretched on a new pair of socks and slipped her feet inside pink cowboy boots.

Her stomach gurgled. As a Cupid, she didn't need much sustenance. Breakfast consisted of exotic fruit, nuts or a poached robin's egg, and a fresh-baked muffin or biscuit.

Unlike most Cupids, at least she could bake. Every Sunday growing up, her mother taught her sisters and her to make muffins from scratch. She'd make muffins for Michael and Rhett.

Michael asked for scrambled eggs—something she'd never attempted. She pushed the side button on her communicator. "In virtual mode, show how to make scrambled eggs."

A holographic cook appeared in front of her. He stood behind a counter with a virtual burner on the left. "Crack a few eggs at the side of a bowl. Add two or three drops of milk for each egg. Whip the contents. Cook everything in a pan."

That's not hard.

Rhett mentioned bacon. "Show how to prepare bacon."

A woman in a cook's hat appeared. "I highly recommend using a cast-iron skillet. You'll also need prongs."

Hopefully, she'd find the displayed utensils in the ranch's kitchen.

The cook spoke with a British accent about turning the burner to a medium-low flame, browning evenly, flipping the strips, laying the bacon on a paper towel.

I can totally do this. "End virtual mode." The holograph disappeared.

She headed outside. At the bottom apartment step, she heard an animal bellow. Startled, she grabbed the railing and looked south. A cow grazed behind a fence several yards away. *Rattled by a silly cow.* Ridiculous.

The dirt road to the house was easier to maneuver in boots. She stopped at the top step, breathed in the cold air, and settled her angst.

"Hey." Michael stepped onto the porch. "Help yourself to coffee in the kitchen."

"I don't drink coffee."

"No coffee, why that's un-American."

She tensed until she saw his friendly grin.

"Left you a basket of eggs on the counter." He walked off.

If only the council had made Michael her assignment instead of Rhett. A knot looped in her stomach. They hadn't assigned her to Rhett. She created this problem all on her own.

She headed through the swinging kitchen doors and into a solid muscular wall. She breathed in a masculine scent and stepped back. "Sorry."

Rhett chuckled as he gazed at her. "Mornin' Cami."

"Hello." She sidled around him. "Breakfast should be ready in about an hour."

"In that case, I'll feed the horses." The front door banged, and her tightly coiled nerves untwisted.

The men had washed the dishes and wiped down the marble-like counter and stovetop. The kitchen wasn't spotless but clean.

Now to find the muffin ingredients. She opened the pantry door. What a disaster! Cans, boxes, and containers filled the shelves with no apparent order. On the bottom shelf behind a box of cereal, she found sugar, vanilla extract, a bag of flour. No ascending crystals to make the batter rise. She pressed the button on her watch, and said, "Substitution for ascending crystals."

"Baking powder," a voice answered.

She stood on a step stool and got the red can from the top shelf, snagged a box of Elderberry tea, and placed the items on the counter.

Ceramic bowls and muffin tins were in a cabinet. Measuring cups, spoons, and a whisk in a drawer. Muffin ingredients etched in her memory years ago, but she'd baked them using a sunbeam-heated oven. "How to bake muffins?" she spoke into the communicator.

"Preheat the oven to three-hundred-seventy-five degrees," a woman's voice chimed.

Yes! The oven knob had numbers.

She creamed half-a-cup of butter and sugar with a spoon. Eggs, three times bigger than robin eggs, sat in a basket. She tried hitting one on the side of the bowl. Nothing happened. Using more force, she smacked the egg on the bowl's rim. It cracked; she dropped in the contents, picked out eggshell, and mixed the batter.

All-purpose flour would have to do since she couldn't find coconut flour. She stirred in the rest of the ingredients. Fruit would make the muffins better. In the freezer, she grabbed a bag of blueberries. As she poured the batter into the six muffin tins, her sleeve accidentally dipped in the bowl. *Oh well.* She set her communicator timer for twenty minutes.

Separating strips of bacon and placing them in a big black pan, she turned the burner to medium, and flames appeared like magic. Had she wasted some of her powers? She checked her emblem. Mostly white with a narrow strip of pink. Darn.

For scrambled eggs, she cracked one, two, three, four, five, six, seven, eight eggs. With no milk in the fridge, she recalled seeing a can labeled milk in the pantry. Yes! She found evaporated milk on the top shelf. The pull-top fought her. Half of the can spilled on the countertop. The video said to add a couple drops for each egg, so the rest of the can should do. She whisked the eggs. A little got on the counter, more on her sweater. What did it matter? This was fun.

With the egg content poured into the pan, she recalled the virtual cook saying to gently turn the eggs every now and then with a spatula. Not sure how long 'now and then' was, she waited two minutes. The eggs thickened. The cook had suggested sprinkling in cheddar cheese. In the refrigerator drawer, she discovered a bag already shredded, took a handful and threw it on top. The cheese melted in seconds.

As she turned the bacon strips, grease sizzled. The prong didn't grip right, and she dropped two slices on the floor. The floor looked clean, so she set them on a paper towel. The next few pieces cooperated with her prong.

She carefully arranged the bacon and eggs on plates she found above the sink.

The timer buzzed. She opened the oven to golden brown muffins and gripped the pan with her fingers. "Ouch."

What could she use? A towel on the stove would have to do, and she quickly set the tin on the stovetop.

Her fingertips throbbed. Instinct told her to use ice, so she shoved her fingers deep into the ice bin in the freezer. The pain diminished.

The front door banged shut.

Show time.

RHETT WASHED up at the outside sink and headed into his house. A sweet baking aroma fueled his hunger.

Michael fiddled with his phone from his usual spot at the dining table.

Rhett sat across from him. "A storm's supposed to pound the area tonight. Dad's helping me patch the old barn's roof. Think you could bring hay to the south pasture?"

"Gotta pass that field on my way into town. Mom's insisting I pick up more balloons and streamers at Party Heaven. You wanna switch jobs?"

"No thanks." Rhett would patch a roof in a lightning storm rather than step inside that stupid store.

Cami set plates in front of Rhett and his brother. An uneven line of egg yolk decorated the front of her sweater. A streak of flour powdered her right cheek. Uncertainty graced her wide eyes.

He tried the bacon. Crispier than he preferred, at least it wasn't burnt. Her fluffy eggs were a bit runny and bland, so he salted and peppered them.

"Be right back." She barreled into the other room, came in with a cloth-covered bowl, and put it on the table. "I'm not used to your, um, oven. Hope the muffins turned out."

Rhett grabbed one and devoured it in one bite. “Scrumptious.”

She smiled at his compliment.

“Don’t hog ’em all.” Michael took two from the bowl and polished them off in seconds. “These are really good.” He snagged another.

“We’re not formal around her, Cami. Join us for breakfast.” Rhett motioned to the end chair.

“I’ve already eaten.”

“In that case, sit and we’ll figure out today’s duties,” Michael gave her a warm smile.

“Alright.” She kept her posture ramrod straight, her eyes on guard. There was something off about her. He couldn’t quite place it, he just knew. Her last job had been with a family. Working for a couple of bachelors must make her uneasy.

“We desperately need clean clothes. Start with the shirts, socks, and boxers by the washer.” Michael said quickly.

“Mind if I borrow this?” She snatched a pad of paper from the center of the table.

“Sure. You’re gonna need this,” Rhett handed her a pen. Their fingertips touched and created an electric shock at the contact.

“Michael, you said shirts, socks, and?”

“Boxers.”

Her cheeks heated as she wrote down the name for men’s underwear. “Got it. Anything else?”

“Throw in some jeans if you have time,” Michael said.

“For lunch, corn chowder, fried potatoes and ham sandwiches will do." Rhett noticed her writing. She dotted her i's with a heart. "Unless you have something else in mind."

"I'll have to see what ingredients you have in stock. If we're done, I'll get busy." She pushed away from the table and dashed through the kitchen door.

"Skittish isn't she?" Rhett whispered. "What'd you think of her cooking?"

"Eggs could be better, but those muffins. Yum."

"Reckon I could've polished off a dozen by myself." The sweet taste made Rhett's mouth water even now. "I'm snagging another coffee before I head out. Want one?"

"That's okay. I'd better deliver that hay."

Rhett went into the kitchen and heard Cami from the laundry room. "What's wrong with this thing?"

He stepped around the corner. She slammed the lid on the washing machine and twisted the knob. "Why won't you work?" She twisted it around again.

"Push on the button in the center." He leaned in and reached for the knob.

Startled, she backed into him, and he stopped her with his hands. A spark charged through his veins.

"Thought you heard me come in."

"Do you need me for something?" She turned to face him.

"Just came in to get coffee. Need you to make another pot."

"Could you show me how?" She gave a damsel-in distress-smile. "My … um … boss used a different device."

"This one's basic. It's the same as the one in your apartment."

"Haven't used it. I drink tea." She gave a flirty smile that undoubtedly worked to get her way.

"Live out here long enough and you'll change."

"I doubt that." She blinked twice.

He'd swear he'd seen her before. "Bet you're drinking coffee by the end of the month."

"What's my prize when I win?" She stepped close to his side.

Desire sizzled. "Hmm … have to think on that." He grabbed a coffee can on the counter. "Empty." He threw it underneath the sink and snatched a can from the pantry.

She watched pensively.

"This is the last one. Better add coffee to this list." He took a marker. "When you get low on anything, write it on the board. We'll be sending you shopping later today."

"Shopping?" She shifted back on her heels and sucked in a shallow breath. "I'm not familiar with the area."

"This town's easy to maneuver." Might be fun to show her around when he had time. He pulled out the coffee basket. "Use three scoops. We like our coffee strong."

"Cowboy coffee?" She eased closer.

"You guessed it." As much as he like being near her, he had chores to do. "I'm up at the crack of dawn. If you promise to double the muffins, I'd be more than happy to make coffee in the morning. I'm not picky. Apple, banana, cinnamon will be fine."

"You've got yourself a deal."

They shook on it, and a buzz shivered up his arm.

CHAPTER 6

The human's attention strained every magical sparkle inside Cami. *Quit thinking about Rhett and find him a soulmate.*

She glanced at the clock. Two hours had passed, and it was already eight. Dishes from breakfast filled the sink. She said into her communicator, "Dish washing."

"I have found twenty dishwasher photos," a virtual voice answered.

Did this place have a dishwasher? The silver panel on the Whirlpool near the sink matched one of the pictures.

"How to use a Whirlpool dishwasher?" she asked.

"Would you like to connect with the first video?"

"Yes. Play in flash mode." A six-inch virtual man in a navy jumpsuit appeared. "Rinse off the dishes and place them inside the machine."

It seemed odd to rinse dishes when the machine did the

cleaning. She paused the video. Since the sponge in the sink smelled like rotten pomegranates, she tossed it in the trash and got a new one from underneath the sink. Rinsing plates with hot water, she opened the appliance's door and set plates on the bottom rack. Glasses and coffee cups on the top.

The bacon pan had a thick layer of grease. Not sure what to do with the mess, she poured it down the drain. Eggs had coated the bottom of the other pan. She scrubbed it and placed it on the bottom rack.

"Play." The video man said to add soap. A bottle of Dawn dish soap was on the sink. Perfect. She added liquid soap into the dispenser, flipped it shut, closed the door, listened to the video, and started the dishwasher as instructed.

Done.

Better check on the laundry.

The washer's cycle finished, and she grabbed the bundle of whites with her right hand and flipped open the dryer front. With the washed items inside, she turned the knob to *dry* and pushed a button. The machine chugged.

A grandfather clocked chimed eleven times. Lunch in an hour.

Rhett suggested corn chowder. With potatoes, carrots, and onions on the counter, she opted for potato soup. She'd never actually made it before, but how hard could it be? Her communicator said to half fill a large stainless-steel pot with water and set it on the burner. Without magic to peel the potato skin, she opted to leave it on. She washed and cut ten potatoes and ten carrots with a sharp knife. Tears filled her eyes as she chopped onions. She sliced her thumb. "Ow." Holding her hand under the faucet, the water washed away the blood, but her thumb hurt. Already, she'd burned her fingertips, now sliced her thumb.

The clock chimed once. She pressed a paper towel to her cut and scooped the onions into the pot with the other hand. While the soup cooked, she added salt and a pinch of cinnamon.

Carefully removing the paper towel and checking her cut, she thanked the gods it stopped bleeding.

Ham sandwiches better not be difficult. According to her communicator, the requirements were bread, cheese, lettuce, tomato, ham, and mayonnaise. The fridge had everything except ham. Roast beef should do. She slathered four slices of bread with mayonnaise, layered the lunchmeat, cheese, lettuce, and tomatoes and set the sandwiches aside.

Her sweater stained with egg, batter, and now mayonnaise. With fifteen minutes to spare, she had enough time to sprint to her apartment and change.

She took a step. Bubbles covered the floor. Automatically she flicked her fingertips. No sparkling flitters or swirls appeared or magical dust, while the foam multiplied.

Rhett and Michael were due back. Holy Zeus, if she got fired on her first day, she'd be doomed.

Think. What to do? Get towels.

She sprinted toward the laundry room and slid. "NOOOOOO!" Airborne she instinctively tried to flap her wings. Momentum pushed her forward. She landed on her knees with a thud and skidded across the floor into the refrigerator. "Ouch!"

"You okay, Cami?" Michael waddled his way through bubbles and kneeled next to her.

"Do I look okay?" She didn't belong on Earth, didn't know what to do, didn't like being helpless.

"Let me rephrase that, are you hurt?" He offered his hand.

She stood, struggling to stay upright in the sudsy mess. "Besides demolishing my dignity, I'll survive." If only she could hide underneath a mound of bubbles.

"Where are all these bubbles coming from?"

"I believe the dishwasher decided to spit them out." This wouldn't be an issue if her magic worked.

He switched off the machine and held up the bottle on the counter." You didn't use dish soap in it, did you?"

"Why wouldn't I?" He acted like she couldn't read.

"We keep the right stuff underneath the sink." He seized a yellow bottle labeled dishwasher detergent.

"Oh. I didn't know."

"You've never been a housekeeper before?" His mouth twisted into a smile.

"Why would you say that?" She batted her eyelashes.

"Because we're taking a bubble bath in the kitchen. Grab towels from the laundry room, and we'll sop up the suds."

They hurried, each carrying armloads of towels, and wiped the floor until all the bubbles were gone.

"That was crazy." He chuckled. "I'll put in a load of towels. Go ahead and set lunch in the dining room. Rhett was a little skeptical about hiring you. Let's not tell him about this mishap, yet."

Mishap. She hated that word. Snagging the sandwiches out

of the fridge, she went through the swinging door and placed them on the table. Back at the stove, she ladled soup into two bowls, grabbed spoons, and put them next to the plates.

Rhett walked in and sat down. "Smells delicious. What'd you make?"

"Um." Her pulse sped fast, making it hard to think. "Potato soup."

"What happened to your pants?" He eyed her jeans. Water soaked the hem and splattered along her knees.

"Spilled some um … dishwater."

"I'd like milk with this." He started to rise.

She planted her hand on his shoulder, his immense muscular shoulder. Awareness jolted through her. "You're all out."

"Water will do. Any idea what's keeping Michael?"

She shrugged. "I'll be right back." Once through the door, she let out a sigh. What was she supposed to get? Water. Snagging two bottles from the pantry, she entered the room. Michael sat across from Rhett.

"Hey." Michael nodded to his brother while ignoring her.

"Great soup," Rhett said.

"Glad it turned out okay. I don't quite have the kitchen appliances down."

Michael winked at her. So what if he knew she was an inexperienced housekeeper. Thanks to him, she made it through her bubble dilemma unscathed. "Sandwiches aren't bad either."

Rhett scraped his spoon at the bottom of his bowl. "Are there seconds?"

"Yes." She zipped into the kitchen and ladled the soup, half expecting to see bubbles.

She set a steaming bowl in front of him.

"You've done alright so far." The corners of Rhett's mouth quivered upward. Not quite a smile, but close.

"I'm trying."

"We need groceries. Think you could take Cami into town this afternoon?" Rhett asked Michael. "In her last job, the supplies were delivered."

"You don't say." Michael actually smirked. "Meet me by my silver truck at three, and I'll be more than happy to take you."

She was sure he'd be grilling her as they traveled, but she didn't care. As nice as he'd been so far, he would make a great ally.

CAMI WAITED by the truck shivering, even though she wore a puffy pink jacket. She stared at the patches of snow covering the ground. Cupid's Corner never had snow, the town never got colder than fifty.

As she waited for Michael, she thought up questions he might ask her. Why was she faking her experience? Easy. She loved horses. Preferred unicorns but would keep that to herself.

"Hey." Rhett's voice made her jump. "Michael couldn't make it, so we're taking my truck."

"Okay." But it wasn't okay. The handsome human unsettled her. Now she'd be alone in a confined space with him.

"Truck's nothing fancy but does the job." She followed him

to the blue truck on her right. The door squeaked as he opened it for her. "Allow me." He offered a calloused hand to assist her. His touch caused a zing to shimmy up her arm.

She carefully lowered herself into the seat. Chariots were easier. All you had to do was step inside and hold onto the bar.

He shut the door and got in on his side. "Buckle up." Reaching for a strap near the roof, he stretched it across his torso and clicked a metal end into a square thing. She copied his actions. Her strap went out an inch and stopped. She tugged. It wouldn't budge.

"That belt sometimes sticks. Let go of it and try yanking hard."

Following his instructions, she managed to click the metal into place.

He inserted a key like the ones she'd seen in the television shows she'd watched. The engine roared. A song about a man demanding his girlfriend bring him a beer made her giggle.

"Not a Luke Bryan fan?" The car lurched forward, and he drove.

"Who's he?"

"You really don't know?" This time he gave her a broad smile, his white teeth contrasting his tanned complexion.

The dirt road bumped and jostled the truck as they passed a red barn and took a fork to the right. "The grocery store's not far. Pretty much a straight shot. You won't get lost when I send you out."

"You expect me to drive?" She'd never even maneuvered a chariot.

"Is that a problem?"

"Yes." Better to say something now.

"Let me guess? You don't have a license."

"A license for what?"

"To drive." He blew air onto his upper lip.

"Of course. Guess I'm a little tired."

"Fresh air here can do that to folks." He stopped at the gate by the Lazy *H* Ranch sign and got out.

She stared at his backside, tingles rippled through her body. He pivoted to come back, and she pretended to check out her chipped fingernail polish.

They turned left and passed the Stone Meadow Ranch, Clearview Farm, and various homes and barns and open space.

"You're from Heavenly Valley. I've stayed at the lodge on Pioneer Street. Had a blast." He glanced over at her. "Great place. Close to the slopes. You snowboard or ski?"

"Neither." She'd seen snowboarding contests on television. It seemed dangerously thrilling. "I prefer warmer activities."

"Next month we're heading to Bear Mountain. Could use your help with the cooking. While we're snowboarding, you'd have plenty of time to take lessons."

Hopefully, she'd be back in Cupid's Corner by then.

"Weird, you grew up in Heavenly Valley and don't like snow?"

"Never said I grew up there."

"Where you from?" He focused on the road.

"A small town to the north."

"I'm curious."

Please don't ask where?

"Why'd you leave my favorite mountain town?"

"For a change of scenery." She assumed that sounded plausible.

"You chose our ranch?" His voice rose a bit higher.

"I'd like to ride one of your horses. Think I'll get a chance?" Over the years, she and Belle would gallop on unicorns in the meadows near the lake.

"Tell Michael. Bet he'll give you a riding lesson on your next day off."

"I'd like that." She focused on the shops and buildings lining the street.

"We're in downtown Cedar Springs. Ralph's is up ahead. Target's to the right." He parked and walked around to help her down. His mere touch made her insides quiver.

The sooner she finished this job, the better.

"You bring the shopping list?"

"Forgot it." She never even thought to create one. "I know we need flour, coffee, milk."

He grabbed a metal cart and pushed it toward the glass doors. The cloud-like doors for her apartment required her to wave her magical dust to part them. The doors at the store magically opened. Amazing. She followed him to a section rainbowed with fruits and vegetables.

Picking up a dark purple object, he asked, "Ever try eggplant?"

"Can't say I have?"

"Me neither. Seems to me, a vegetable that purple can't be good."

"I happen to like purple." She flipped her braid behind her.

"Along with pink."

Uh-oh. He should be noticing details about his future soulmate's clothing, not hers. Her pulse grew faster.

"You want any other lettuce besides iceberg?" He placed a head in a plastic bag and set it in the cart.

"Romaine, red leaf, and cabbage."

He added one of each into the wire basket and pushed the cart forward. "If you see anything you like, grab it."

She picked mushrooms, celery stalks, garlic.

"You're not much of a talker." He rewarded her with a brief smile and hefted a ten-pound bag of potatoes into the cart.

"I suppose not." She concentrated on reading the labels. "I can't believe they have red dragon fruit."

Rhett came up behind her. "What's that?"

"Really sweet. It's delicious in a tart."

"If your tarts are as good as your muffins, I'm in." His eyes danced.

She could get lost in his whiskey-colored eyes.

He picked up a tomato. "Do you prefer roma or vine grown?"

"Depends on what I'm making." As if she had a clue about the difference.

He stood inches from her and helped her bag several varieties. His nearness undermined her ability to reason rationally, aware only of him.

In the next section, he lifted a thirty pack of *Budweiser, King of Beer,* and stuffed it under the cart.

Heart-shaped cookies, angel food cake, and cherry cheesecake were on a table under the bakery sign. He grabbed loaves of sourdough and wheat bread from a nearby shelf.

They stepped to a glass counter filled with assorted meats. He ordered sirloin, ground beef, and ham. A man wrapped the items in white paper and handed them to Rhett. "You need anything here?"

"None for me. I don't eat meat."

"You all right cooking it?"

"I'll manage." She moved in close to an enormous glass tank. A dozen clawed creatures crawled along the bottom.

They slowly ambled through the aisles. "What do you like to eat?"

"Cheese, nuts, vegetables, fruit, eggs." In her community, they had goat's milk, robin's eggs, various nuts, and lots of fruits and vegetables.

"Eggs. That's good. Had a vegan girlfriend who drove me insane. Wouldn't eat anything even closely related to animals."

Don't set him up with a vegan.

"Is there something specific your diet requires?" he asked.

"Almonds, walnuts for protein." She found his concern sweet as he brought her to the nut bins and helped her fill baggies with different varieties.

"Let's check out." At the register, he took his phone and held it up to a device in front of the cashier. "Love this shopping app."

They loaded the bags into the backseat of his truck. He checked the time on his cell. "It's still early. Can I buy you ice cream?"

"I'd like that." She followed him to a shop kitty-corner to the truck.

They stepped up a curb, and he held the door for her.

Behind a glass counter were round containers with dozens of choices. Rocky Road. The name resembled her life lately.

The girl behind the counter recognized Rhett. "The usual, cherry vanilla on a sugar cone?" she asked.

"You bet." He turned to Cami. "What'll it be?"

"Chocolate fudge."

"A safe choice." His hand touched the middle of her back and heat shimmered across her shoulder blades.

The clerk made the cones.

"Here you go?" He handed her one.

She licked the ice cream. "This is exquisite."

They took a round table with red and white cushioned chairs. On the wall, she appreciated the old-fashioned painting of a couple sharing a milkshake with a straw.

Rhett stared at her. "Why do you seem so familiar?"

"I have no idea."

"It's your eyes. They're such a unique blue shade."

"Lots of people have turquoise eyes."

"Well, they're pretty."

His attention made her a little bit lightheaded.

CHAPTER 7

Cami snagged her puffy pink jacket from a hook on the wall, stuffed her arms into the sleeves, and stepped out the sliding glass door to her apartment balcony. Rays of sunlight slipped between the mountains as she sat on a plastic chair. The black shadows lightened into dark green pine trees and shrubs, angular and rugged compared to the lush fauna surrounding Aphrodite Lake. The sky turned blue with a splattering of white clouds, as the Earth awakened with its colorful spectrum.

The market experience piqued her curiosity about the human lifestyle. It amazed her that so many choices were available on Earth. None were created with a single speck of magic. And that chocolate ice cream had tasted heavenly. Earth was a marvelous place, but a place she'd have to leave once she'd found Rhett his soulmate.

So far, she hadn't met any eligible women to match with

him. Where did single women hang out? The saloon, not that she ever planned to go inside there again if she could help it.

As she headed for the house, her boots stepped on the ground in a rhythmic tempo. Rhett leaned against the railing along the front porch. Steam rose from the cup in his hand.

He tipped his hat. "Mornin'." A smile lifted the corner of his lips.

A fluttering rippled inside her stomach. "Hello," she said, and quickly went inside. Her thoughts jumbled. Rhett's smile shouldn't be turning her mind to mush. She opened the fridge and spotted the dragon fruit.

"If your tarts are as good as your muffins, I'm in," he'd said at the store. By golly, she wanted to impress him.

"Find tart recipes," she spoke into her communicator watch. She opted for a page with 4.5 stars. In no time, she kneaded the dough, formed it into greased muffin tins, and let them bake. As she prepared instant vanilla pudding, she folded in the fruit.

While the eggs and bacon cooked, the timer dinged. She pulled out the tins from the oven to cool on the counter. Flipping the bacon, she divided the eggs into two plates. Using a spatula to get the tarts out, she placed three on each plate, spooned the fruit filling inside, and added the cooked bacon in an empty space on the plate. She'd orchestrated the meal perfectly.

She brought their in breakfast, humming.

"Tarts. You used the devil's fruit we bought yesterday." Rhett's eyes met hers, and she could've sworn they twinkled.

"It's dragon's fruit." She giggled.

"I get points for being close, don't I?" He popped one in his mouth.

"I suppose. You are the boss."

Once the men left, she washed the dishes.

Now, for the laundry. Inside the cramped room, jeans overflowed in one of the baskets on the floor. She picked out six pairs caked with mud, threw them in the washer. Since the pants were extra dirty, she filled the powdered detergent cup to the line and added two more cups into the machine. Twisting the knob, she remembered to push in the center like Rhett had shown her.

A flawless morning so far, and it was only ten. Might as well vacuum. "How to vacuum?" she asked into her communicator.

A picture of a square machine with a long thin handle appeared on a virtual screen in front of her. Hadn't she seen something like that in the hall closet? She quickly read the instructions and closed the screen. Finding a red and silver Hoover, she wheeled it out and brought it to the living room. The instructions said to push the power button near the bottom. Nothing happened. She tried three more times. Still nothing.

"How to turn on a Hoover vacuum?" The screen popped up. She'd missed the cord that wound around the side with a prongy plug at the end. She spotted an outlet in the wall and pushed it in. The vacuumed roared louder than a gryphon's call. She moved it back and forth, but nothing seemed to happen, so she called into her communicator. How brainless—she needed to release the foot pedal and recline the handle back.

Pieces of debris were sucked into the chamber. She ran the

machine over a sock and it groaned to a stop. Not good. It smoked and smelled like burning leaves. She yanked the plug to shut the power off. It took all her strength to tug the sock out of the bottom.

By this time, sweat dripped into her eyes. "So much for vacuuming." She put the machine back in its place, went into the bathroom, washed her face, took several deep breaths, and collected herself.

Then she started on lunch.

AT PRECISELY NOON, Rhett strutted into the dining room. An odd burning scented the air. He hoped it wasn't lunch, but as hungry as he was, he could eat just about anything.

Cami brought in two plates with sandwiches and chips and set one in front of him. "You want milk with that."

"Please. Michael's gonna get lunch at my folks. Since it's just the two of us, why don't you join me? Give me a chance to know you a little better."

"Okay." She hurried into the kitchen and came back with his milk and a glass of water for herself, took the chair at the end of the table, and folded her arms.

"Aren't you eating?"

"I already did."

"At least have the chips on Michael's plate. Then I can pretend to be having lunch with you." He wondered what it'd be like to take her out, but since she was his employee, he nixed that idea. "I'd offer you his sandwich, but I know you don't eat meat."

"You remembered." Her eyes glittered as blue as the center of a peacock's feathers.

"Plus, you like plain boring chocolate ice cream."

Her smile wavered, reminding him to stick to work topics. "You make a dent in our laundry?"

"Since yesterday, four loads." Why wouldn't she look him in the eye? He took a bite of his ham sandwich. Dry, it could use more mayonnaise, but he liked that she'd toasted the bread.

"I forgot to make soup, sorry." She took a gulp of water.

"That's fine."

She crossed her leg and jiggled her foot. Her boots were bitty compared to his.

"Is something wrong?"

"I broke your vacuum." Her shoulders slumped, and she gazed at him with wide eyes. "It started smoking."

He couldn't help chuckling. "My sister borrowed our good one last week. The one in the closet isn't worth shit. Should've tossed it out years ago."

"Oh." Her eyes remained downcast.

"You think I'd fire you for breaking a machine?" He covered her hand with his and a spark arced to his fingertips. Must be static electricity.

"I guess not."

"I'm not an ogre."

"No?" she giggled. Cute.

And off limits he reminded himself. "Besides dealing with our messy home, what do you think of the ranch so far?"

"I haven't seen much of it, but I like the open feeling. Does anyone else live nearby?"

"My parents and sister have separate houses on the property, and there's the bunkhouse for our wranglers."

"Are you close with your family?" Her eyes got wide. "Sorry. I know it's not my place to ask."

"It's fine. We've all been busy preparing for a party my folks are hosting next week. I imagine you'll meet most of the town then. Mom's already planning on recruiting you to help out, so beware."

"A Valentine's Party, here, really?" Her voice sounded dreamy, opposite to his own opinion.

"Unfortunately, there's been one every year for as long as I can remember." He finished his sandwich and Michael's, too. "Take your break now, and I'll give you a tour of the stables."

"I still haven't decided what to make for dinner?"

"We'll discuss options as we walk." He wasn't ready to give up his time alone with her yet.

"Works for me." She took off her apron, put on her pink jacket, and followed him outside. He glanced sideways at her, appreciating her profile. She had a pert nose. Her bow-shaped lips appeared devoid of lipstick. Her blonde hair looked natural.

"You must love working here."

"At times. It's hard work, but ranching's always been in my blood."

"What's your favorite part of the job?"

"Working with horses? I've been told I'm better with them than people."

"That's funny."

He led her to the stables and held the door open for her. "We're holding the first few stalls empty for our expecting mares."

A palomino hung her huge triangular head over a stall gate and whinnied.

"Hello, sweetie." The horse nudged his shoulder. "Sorry, girl. I forgot to pack an apple." He turned to Cami. "When you go riding, we'll put you on Buttercup."

"She's divine." Cami gazed at the mare with adoration.

Forget his brother taking her out riding. He wanted the job.

"Have you decided what I should make for dinner?" Her hand went to her hip.

"Stew or soup should suffice." What he wanted to say was, kiss me and forget about cooking.

A WEEK LATER, Rhett brought Cami to his parent's home for dinner to discuss her duties at the Valentine's party. The fact he still couldn't figure where he'd seen her before annoyed him. She gazed out the window, her posture stiff.

"You okay?"

"I get nervous meeting new people."

"Don't be. My mom's ecstatic to have another set of hands to help." If only she could replace him at the party.

Another dumb love song played on the radio. He parked his truck behind Michael's on his parent's circular drive. The massive ranch style house had been his home growing up. He'd always liked the hunter green color. He glanced sideways at Cami. Her shoulders stiffened. "You'll do fine."

"I hope so."

They walked up the two wide steps to the front door. He didn't knock but opened the door and held it for her. Country music twanged from speakers spread throughout the house.

He took her jacket, hung it on the entry coat rack and added his own. Her pink sweater molded to her petite frame. Sexy, hot, and his employee.

Voices chattered in the living room. Michael and his brother-in-law, Jason, shot pool at the table toward the back. His sister, Heather, held her toddler son on her lap. Her four-year-old twin girls colored at the coffee table. Dad sat in his chair with Rhett's five-year-old nephew on his lap, reading a picture book.

His mom walked over. "I'm Lilly. You must be Cami." She extended her hand.

"Hello." Cami gave a guarded smile as she shook hands with his mother.

"Are my boys treating you right?"

Cami nodded.

"You're brave taking on that messy bachelor pad." His mom ushered her over to the group as if Rhett were invisible. At least the focus was off him. "Cami's helping with the party," she stated.

"We'll keep you busy," his dad said. "But not so busy you can't sneak in plenty of dances."

"Okay," Cami spoke with a soft tone.

The group walked into the dining room. The narrow room

filled with people. Cami would've been last if Rhett hadn't been behind her. He took his usual spot to the right of Mom and Michael. Cami next to his brother. The twins' chairs with booster seats were on the end.

"What brings you to the area?" Heather spoke as she added mashed potatoes to her toddler's plate.

"I thought working on a ranch would be exciting," Cami said, without taking a slice of ham from the platter and handed it to Michael.

"You don't like ham?" his niece, Zoe, asked Cami.

"Mom says we're 'sposed to try everything," the other twin, Zia, whined.

He could see Cami squirm. "I'm a vegetarian. That means I eat vegetables, fruit, nuts."

"Supposedly, it's a healthier diet." His mom chimed in.

"Don't be getting any ideas, dear," his dad groaned. "Stop serving me beef and you'll have a mutiny."

"Not if I season tofu the right way"

Rhett had an urge to sweep Cami away from this nonsense. Instead, he concentrated on his meal.

"What's your name?" his niece asked.

"Cami. And you are?"

"Zia."

Cami shook Zia's tiny hand.

"I'm Zoe. We're twins." She gave a lopsided grin. "You Michael's girlfriend?"

Cami wasn't Michael's anything if he had a say in this. He found himself clenching his jaw which was crazy.

"I'm Rhett and Michael's housekeeper."

"You clean house like mommy," Zia said.

"I do. Except I'm not as lucky as your mother. I wish I had two great helpers like you girls."

Heather snickered.

"Your face sparkles with pink and white glitter like Tinker Bell," Zoe reached out, touched Cami's face, and outlined an imaginary heart on her cheek. "You a fairy?"

Cami gasped. Coughing, she grabbed a glass of water and took a long drink.

Heather mouthed, "Sorry."

"Don't be. They're adorable." Cami kept her eyes on the girls.

"Hope you're ecstatic about the party." Heather laughed. "On this ranch, we celebrate Valentine's Day in grand style."

"My favorite day." Cami's wardrobe in shades of white, red, and pink screamed the dreaded valentine theme.

If he hadn't already swallowed his food, he would have choked. Valentine's. He figured a woman started the event to torture men to buy flowers, candy, cards, jewelry. And God forbid if you ask some gal to marry you that day.

His mom leaned forward and talked to Cami. "Michael said you're quite a cook. You can assist Heather with baking."

"I'd like that." Cami's fork made a pattern in her mashed potatoes.

Michael and Cami chatted, but Rhett couldn't hear what they said. She seemed more relaxed than she did with him. He could care less how she interacted with Michael. What mattered was her performance as their housekeeper.

His mom nudged Rhett. "Think one of you can bring Cami at nine tomorrow?"

"Michael will. I have … things to do." He couldn't think straight with Cami's pretty eyes gazing at him.

"I'll be happy to bring her," Michael said a little too quickly.

His mom got up and tapped Rhett's shoulder. "At the party, I expect to see a smile on your face."

"Of course, Mom." As if he had any other choice.

The meal ended, and Rhett turned to Michael, "Think you can take Cami back so I can head into town?"

With his brother's nod, he was off for a beer at the Last Call Saloon.

Ten minutes after Rhett left his parent's home, he drove along the ranch's rutted dirt road toward the town. Two nights ago, he'd drunk far too many whiskey shots. Maybe the bar wasn't a good idea. He turned around, deciding to have a beer at home. His thoughts drifted to Cami. Serious and guarded, and full of secrets.

Once inside his home, Rhett snagged a beer from the fridge and sat on the couch in the living room, taking a long swig.

MICHAEL LED Cami to his shiny silver truck and opened the door.

"What's up with Rhett?" She sank into the plush seat, pulled out the buckle, and snapped it in place.

"This time of year's not exactly his favorite."

"Why not?"

Michael started up the car and drove. "It's up to him to share."

In other words, mind your own business. Well, she certainly didn't want either him or Rhett nosing around her personal affairs. "I liked your family. You're mom's an absolute doll. She went out of her way to make me feel welcomed. And your dad was nice, too." His dad had been warm and friendly.

"You seem tense. What's up?"

"I'm a little anxious about the party." As a Cupid in the mortal world, the event had her more than anxious. She was pretty much terrified. "The whole town will be there."

He glanced sideways at her. "Folks are friendly."

"Easy for you to say." Finding Rhett's soulmate and shooting her arrow when they both made eye contact wouldn't be easy.

"The party's pretty casual. Potluck. Everyone will be bringing their favorite dishes."

She took in a deep breath and let it out.

"Once you bring out food from the house, you can hang with the women, even dance if you'd like." Michael's jovial tone failed to ease the dread knotting her stomach.

"I'm not much at socializing."

"Then don't. At the end, you clear off tables, throw away trash, bring dirty platters into the house. It's not hard."

She hesitated. "Thanks for not telling Rhett about the dishwasher. I want to keep this job."

"We both hired you. And since you're cooking isn't bad, I'd like you to stay on. But you need to tell me when you don't know how to do something. Yesterday, I noticed soap crusted on the jeans you hung up and rewash them."

"Sorry." So much for staying under the radar, competently doing her job until she matched up Rhett.

"You're obviously not a housekeeper. Are you in some kind of trouble?"

"No. I saw the ad and thought a ranch would be a nice change of pace." If only she could confide in him about her real mission. Somehow, she had to keep him on her side.

He shrugged. "If you say so … but if you're in trouble, please tell me now."

"It's nothing like that. Honest." Time to switch topics and get some info about Rhett. "Either of you have girlfriends?"

"Had a wife. Never again." A deep sadness mirrored his eyes.

"And Rhett?"

"Rhett likes women plenty but isn't lookin' to make a committment."

"Oh." Had she accidentally shot a human who might never fall in love?

"You like him."

"Not me."

"Your eyes don't go soft every time I enter the room."

"That's ludicrous." Rhett fascinated her because he was different from male Cupids. She liked how she had to look up to see him, whereas most Cupid males were a few inches taller than her at most. She liked how his suntanned face brought out his whiskey-colored eyes, where the blue or green eyes of Cupid men seemed, well, rather boring. While Michael and his brother were similar in looks, there was something about Rhett that captivated her. She shrugged. No sense pondering about such a silly notion.

Michael parked behind Rhett's truck. "Looks like my brother decided not to go into town. Wanna come inside and have a beer?"

"Okay." She might gain a little insight into Rhett's interests and use it to find his soulmate at the party.

MICHAEL STROLLED IN WITH CAMI. "Cami's gonna have a drink with us." He motioned to her to take the leather chair.

"Unless you'd prefer Pepsi, Bud's all we've got." Rhett said, waiting for her answer.

She eased into her spot and crossed her legs. "To be honest, I've never had beer. I drink ambrosia and, occasionally, champagne."

"Ambrosia?" Michael chuckled. "Must be a fru-fru drink."

"And we're plumb out of champagne." Rhett shook his head.

"Bud it is." Michael strutted toward the kitchen.

Cami's foot wiggled. "You left in quite a hurry."

"Yep." He turned on a hockey game, ignoring the scent of her sweet perfume that lingered in the air.

Michael carried two bottles, unscrewed one and handed it to Cami. "Here you go."

She took a sip. "Interesting flavor." She focused on the game. "About time Vanrazzo got the puck."

"You like hockey?" Rhett would have never guessed.

"Dad's a Silver Wings fanatic. We used to sit on a cloud and catch the game. He got me hooked." Her eyes stayed glued to the screen.

Sit on a cloud? He must've heard wrong.

She took a swig, her attention on the television. "Block it. Yes!" Her eyes glowed with excitement.

Rhett smiled. "No offense, but I'm rooting for the Jackals."

"You'll lose."

"Care to wager a dozen cinnamon muffins when the Jackals win."

"And you'll mop the kitchen floor when your team loses?"

"You drive a hard bargain." He shook her hand, and a jolt of awareness sparked.

She finished off her bottle, smiling as she set it on the table. Her cheeks flushed.

"Want another?" Michael pointed to Cami.

"Yes, please." She stood when Skipwyth brought the puck down the rink. "You're clear. Shoot!" The puck crossed the goal line between the two posts. "Goal! Rhett, the mop's calling you."

"No it's not. Silver Wings will be the victor."

Her jibe stirred emotions he'd preferred buried. He didn't want to be attracted to her. He wished he could fire her, but what would be the reason? Being beautiful and tempting. That would never work.

The Jackals got possession, passing the puck toward the goal. "Knock it in, Drayton. Yes."

The television announcer said, "Jackals tied the score."

"Not so sure of yourself now?" Rhett laughed as he contemplated his prize. "Hope you bought plenty of cinnamon."

"Silver Wings will be victorious."

Hot damn, she was cute acting defensive.

Michael handed her another open beer.

She took a swig, putting it down when a hockey fight erupted. Thomas slammed into Vanrazzo. Vanrazzo threw a hook. Her hands folded tightly together as she watched the screen.

The referee continued, "Double-minor on Silver Wings for unnecessary roughness."

"Unfair!" she shouted. "Thomas started the fight."

"The referee's just doing his job." Rhett couldn't resist chuckling.

"Then he needs glasses."

"What's up with you two?" Michael asked.

"A little bet, one I plan on winning." Rhett smiled at Cami.

"His team is losing." Her lips were tight, her stare direct and satisfied.

Michael snickered. "Hope you're right. My brother tends to be a tad competitive."

"Who me?"

"Block Thomas. Don't let him pass to King." She shrieked, "Nooooo."

Another goal. The scoreboard on the television showed Silver Wings 4. Jackals 6.

Her head dropped. "The muffins will have to wait 'till after the party."

"Don't mind waiting." He longed to pull her into his arms and kiss her senseless. What's wrong with him? He had to fight this temptation to do something stupid.

"It's getting late, and I have a busy day tomorrow." She got up and walked to the door.

Rhett stood. "I'll walk you home."

"That's not necessary."

"Maybe not, but I'm escorting you." He held the door open for her, grabbed a flashlight from the outside wall, turned it on, and offered his arm. Surprisingly, she took it. He guided her up the stair to the platform and unlocked her apartment. "Good night, Cami."

She turned and their eyes locked.

"You have the prettiest eyes." Unable to resist her any longer, he leaned in, and pressed his lips to hers.

Cami darted inside her apartment. Her pulse tatted, and her legs wobbled. Holy Zeus. A mortal just kissed her. She stripped and put on her nightgown, all the while trying to forget his mouth against hers.

"A-choo," she sneezed.

Her right eye twitched. Her eyes never twitched. She sneezed again. Green heartbumps formed on her arms.

Oh, no! An allergic reaction. Think. What had she eaten? At the parent's home hours ago—scalloped potatoes, steamed vegetables with a buttery sauce, apple strudel. Since her reaction usually occurred within the first hour, she thought about what she consumed at Rhett and Michael's. Popcorn and beer.

What's in beer?

She called into her communicator to list the ingredients.

"Water, hops, yeast, barley malt," a voice said.

Barley.

She was allergic to barley. At the age of five or six, she had barley soup. Staring into a mirror, a bright yellow face with purple spots reflected back. As a teen, she ate a barley muffin, and her fingernails turned orange. A year ago, she'd nibbled an appetizer with barley. Her body shrunk to the size of a dragonfly.

A teaspoon of orange blossom honey cured imbalances. She'd forgotten to bring any.

Her eye twitched.

Searching the cabinet above the sink, she found a can of split pea soup, crackers, kitchen trash bags, baking soda. Behind that box a nearly empty bottle of maple syrup. Might as well give it a try.

She got a spoon from the drawer, tilted the bottle, and took a spoonful. Both of her eyes twitched, and she sneezed three times in a row.

Not good.

Aaaa-choo. The mustard-colored fairy dust that discharged from her nose and encircled her body. She shrunk to her Cupid stature. Wings fluttered. Even though her green heart-bumps disappeared on her arms, she took off her nightie to check for sure. Darn it. Her belly had yellow and blue splotches.

Now what?

The ranch house had honey in the pantry. She turned the front doorknob, but her small stature didn't have the weight to yank it open. Great.

A soft breeze came from the patio. She'd left the door ajar a few inches, so she slipped through the crack, flew outside, and zoomed above the path to the front of the house.

The windows had screens. The slider shut tight. She floated upwards and circled the place.

An open vent on the rooftop. *Please lead to the kitchen.* She squeezed inside the vent and fell, wishing she'd thought to put on clothes because the metal felt cold on her butt as she plummeted, pushing through the bottom guard into a steamy room.

Omph! She held out her hands and landed belly down on the tile floor and stared at a toilet, the sink, a foggy mirror.

The bathroom.

Water from the shower splashed. The glass door steamed with a man's silhouette. She fluttered up to the top and peeked over the glass. A naked Rhett rinsed off shampoo. Suds flowed down his broad shoulders rippling with muscles.

He turned and reached for a bar of soap, and she glimpsed his profile. Instead of figuring a way out of this mess, she dared to glance down at his narrow waist and check out his firm and sinewy buttocks. Her fingers longed to stroke his muscles to see if they were as firm as they appeared. Her pulse quickened. The thought of touching him made her insides quiver with anticipation.

A foot-long red scar marred the perfection on his left shoulder. Fascinated, she wanted a closer look.

"Hey, sweet girl," his deep voice sang.

Did he see her?

"A-choo." Her body shook.

"Is someone out there?" He called out and turned off the water.

Oh hades! She had to hide. Where?

She fluttered to the farthest towel on the rack, furled her

wings, flattened against the wall and hung onto the middle of the towel. The towel started sliding with her weight pulling it down. If she tried to open her wings, the towel would flutter.

Rhett yanked the other towel. Hers tumbled to the floor, and she fell flat on her back. She snapped her lips together to keep from crying out in pain. At least the towel covered her.

The door squeaked open.

A sneeze tried to slip out, so she held her hand over her mouth and nose. Only a muffled, "Choo," came as he closed the door. He must be gone, she peeked out from under the towel. No sight of him.

She stood and sneezed again.

Yellow dust particles floated and surrounded her. She turned back into a human, a naked human.

Oh, my gosh! If she got caught here, she'd get fired. Wrapping a towel around her body, she yanked down a robe from the back of the door, rolled up the sleeves and tied the belt.

Opening the door a crack, she peered out. Nobody in the living room.

Should she wait a little longer? Never patient, she opted to go out. Even though the reaction seemed to settle itself, she'd better get that honey just in case she sneezed again. The floorboard creaked. She stopped. Her heart thumped hard and fast as she turned into the kitchen, opened the pantry, and grabbed the bottle of honey shaped like a bear from the second shelf. She tiptoed through the living room, heard snoring from one of the bedrooms, let out a soft sigh, turned the knob of the front door, and stepped out.

The wooden planks on the porch hurt her feet. Against the

wall, she spotted a pair of muddy boots. The boots came up to mid-thigh. Her feet swam inside them. Holding the sides of the robe up, she clomped down the steps and walked to her place.

Outside her apartment, she yanked off the blasted boots, threw them over the railing to the ground, and rushed inside. Hot and sweaty, she went into the bathroom and splashed watered on her face.

Beep-beep-beep. Her communicator flashed. "Darn it." She'd left the device here this morning when she showered.

She tapped her watch. Four messages.

7:00 p.m.

Miss Calypso, the council requests your presence in our chambers. Hold your finger on the flashing button.

8:00 p.m.

Why haven't you responded?

8:30 p.m.

Where are you? The council is waiting.

9:00 p.m.

Come to the council chambers.

Really, now. Perfect end to an already dreadful night. Might as well get this over.

She pressed the button. Pulled upwards at warp speed, she landed on the hard marble in her Cupid form wearing a twinkling white gown. Four solemn council members stared at her.

"We've been trying to reach you." The captain spoke, his lips curled down.

"Um … Serenity said to not get my communicator wet. I took it off when I showered and forgot to put it back on."

"See that you don't forget again," Andre snapped. "What progress have you made since you arrived?"

"Actually, I'll be working a Valentine's party tomorrow night. I will find Rhett's soulmate there."

Andre folded his arms. "Do not fail. Your well-planned future is at stake." He meant her presumed future with Zander. Everyone in the community assumed with their prestigious families and archery talents, their friendship would turn serious. Marriage was a logical step to unite the Eros and Calypso line.

Stop focusing on Zander. She had a human to worry about. "I will fix this, I promise."

"You'd better. Remember to shoot the red arrow we gave you," Andre growled. "Would any council member's care to add anything?"

"Don't disappoint us." The captain fiddled with his shirt's collar.

Cami was propelled back to Earth and landed on the floor of her apartment with a thump. Falling must be her penance for kissing a human.

CHAPTER 8

Valentine's Day

TONIGHT WAS the damn barn dance at his parents' place. If only the holiday could be stamped out, cancelled, eliminated forever.

Rhett made a cup of coffee and sat at a chair on the front porch to watch the day break.

Cami ambled up the steps. "Hi." She flipped her long braid with a bright pink ribbon on the end over her shoulder. The ribbon matched her pink beanie, jacket and boots. She had a serious obsession with pink. Not that he had any objection to pink, especially on her. Pink brought out the rosiness in her cheeks and made her eyes bluer. Pink wasn't the problem. It was the idea the color represented.

"Mornin'," he said, wishing he weren't so tired.

"I'll have breakfast ready within the hour." She bolted inside the kitchen.

Last night, betting against her team had been fun. And then he kissed her. Dammit, he wanted to kiss her again.

Mucking out stalls would set his mind right. He went to step into his rubber boots under the eaves. They weren't there which aggravated him. He always kept his boots in that exact spot. Borrowing Michael's, he headed for the stables.

"Hey, Starlight." He held out an apple over the railing. The horse neighed, and Rhett rubbed his hand along the animal's nose. He shoveled manure into the wheelbarrow and dumped it into an outdoor spreader. Next, he swept the stall, grabbed a pitchfork, and covered the area lightly with hay.

"Sorry boy. Won't have time for a ride." The dang party. "Tomorrow, I promise."

The horse's ears flicked as he pushed his head against Rhett's shoulder. Horses he understood.

At the outdoor sink, he washed up with frigid water and went inside the dining room. Michael sat at the table scrolling on his phone. Rhett caught an image of his brother's ex. He wanted to say, *"Move on. You guys are divorced,"* but kept those thoughts to himself. After all, he still struggled with lingering issues of his own. "Gonna be a long night."

"I reckon." Michael put down his cell.

Cami came in and handed them plates with fried eggs, a square tart in the middle and three slices of bacon on the bottom. "Anything else I can get you guys?" When she glanced at Rhett, her cheeks flushed.

"O.J."

She bolted into the kitchen and quickly came back, setting his drink on the table, more fidgety than a dog full of fleas.

"Everything okay?"

"Just anxious about the party." She rocked on her feet and gave him a wary look.

"You're not the only one." The words were out without thinking.

"Rhett doesn't care for Valentine's Day." His brother chuckled.

She glanced at her pink blouse. "I suppose you don't care for pink?"

"Not particularly."

Michael kicked his shin under the table.

"I mean on you it's nice."

She flashed him a smile. One that didn't reach her eyes.

"Ready to get dropped off at my folks?" Michael said.

Rhett opened his mouth to offer to take her himself. Crap, he still had a few chores to finish.

"I'll need to clean up in here first."

"An hour give you enough time?"

"Plenty." She sauntered towards the kitchen.

Rhett watched her hips swaying in her tight-fitting jeans. A hot and sexy bit of trouble.

CAMI TREADED SLOWLY through the open door of the new Double H Barn. The building rivaled Aphrodite's ballroom in size and height. Pink hearts blinked from the rafters.

Red and white lights spiraled around posts like candy canes.

Six women draped red tablecloths over round tables. Rhett's dad and his sister's husband stacked bales of hay at the sides of the building.

"Glad you're early." Rhett's mother, Lilly, rushed up to Cami. "Heather's ready for you in the kitchen."

"Okay."

Out the door, Cami veered to the right. The twins waited on the porch bench. Dressed in matching red polka-dot dresses, white dough coated one of the girl's pigtails. The other had batter splattered across her dress' bodice. Obviously, banned from the kitchen.

"Hi Cam-eee," one twin said.

"Cam-eee," the other one echoed.

At dinner last night, Cami had been too nervous to pay the twins much attention. Now, she didn't mind the distraction. She got down to eye level. "Tell me your names again."

"I'm Zia." She smiled with a round face and root beer-colored eyes.

"I'm Zoe." Cinnamon eyes flashed. A bright blue aura surrounded the girl. Her psychic abilities were developing. Cami had better be cautious around this one.

"Do people always get you mixed up?"

"Always, even Mommy," they spoke in unison.

"You're a fairy." Zoe stood and hugged Cami, mashing batter into her apron. "Teach me to fly."

"I wish I could. It would be fun to soar above the guests at the party." Cami put her arms out like wings, and so did the girls. "It's Valentine's Day so why don't you think of me as a Cupid."

Heather walked outside. "Are my girls bothering you?"

"Not at all. I find them delightful."

"And a mess. Look at you two." Heather said to Cami, "Already put several cakes in the oven. Help yourself to a cup of coffee, and I'll meet you in the kitchen after I clean up these two."

"Bubbles, mommy, lots of bubbles," both twins chimed.

Cami cringed remembering the dishwasher bubbles. Heather held the twins' hands and disappeared inside, while Cami strolled into the living room. Photo's lined the wall. A sweet baking aroma filled the air. Here to bake not lollygag, she stepped into a kitchen, five times as large as the kitchen at Michael and Rhett's place, with three oversized ovens and four dishwashers. A mixer bowl with beaters sat on the counter. Running her hand over the machine, she must've touched a button. The thing groaned, and the beaters spun. Flour floated in the air. Not another disaster. Spotting the stop button, she pressed it, and the thing quit whirling.

Heather walked in. "Couldn't resist playing, huh?"

"Guilty. Hope I didn't ruin anything."

"Not likely." Heather's tone seemed non-judgmental. "My mom took the girls to decorate the barn. As much as I love them, they can be quite a handful."

"You love every minute with them."

Heather laughed. "You have a smudge of white on your nose."

Cami rubbed the bridge. "Did I get it?"

"Yep." Heather unwrapped four sticks of butter and dropped them into the bowl, measured sugar, added it and turned on the machine. The beaters spun and mixed the batter. "Love, love, love how easy this is." She added the other ingredients.

In minutes, Cami and Heather spooned cookie dough onto metal sheets.

"You like working for my brothers?"

"I do."

"Then you're one brave lady. I saw their pigsty of a house before you came." The timer beeped. They used potholders to remove five red velvet sheet cakes and set them on the counter to cool.

An older woman walked in holding two grocery bags. "Hello."

"Maddie, this is Cami. She works for my brothers." Heather's eyes sparkled with affection as she took the bags out of her hand and set them on the counter.

"Seems like yesterday when those boys traipsed into the kitchen with their muddy boots. Imagine you'll earn every penny working for them."

Heather giggled as she unloaded bags of powdered sugar. Cami took it upon herself to start on the other bag filled with containers of sprinkles, candy hearts, and bottles of red food coloring. The Valentine theme made her homesick.

"Don't get me started on you, missy." Maddie's stern tone contrasted to her beaming grin.

"Maddie's been here since I was a baby— knows all our secrets." Heather hugged her.

"And don't you forget it." Maddie laughed as she grabbed

covered trays from a counter. "I'll fill phyllo crusts. You girls decorate the cookies on the sideboard."

Heather threw sugar, butter, and red dye in the mixer. It whirled, creating pink frosting in seconds. Cami should talk her employers into one of these machines that worked almost as easily as magic.

A redhead and brunette strolled in, each carrying platters of food.

"Cami, this is Violet, my husband's sister." Heather motioned to the redhead. "She brought along her friend, Lori."

"You're the new housekeeper?" Violet's brows rose in interest. Was she considering Cami competition? If only she could tell her the truth.

"Think Rhett and Michael will make it tonight?" A blush spread across Lori's cheeks.

"Sure will. Mom didn't give either of them a choice." Heather scrunched up her nose. "It seems she's determined that tonight each of them will find a girlfriend.

"I'll volunteer. Rhett's hot." Lori fanned her face, and her love-light brightened.

Lori liked Rhett. Cami nonchalantly checked out the woman's features. Her nose might be a bit bird-like, but she had stunning green eyes. Lori was tall with wavy mahogany hair that touched her shoulders. Rhett's tall. They'd make a good match.

Maddie snapped her fingers. "The cookies won't decorate themselves."

"Yes, ma'am." Heather said, and the women got busy. Since Cami needed information about potential soulmates for Rhett, now seemed like a good time to probe. "Have you ladies always lived in Cedar Springs?"

"My brother and I were young when we moved to Stone Meadows Ranch," Violet said.

Cami had passed the ranch on her way into town with Rhett.

"Violet was my roommate in college, so I came home with her a few times. Her parents hired me to train horses last summer, and I decided to stay." Lori thought Rhett was hot. She liked horses. Another plus.

Heather frosted cookies. Cami outlined a smaller heart in red. Violet filled the inside with sprinkles. Lori arranged the cookies on a heart-shaped crystal platter.

The day went by quickly. Around three, the women finished in the kitchen.

"You wanna join us here while we get ready for the party?" Heather asked Cami.

"What I have on is fine. I'm working tonight and will be wearing an apron."

Violet crinkled her eyes together. "Everyone helps out."

"She's right." Lori nodded. "Everyone dances, too."

Cami had no plans to dance. Her only goal was getting Rhett and Lori together.

"Love the jeans, especially the rhinestone heart on your back pocket. Lose the blouse." Violet's eyed eyes gleamed determination.

"Something that screams sexy. Let's check the closet in my old room." Heather didn't ask, she commanded.

"But—" This seemed like a waste of energy.

"Quit arguing, or I'll tell your boss." Heather linked arms with Cami.

"Which one, Michael or Rhett?" Violet giggled. She and Lori headed to their cars for their outfits.

Cami spotted family photos lining the walls, but Heather's brisk walk left no time to really look, and she ushered her into a bedroom. "Have a seat." She motioned to a twin bed, opened the closet and flipped through hangers. "Mom kept some of my clothes from high school." In seconds, she'd snatched a cashmere sweater, a silky red top, and a green blouse.

"Try these on while I get my outfit I left in the hall closet." Heather shut the door.

Cami's instinct was to fly as far as she could go. If only she had the use of her wings. She tapped her front pocket for her pouch with the magic vial and her miniaturized bow and arrow and breathed relief.

She didn't want to try these blouses on. Reluctantly, she took off her top, slipped the sweater over her head and stared into the mirrored closet doors. A bit loose. She swam in the red top. The sea green blouse had lacey sleeves and a low-cut V-neck. The tight bodice gathered to enhance her small waist. A vampish style. About to switch back to the sweater, she heard two knocks.

"You decent?" Heather called.

"Yes."

"Love the blouse. The color's perfect." Heather unzipped her garment bag.

"Wow." Violet plunked on the empty twin bed and gave her a thumbs-up.

"I like the sweater better." Cami lied, determined to persuade the others.

Lori adjusted her knee-length skirt. "Let's see."

Cami modeled the sweater. "This is perfect."

The women shook their heads.

"It's three to one." Heather gave her don't-argue-with-me look.

Cami changed back into the blouse. As the others dressed, she decided to get some insight into how couples met around here. "Besides dances, what else do you have for entertainment?"

"Riding. There are tons of trails," Lori said. "In town, you can catch a movie, bowl, eat, go bar hopping."

Violet plugged in a curling iron. "Love line dancing at the Boot Scoot or getting a drink at the cowboy's hang out—Last Call Saloon."

The dreadful bar. It took effort to stifle a groan

"Met my husband there." Heather gave a wistful look, buttoned her white blouse embellished with colorful beadwork, and tucked it into her jeans waistband.

"Violet you should fix Cami's hair." Heather turned to Cami. "She's good with curls."

"I guess." She'd rather they left her alone.

"Sit here." Violet motioned to a chair by a mirrored vanity. Cami stared at her reflection as Violet undid her braid and wound Cami's locks around the barrel, heated her hair to form a perfect curl, and continued until every strand spiraled. "Close your eyes."

Cami breathed in a bitter, nasty hairspray and coughed.

"Sorry. Forgot to say hold your breath."

Heather unscrewed a water bottle and handed it to Cami. The water barely washed away the awful taste.

"Did you bring makeup?" Lori asked.

"No." Cami only used magical enhancements at competitions.

"No worries. I brought my case." Lori picked up a black box. "In college, I earned extra money doing makeup for bridesmaids. Would you like me to do yours?"

"Why not." She hoped to look *'Easy, Breezy, Beautiful'* like the Covergirl cosmetic commercials claimed.

Lori gobbed cream onto Cami's cheeks, spreading it out with her fingertips. Brushed black stuff on her eyelashes. Painted aqua on her eyelids. Added a ruby gloss to her lips. "You were pretty before, now you're smokin'."

Cami stared in the mirror. Her hair perfectly coiffed with curls cascading down past her shoulders to her waist. Her eyes appeared bluer, her lashes longer, her lips too red, her cheeks pink. She shook her head. Her curls barely bounced.

"We're gonna have a blast tonight." Violet stood, bouncing on her toes.

Blast. Hardly, Cami had a much bigger mission to accomplish.

CHAPTER 9

Cami carried platters of cookies into the barn, dodging the two children who darted in front of her. She concentrated on her destination, the long dessert table at the far left. Country music blared. Fast and lively. Different from the classical waltzes played at the balls she attended. Different from rock and roll that she and Belle adored.

She put down the tray of sweet confections and tried to settle her runaway pulse. A fish out of water would be more comfortable than she was in this mortal setting. If only she could be invisible here. She could float above the crowd and zero in on Rhett and Lori. Why'd she have to be in human form?

The answer was simple. She'd hit the wrong man. The standard Cupid tactics were invalid. Her penance, she must get into the mortal's psyche and figure out who would be a proper soulmate.

A hand snagged a cookie from the closest platter. She turned and looked up.

"Hey, Cami." Rhett eyed her low-cut blouse. "Nice top."

"Thanks."

"Gotta help my dad. Save me a dance." He strode across the room and stepped up the ladder to a hayloft stage. His jeans fit his firm buttocks. Her face became warm. What was she doing? She switched her focus and glanced toward the front of the barn. Three little girls twirled on the wooden dance floor. Streamers hung from the rafters. A song twanged about swinging doors. Hay and sweets and crockpot chili filled the air. The setting—homey and comfortable.

Lori set a tray with four pies on the table and eyed the loft. "Rhett's one handsome tall drink of water. Makes me mighty thirsty." Her eyes fixed on Rhett with hunger. Those two would make a good match. This dance was a perfect place for their courtship. If things went well, Cami would shoot her arrow and resolve her issue with Rhett tonight.

Along the barn's perimeter, heart-shaped lights twinkled. Friends and neighbors clustered to chat. Cami people watched. Statuesque, medium, short people. Skinny, muscular, rotund people. Blonde, turquoise, maroon, brunette, or red-haired people. Women embraced. Men shook hands.

"What's over there?" Cami pointed to a line forming across the way.

"The beer line," Lori said. "Wanna cup?"

"No thanks. Beer … well … it doesn't agree with me." After last night's disaster, beer became Cami's enemy. "Snag me a bottled water if you see any."

"You've got it." Lori wandered across the room and stood in line.

Michael moseyed next to Cami and handed her a steaming cup. "Here."

She smelled apple cider and took a sip. It had a kick that burned as it went down her throat. "What's in this stuff?"

"My old friend, Captain Morgan." He grinned from one side of his mouth.

"Never met the guy." No doubt a kind of alcohol. "Please tell me it doesn't contain any barley?"

"It's rum." He scrolled his phone. "Nope, just molasses."

She checked her wrist emblem anyway. No greenish tint. Keeping her wits sharp, she readied herself for her mission.

"What'd my brother do now?" Rhett appeared next to her and looked into her cup.

"Gave her a hot toddy." Michael flashed an I'm-so-innocent smile.

"Probably a good idea. She's wound tight."

And alcohol would cure her ails? Not likely.

Lori waddled over, holding three cups in her hands. "Couldn't find water," she said to Cami. "Want one, Michael? Rhett?"

"You're a sweetheart?" Rhett took a beer, and so did Michael.

"To Valentine's Day." Lori held up her cup.

The corners of Rhett's mouth dropped—agitation flared in his eyes. What caused him to despise Valentine's Day? If only she could access his past relationship records, but her mistake locked the system.

The crackle of piped-in music stopped. “Howdy folks.” A white-haired man spoke into a microphone. It took a moment to realize the man’s location up in the loft.

The audience’s chitchat diminished to silence.

“Let’s give a round of thanks to Frank and Lilly Holloway. Not only are they hosting this wonderful shindig, but they’re also celebrating their thirtieth wedding anniversary.”

The couple waved from the side, and the crowd clapped, whooped, and hollered.

Lori scooted next to Rhett and gazed at him like he was a delectable cheesecake drizzled with caramel. For some reason, the gaze irked Cami.

“Grab your partner for our first number, “Save a Horse, Ride a Cowboy.”

“Let’s show the folks how it’s done.” Lori leaned her torso toward Rhett and playfully hit his arm.

“That’s okay.” Rhett quickly glanced over at Cami.

“Please.” She gave him a mock frown.

“Go on,” Michael said. “It’s not polite to leave a woman waiting.”

“Fine.” Rhett followed Lori. Together they weaved to the dance floor.

Lori was personable, pretty, and tall. Rhett charming, handsome, tall. They looked like soulmates.

Michael offered his hand. “Wanna dance?”

“I need to serve refreshments.” She didn’t want to draw attention to herself here. She could waltz and cha-cha, knew a few popular dances but not many country ones.

He tilted his head. “What’s the real story?”

"Don't know how." That should get him to leave.

"I'll show you." Michael led her to the floor, assumed the position, his right arm elevated, his left reaching for her waist. "It's easy, step together step, walk, walk. You'll be going backwards. Start with your right and shift with your left."

It didn't sound difficult. "I suppose I could try." Cami put her left hand on his right shoulder. Her right hand clasped with his left. The position similar to a waltz.

"Think quick, quick, slow, slow." Michael kept his voice low.

The fiddler played. Michael stepped forward with his right foot, and she her left. She said the steps in her head a few times. He turned her under his arm and spun her into an older couple.

"Sorry," she said to the couple, and whispered to Michael, "You did that on purpose."

"Who me?" His tone was not the least bit innocent.

Rhett and Lori moved past. Cami couldn't deny the couple had charisma.

The music stopped. "Thanks for the dance." Michael bowed.

"Sure." She pivoted to head for the refreshment table and ran into a solid wall.

Rhett laughed, his eyes lit with interest or more like curiosity. "May I have the honor?"

She tried to get around him. "I need to get more cookies from the house."

"Dance first." He put a hand on her shoulder and heat coursed along her spine.

"Our next number is a two-step favorite, "Holdin' Heaven," the band announced.

A favorite in Cupid's Corner, at least Cami knew the steps.

Rhett's grin widened as he held her right hand and looped his arm to grasp her left. Sparks shot through her heart emblem. She heard her friend, Serenity, talk about how her last boyfriend made her all quivery inside. That couldn't be happening to Cami. Not with this mortal.

"See, this isn't so bad." He brought her closer reminding her of last night.

Their bodies touched and formed strange tingles deep in her womanly core. "It's okay." She glanced at his strong chin highlighted by a five o'clock shadow.

His mouth turned up at the corners. "You're different tonight." His deep voice soothed. "You mad about the kiss?"

"No." The kiss had her heart fluttering, and as much as she'd liked it the contact had been a major gaffe.

"Good. I'd like us to stay friends."

Friends don't kiss each other on the mouth, but if he could remain unaffected, so could she. "Fine with me." She didn't dare look at him and quickly changed the subject. "Lori's nice."

"Yep." He spun her under his arm, and again they were side by side.

"Relax," he whispered as they did a fancy double and several clogover vines.

"I am."

He laughed. "No, you're not."

"Are you always so bossy?"

"Most of the time." Again, he spun her under his arm. "You're a good dancer for a city gal."

"Thanks." She felt her cheeks warm.

"I like it when you blush. You look pretty."

Holy Zeus. He should be noticing Lori and not flirting with her.

The song ended. He tipped his hat. "Thanks for the dance."

She couldn't help watching him walk away. The man had a well-sculpted body. His shoulders were broad, his hips narrow.

Then the devil looked over his shoulder at her.

RHETT GOT in the keg line behind his buddy, Ace.

His stocky friend smiled. "Who's the new gal?" He motioned to the other side of the barn where Cami chatted with an older couple. Her golden hair coiled down to the middle of her back. Rhett imagined trailing his fingers through her soft curls.

"My new housekeeper."

"Really." Ace handed Rhett a beer. "Bro, she's hot. What's her name?"

"Cami."

"Think she'd go out with me?"

"Don't know?" Rhett shrugged and listened to the band play, "Boot Scootin' Boogie."

"You like her?"

"She's my employee. That's it." He didn't want to admit that the woman drove him to distraction.

Violet and Lori coerced Cami to the dance floor, and they joined in a line dance. Cami did a quarter turn in the wrong direction. She caught her error and pivoted, stepped forward and back, hitched up her knee and stomped her foot. Sexy as hell.

The song ended, and people clapped.

"You've gotta introduce me to Cami." Ace put his empty cup on the table.

Cami had hearts and flowers written all over her. With blonde hair and blue eyes, she spelled heartache to any man, yet, she seemed to be reeling him in. That kiss they shared had been oh-so-wrong, primarily since she was his employee. "Fine. But you have to promise to be on your best behavior. Cami's a good cook. Don't do anything to scare her off."

"Why are you so huffy? I just want to meet her."

"Fine." He and Ace maneuvered through the crowd to the dance floor.

Lori's eyes brightened as Rhett stopped near her. "Hey, Rhett. Ace."

Cami glanced up. Rhett tried not to get lost in her bewitching eyes. It was as if the woman cast a spell over him.

Ace nudged Rhett's shoulder.

"Ace, this is Cami."

"Hello." Cami rocked on her heels for some odd reason.

The band announced another two-step number.

"Would you honor me with this dance?" Ace tipped his hat and gave her a ten-dollar smile.

"Go on," Lori said, "He's a good guy."

Ace whisked Cami off to the dance floor. Being shorter than Rhett, Ace and Cami's heights were a good match. Rhett's stomach twisted. This fixation on his housekeeper was crazy.

He noticed Lori next to him. Just the distraction he needed. "Care to dance?"

"Absolutely." Lori didn't hesitate.

He took her hand. Only a few inches shorter than him, her height complimented his. He should be attracted to the leggy brunette, but when he spotted Cami in Ace's arms smiling, Rhett wanted to snatch her away from his friend.

Air, fresh air would clear his mind. "It's stuffy in here," he said to Lori. "Wanna step outside for a minute?"

"All right." She moved closer and smiled a bit too broadly.

Based on the enamored look she gave him, he might have been too quick with his offer. He took her hand, moved around people to the open barn door, and didn't once glance back at Cami. Outside, he breathed in the cold, crisp night.

Lori shivered in her thin coat.

"You're freezing. Take my jacket." He draped it over her shoulders. "How's the Arabian's training going?"

"The ligament injury below the hock is slowly healing. Heard your dad's new mare's quite a find. Let's go see her."

"Absolutely. This noisy party might unsettle her."

Lori was smart. A natural with horses making their conversation easy.

They strolled to the stables kitty-corner to the barn. He unlatched the door, glad to be away from the smothering crowd at the party. Horses made sense. The smell of hay and manure calmed him.

"I forgot how big this place is." Lori looped her arm through his elbow.

A bald-faced roan leaned its head over the top of the stall. "Hello, General." Lori rubbed her hand along his forehead. "See you're still as handsome as ever."

"Why thank you." Rhett laughed.

"You feeling neglected, handsome?" She kissed his cheek.

He tried to muster desire for her, but it wasn't there. He had taken her out a couple of times, liked her enough, but she didn't make his pulse sped or his heart pound.

He thought of Cami—and all that pink.

LORI AND RHETT WERE TOGETHER, arm-in-arm, heading outside. An excellent sign.

Cami ignored the lump in her throat. If fate was on her side, they'd find an isolated spot. She tried to forget his tantalizing kiss, tried to concentrate on her task.

Tapping her pocket, she felt the pouch. Still there. The antidote arrow would correct her mistake. Due to the crowded room, she cut to the right and a man stepped on her toe. A little girl ran straight into her leg and held on until her mother pulled her off. A young couple stopped in front of her. She darted around them and made it outside. The cold wind seeped through her thin blouse sending a chill clear through to her bones. She couldn't waste this perfect opportunity to fix her mistake because she was cold.

Cami kept close to the wall as she pursued Rhett and Lori. They ducked into the stables, and she followed them inside. The first stall stood open and empty. She went in, shutting the gate in case anyone else was in the vicinity.

Rhett's voice carried from several yards away, "Our new mare's three stalls down."

Cami sat ontop of a haystack, carefully opened her pouch

and placed her bow and quiver on her shoulder. She gripped the vial and sprinkled dust over herself. Fuchsia sparkles swirled around her. Her body shrunk and her borrowed clothing dropped to the hay. A long silvery gown swirled around her body and her glittering wings formed. She jetted up to the rafters.

Patience and precision. Patience and precision. Patience and precision. I can do this.

"Is the mare a stock quarter horse?" Lori's voice wafted up clearly.

"Yep." Rhett smiled. Even from this distance, his smile made Cami's heartbeat quicken.

Lori stroked his arm.

Quit dallying and complete the task.

Rhett and Lori were facing each other. Lori's love-light glowed a deep ruby. Cami circled, floating down to secure a clear shot. She nocked her arrow, checked her aim and released. It hit Rhett straight through his heart.

"Ouch." He slapped his hand over his chest.

Cami thought she saw a glowing light through his fingers. She almost shouted, "*Success!*"

"You okay?" Lori gazed at him.

"Had the weirdest feeling like something lodged in my torso."

"Poor thing. I can make it better." Lori roped her arms around Rhett's neck and the two kissed. He'd found his soulmate.

A sense of melancholy hit her as she flew back to the stall.

The barn seemed dark and gloomy like her mood. There'd be no more searing kisses. The mortal belonged to another.

A horse snorted, reminding her she was still inside the stables. With her job finished, she sat at the edge of the haystack and counted her blessings. She'd grown up in an affluent archer family with plenty of privileges and lots of friends.

Her legs swung back and forth. They could pass as toothpicks. At fourteen-inches, the straw reminded her of elongated chopsticks. The human clothing could fit a giant. Her Cupid body made her feel small and insignificant.

Quit pondering. Someone could walk in and catcher her wallowing in her personal pity party. She carefully added her bow and arrow into the pouch, clutched the edge of her jeans and blouse, and sprinkled the remaining dust over her head. The swirling magic transformed her into a five-foot-two woman. Brushing off straw with her hand, her size fit the space —her boots touched the ground.

She liked being a human. She liked the people. They were friendly and welcoming. She'd been taught that Cupids were superior to humans. Based on her few days on Earth, magical powers seemed to be the only advantage Cupids possessed.

Once she completed her task, she'd have to say her goodbyes. This irritated her because she had just started to fit in.

She opened the stall's gate and peeked her head down the aisle. Rhett had his back to her on the other end of the stable, so she sprinted out the door and kept going until she reached the barn's entrance.

The band played, "Home on the Range," as she went inside.

Home on the *ranch.* That's what she'd found here. Her eyes blurred with tears.

RHETT COULDN'T BELIEVE Lori locked lips with him. Normally, he enjoyed an aggressive woman, but not tonight and not with her. For the past year, he'd socialized with Lori at parties or town events. The leggy brunette was fun and spirited and smart. A couple of weeks ago, he'd taken her out to dinner. Sparks on his side never fully surfaced.

It'd been a mistake to take a breather with her. The truth was seeing Ace holding Cami as they danced had him riled. When he got riled, his brain misfired.

He pulled away. "Guess we'd best head on back."

"We don't have to." She batted her lashes, took a step closer.

He took two back. "I was counting on another dance with you." Of all the times to be tactful? He should say he wasn't interested period.

She sighed a wistful sigh and took his arm. "In that case, let's go, cowboy."

As they crossed the courtyard, he spotted Cami slipping inside the door leading into the barn dance. The bitty female shouldn't stir him. He stifled a groan and turned his focus to Lori. "You're good with horses. Have you ever thought about starting your own business?"

"At one time. Yesterday, I was accepted into vet school," Lori said.

"Congratulations." Okay, this was his chance. What should

he say? *Seeing as you'll be leaving, there's no sense in dating again.* Yeah, right. What if she caused a scene and ruined his parents' party?

"You'll have to visit me." She coyly smiled. "There's lots to do."

"Doubt I'd have time." Rhett had no inclination to see her in another state.

He caught her eyes misting. Dammit. Rhett hated tears. They made it to the dance floor when the band announced, "That's it for tonight. Me 'n' the Brahma Busters want to thank everyone. Catch us at the Boot Scoot every Friday and Saturday. Come on out and say, 'Howdy.'"

She took off his jacket and handed it back. "We on for the Boot Scoot Saturday?'

"Look, Lori, I don't think—" Someone grasped his calf. He glimpsed down and spotted his toddling youngest nephew. "Hey, fella."

His brother-in-law walked up shaking his head. "Seems Jamie's found his favorite uncle."

"I'm his favorite." Michael clapped Rhett on the shoulder.

"You've been eating locoweed, bro."

"Speak for yourself," Michael chuckled.

Lori cleared her throat. "I'm gonna help Violet clear tables. See ya guys later." She stomped toward the front of the barn.

"What's up with her?"

Rhett shrugged.

Folks headed for the door. People he'd known all his life like the pastor's family, Old Doc Findley, friends from grade school, most married with families. Several of the remaining men stacked hay in the corner. Others loaded chairs on wheeled carts. Rhett and Michael folded tables and set them off to the side. Once they were done, Michael headed toward Violet.

Lori approached Rhett. "I'm leaving."

"I'll walk you out."

Lori wove her arm through his. "Tonight was fun."

At her Chevy pickup, Rhett opened her door. "I don't want to mislead you, especially since your leaving for Colorado, but in my experience long distance dating doesn't work."

"If you say so." Her lip quivered. She started her truck and zoomed off.

Inside the barn, he stacked the remaining tables.

"What'd those tables do to you?" Michael's voice startled him. "Is this about Lori?"

"Guess I hurt her feelings. It's this blasted Valentine's Party." He could wrestle the toughest calf to the ground with his bare hands. Corral the most cantankerous Brahma bull. Hold his own in a barroom brawl. But when it came to this holiday, he became as useless as a newborn kitten.

"Or is it a gorgeous blonde."

"Shut up." He never should have kissed Cami last night. Not that he'd tell Michael.

Michael motioned to the side of the room. "Think Cami could use some assistance?"

Her blonde curls bounced against her back as she carried an armload of platters and stepped out the door.

"If you don't help her, I will," Michael said.

Not about to be bested by his brother, he sprinted and caught up with her. "Hey."

Her dishes clattered. "Rhett?"

He reached out to steady her. "Hold still. I'll take the top dishes" He lifted off three platters.

"Thanks. These turned out to be heavier than I first thought." Her bottom swayed as she headed toward the kitchen

"What'd you think of today?" He walked beside her up the steps leading into the house.

"I liked the music and learning new dance steps."

He transferred the platters in one hand and held the door for her. "My toes'll never be the same after a spin on the floor with you."

"Wasn't my boots." He expected her to laugh, not gawk at him and say, "You and Lori look good together."

"About that—"

They reached the kitchen. His mom sipped coffee at the table.

He hugged her. "Great party, Mom."

Cami set the dishes in the sink, rinsed a platter, and placed the item in the dishwasher.

Lilly's dark eyes twinkled, as she said, "Cami, you've already done plenty. I'll have my help finish up in the morning."

Cami yawned as she wiped her hands on a towel. "I am exhausted."

"We're gonna call it a night." He kissed his mom.

"I like that girl. Fits in well," she whispered.

As he walked Cami to his truck, he itched to put his arm around her, itched to kiss her, but played it safe and opened her door.

CHAPTER 10

Rock music blared on the clock radio. Cami reached over to her nightstand and pushed the sleep button. "Five already?" Morning came excessively fast. She flopped on the mattress and covered her head with her pillow.

A drum solo pounded from the radio. "Okay, I'm up." Bleary eyed, her mind foggy, she switched the tiny knob to off.

Quarter to six. Twenty minutes to dress. Her father's words played inside her head, *"Cupids arise early, alert and ready for their commitments."*

Usually, she woke on her own. Why not today?

The party. Cleanup kept her out until midnight.

She jumped out of bed and immediately texted, "Mission Completed." The council would be pleased. Her arrow successfully hit Rhett's heart, and he'd kissed Lori afterwards. Further proof of their love chemistry.

Rhett kissing Lori gnawed at her mind like a puppy gnawed at a shoe. *Quit thinking about him. He's not for me—he's forbidden.*

She dressed in jeans and a pink sweater. With her task completed, she should return home in a day or two. The thought of saying goodbye made her sad. She enjoyed working for Michael and Rhett. A tear slipped down her cheek. She blamed her leaky eyes on lack of sleep.

She glanced at her communicator.

Nothing.

She shook it. Banged it on the table.

Not a single word.

She sent another missive.

I hit Rhett Holloway with my arrow. Mission completed successfully.

As she finished her tea, a message from the captain flashed.

Don't be hasty in your judgement. Check for certainty with the following questions.

Does the subject's eyes light up when he says the love interest's name? Does he seek her out in a crowd?

Rhett sought Lori for alone time in the stables.

Does he create ways to make contact? It could be a kiss, a brush of his fingers along her arm, hand holding.

She'd seen them kiss.

Has he called her? Asked her out?

She assumed he would soon.

Does he take extra time primping for his date? You know, fancy clothes, cologne, gelling his hair.

Rhett doesn't primp. It's not his style.

A word of caution. Males are often reluctant to show an emotional connection.

No surprise there.

If nothing happens within a week or two, a second love dose may be required.

There's no need to panic. In her heart, she knew that the first arrow would fix everything. She let out a deep breath. Soon, she'd be heading back to Cupid's Corner a success.

Not really a success. Not after she made a huge blunder.

A couple more weeks on the ranch would give her plenty of time to prepare for her return.

A part of her wouldn't mind staying on Earth indefinitely.

She didn't mind Earth. The people were friendly. Nobody judged her archery skills.

She didn't mind her human body. She liked being taller, wearing jeans and T-shirts.

She didn't mind her new job. Cooking without magic had been challenging at the beginning, but she'd done all right.

Her steps seemed lighter as she headed to the ranch. Rhett sipped coffee and leaned his elbows on the front porch. He was okay, nothing special. Nothing special except for the way his muscular arms and broad shoulders filled his shirts. Nothing special except for how his eyes sparkled when he taunted her.

"Mornin'." He rubbed his day-old stubble chin. "You could've slept in."

"I don't mind getting up to cook."

"Then if you're up to it, please make your delicious blueberry muffins. They're my favorite."

"You'll have to wait and see what I decide to create." She put an extra sway as she went inside, quite certain his eyes were following her.

TWO NIGHTS LATER, Cami squeezed in the middle section of Michael's truck to head for the bowling alley. Hot air blew from the heater vents keeping her toasty warm.

Rhett slid into the seat's bench on her right. "This is cozy."

"Try sitting in the middle wedged between the two of you." She breathed in his woodsy scent.

"You don't mind." Rhett crooned wickedly seductive.

She knew better than to react, but her foolish heart didn't listen.

The truck turned left onto the main highway. Rhett's thigh pressed against hers. Even with fabric separating them, the man radiated heat. "Ever been bowling?"

"A time or two, but I'm not very good." At Aphrodite's Lanes, she'd thrown diamond bowling balls at titanium pins.

Rhett swathed his arm along the bench seat. "Bet you throw all strikes." His confidence in her might be misguided still her pulse sped. He turned up a song about a lying cheatin' husband.

"You guys ever listen to rock? You know the Stones, Led Zeppelin." In her world, Cupids adored "Stairway to Heaven."

Michael snickered. "Name a rock song that can beat "All My Ex's Live in Texas" or "Don't Cry on My Shoulders 'Cause You're Rustin' My Spurs."

Cami giggled. "You guys need to expand your listening horizons ... um ... channels."

A bright sign flashed for Thunder Lanes Bowling. They parked next to Violet's car as she and Lori got out.

The group walked inside. Cami tried not to gawk at her surroundings. It wasn't easy. The cocktails sign sparkled. The walls were decorated with a gigantic bowling ball and pin silhouettes. On one of the wooden lanes, a man threw a red ball toward white pins.

Rrrrrrrrrr. Cling.

The shouts of "Aww" and "ha-ha" meshed together.

In Cupid's Corner, bowling on white clouds lacked the imperfect charm found in this establishment.

"Shoe rentals are over there." Rhett pointed to the left. "I'll get us a lane." He veered right. His brother and the other two women followed.

Cami waited at the counter.

Ace strolled next to her and clunked his black bag on the floor. "Rhett sent me over for support."

"I take it drab brown's the owner's favorite color."

"Could be." Cute with wavy blond hair and dark eyes, he reminded her of Zander.

"What size shoe ya need?" A heavy-set man behind the counter asked.

"Size? I think a five-and-a-half or a six." She took off her pink boot and handed it to him.

"Smallest woman's we have is seven." He compared the soles. "Too big. Might find something in the kids' section." The clerk set out brown shoes with lime green soles and orange shoelaces. "These should fit."

The clashing tones hurt her eyes. "You have anything less

colorful?"

"Sorry, miss."

She reluctantly left her boots as collateral and sat at a bench.

Ace stood. "May I tie your shoes?"

"Sure." The less she had to look at the dreadful colors, the better. Once he was done, he offered his hand to help her rise.

"Hope you're not superstitious. Rhett secured lane number thirteen."

"Nope." Born on that day, she considered it blessed.

They took the carpeted aisle to the right and stepped down the slope to their lane.

Violet stood behind a table with a screen and punched the keys. "I've partnered everyone. Rhett you're with Lori. Ace's with Cami. Michael, it's you and me. Cami. Do you spell your name with two *m's* and an *ie*?"

"No. One *m*, no *e's*."

"Got it." Violet slunk in beside Michael.

Rhett cruised by Cami and pointed down. "Nice."

"I know. Aren't my shoes vibrant?" Cami took a seat kitty-corner to Violet.

Ace plopped next to her, his spicy cologne drifted.

A pink-haired waitress in a short polyester dress and high heels stilettoed over toward the men. "The usual?"

"Of course." Michael gave a boyish grin and turned to Violet. "You ladies want beer?"

Violet nodded, as did Lori.

"No beer, here." Cami wanted to try something fun. "What fizzy drinks do you have?"

Rhett spoke up. "She likes champagne."

She'd asked for champagne the night they'd watched the hockey game. The night she'd drunk beer and later experienced an adverse reaction to the barley.

"Don't carry champagne." The thirtyish woman put her hand on her hip and twirled her empty tray on her pointer finger. "Will wine do?"

"You have anything sweet like ambrosia, but non-alcoholic?" She planned to keep her wits intact tonight.

"Cherry Coke." The waitress said, snapping her gum.

"I'll take it."

"Five beers and one soda. Want dogs and fries with that?"

"Yep," Michael answered, and the waitress scurried toward the bar.

Rhett's eyes held Cami's for a second.

Lori pressed her lips together.

He turned to Lori. "Our team's up first."

She took a baby-blue ball out of her bag.

Ace said to Cami. "Bet you're good at this game."

"I wouldn't say that." In cloud-covered lanes magic resets the pins, strikes created thunder and lightning. Unlike her friends, Cami's demanding archery schedule gave her little time for recreation.

"I'll give you some pointers."

"Okay."

"See how relaxed Lori is, her knees bent," Ace spoke in an instructive whisper.

Cami nodded, admiring how Lori's baby blue shoes matched her ball.

He stretched his arm around the back of the bench. "Notice how Lori stays focused when she throws."

Cami had mastered focusing on archery, well, almost mastered it.

Lori's first ball knocked down all the pins. On the overhead TV screen, an animated bowler appeared and said, "Strike," and drew an X by her name. She rushed over to Rhett and high-fived him.

"The key is a straight release," Ace kept his voice lowered.

It made sense. Cami watched Rhett stand. Lori's eyes were riveted on him.

"I wouldn't copy Rhett's style. He's a power player, uses his upper body strength to generate the ball's speed." Ace mentioned Rhett's upper body strength, and Cami recalled his muscular shoulders in the shower. The idea caused her face to heat.

She shifted her attention to Ace. "How 'bout you?"

"I'm not into hot-shotting. Prefer consistency."

"So do I." Consistency without errors had been drilled into her brain for as long as she could remember.

Rhett strode toward the lane. His lithe body moved with elegance as he released the ball. It spun and veered to the right.

It's going into the gutter. Her fingers clenched tightly together. The ball spun toward the center pin.

Rrrrrrrrrr. Cling.

"He did it." A teeny shriek escaped as she stood.

"You doubted me?" Rhett called, beaming a smile.

"Of course not, boss." A giggle slipped out. "But I assume you can't do it again."

He chuckled as he sat next to Lori while watching Cami.

Lori put her hand on Rhett's shoulder and whispered into his ear.

The arrow she shot a few days ago contained an exceptionally potent love potion. He should be as smitten with Lori as she seemed to be with him. The potion didn't appear to be working. Why not? Cami had followed the directions perfectly, hadn't she? She blinked several times and gazed at Rhett. He must be one of those people who could mask his love-light.

Ace talked continually as Violet and Michael had their turns.

Cami tuned him out and watched the other lanes. The concession stand glowed with blue lighting. Rock music played. A father assisted his little girl. A group of teens high-fived. A team of adults in bright yellow uniforms applauded a white-haired man's strike.

"Your turn," Ace said, his dark eyes shone as he held up a ball. "Think this pink one should work for you."

Cami placed two fingers and added her thumb in the holes, took four steps, and let the cotton candy colored ball go. It rolled along the center arrow, straight for a few feet, and went into the gutter. Holy Chaos, her bowling skills were pathetic.

"You'll get it next time." Ace's encouragement was nice..

She grabbed her ball from the return tray, breathed in slowly, relaxed her fingers, wrists, and stance. She let go of the ball. It went straight from the second arrow on the left and knocked down five pins. Progress. Not perfection.

"Almost had it." Violet snapped her fingers.

Almost! Cami despised that word. Losers *almost* made their shots. Losers shot the wrong person and had to fix their mistake.

Ace took his turn, his head high. A blond wave fell into his eyes as he threw a strike.

She checked on Lori and Rhett. Rhett didn't hold Lori's hand or put his arm around her, but she would touch his arm and smile brightly as he spoke. He acted like they were just friends. Friends could become lovers, couldn't they?

The captain said men were slow to show emotional connection. No need to worry. She sipped her cherry Coke, got a sugar rush, and caught Rhett smiling at her. A shiver of desire tingled up her spine.

The game finished. Rhett and Lori won.

They played a second game. Violet went first, hit nine, and got a spare. Michael threw a strike.

Cami went next. She tuned out her surroundings, concentrated and let the ball go. It veered from the left to the center and knocked down nine pins. The one pin standing at the back wobbled and fell down. Everyone cheered. She should be ecstatic as she headed for her seat but couldn't let go of the last game.

"You did it." Ace hugged her, reminding her of a supportive older brother.

Rhett gave her a thumbs up.

Ace took his turn, threw another strike, and high-fived her.

Lori's next ball knocked down seven pins. The animated bowler on the screen added a seven and totaled seventeen in her box.

"Lori had that one. Why'd she miss?" Cami needed clarification.

"She added a spin when she let the ball go."

"I see." Mastery of this game wouldn't be easy.

Rhett took his turn. She held her breath and watched all the pins fall. His fist went into the air as he glanced her way. "Thought I couldn't do it."

"I have faith in you," "Lori said with an adoring sigh.

"Lori and Rhett took first," Violet announced. "Michael and I came in second."

"We'll get it next time," Ace didn't have any agitation in his voice. Losing didn't appear to be a big deal. He walked next to her as she turned in her shoes. "Would you like to go to the movies tomorrow night?"

"Ace, you're a fantastic guy, but—"

"You're into Rhett."

"No way. He's my boss. Besides, he's with Lori."

"No, he's not." Ace laughed. "You're blind if you can't see it. He likes you."

The guy was delusional.

They caught up with the group. Violet and Michael held hands. Lori and Rhett didn't. Cami would have to use the second arrow dose soon.

"Tonight was fun." Ace hugged her, brought his mouth inches from hers but pulled away. "That oughta make Rhett jealous," he whispered. As he strutted to his truck, he turned back toward her and waved. His turbo engine vroomed, his tires squealed as he raced off.

Rhett and Lori parted, her eyes fixated on Rhett as he

strolled toward Michael's truck. Rhett never noticed the poor woman.

"What's up with you and Ace?" Rhett quirked an eyebrow as he unlocked the truck's door and held it open for Cami.

"Nothing." She shrugged.

"Shot him down?" The corners of his mouth lifted.

"Why would you think that?" She slid inside the cab.

"No reason." His eyes darkened as he gazed at her. He wasn't into Cami.

Lori was his soulmate. Another love arrow dose would prove the point.

CHAPTER 11

The next day, nothing went right. Cami burnt her wrist taking muffins out of the oven, overcooked the eggs, undercooked the bacon. When she served breakfast, neither man complained.

During cleanup, as she poured bacon grease into a can, her grip of the iron skillet slipped. Grease spilled down the front of her jeans and onto the toe of her boots. Her only consolation, if you could call it that, was little grease dripped on the kitchen tiles.

Following her routine, she added a load of jeans into the washer. The machine gurgled, sputtered, groaned, and quit. "That's it. I'm taking a break." She stomped toward her apartment to change her clothes.

Lori drove up, and she rolled down the truck's window. "What happened to you?"

"I wrestled a greased pig. It won."

Chuckles broke out from both women.

"Need me to hose you down?" Lori motioned to a hose on the ground near the stables.

"Not today. You here to see Rhett?" Cami asked.

"Michael called. Buttercup's showing signs of colic."

"Is that serious?" She knew nothing about diseases.

"It can be if not treated properly. Anyway, I'd better run."

As Lori pulled away, Cami's mind whirled. Rhett should be showing signs of love, a flickering love-light, or at least a radiating aura. Could his head be overruling his heart? She needed to hit him with another arrow.

With Lori here, she'd could get the two of them together alone.

Now for the magical dust. Inside her apartment, she grabbed a vial from her suitcase, slipped it into her pouch, and changed her grease-covered pants.

Shooting stars. Rhett left a few hours ago to pick up a stallion from a neighboring town. He would be back before dark. What if she invited Lori to dinner and cooked them a romantic meal?

She called into her communicator, "Foods to enhance romance."

A list appeared on the face of her smart watch. "Oysters?'

Disgusting.

"Cayenne pepper?"

I'll make Fried chicken coated with flour and a smidgen of cayenne.

"Asparagus, garlic, olive oil."

Asparagus simmered in olive oil. Perfect.

Chocolate, whip cream, cherries, liquor."

Dessert—chocolate with whipped cream and *cherries.* Layered mousse, sneaking in several shots of brandy from the bottle in the pantry. Brilliant.

I can totally do this.

Now to put her plan in action. She hurried toward the stables as Michael and Lori walked out.

"Take the money." Michael attempted to push bills in Lori's hand. "You've more than earned it."

"Not necessary. If I ever become a certified vet, I'll be sure to charge you double."

"Is Buttercup okay?" Cami asked as she walked up.

"She seems fine, but I'm taking her stool sample to the lab to be certain."

Oh no. Lori's not gonna stay for supper. "Is the lab far?"

"In town near the bank."

"Since you won't take a dime, at least stay for dinner. Come over about five." Michael said.

Cami wanted to hug the man.

Lori's face brightened. "I'll be here."

RHETT SPENT the better part of his day picking up a stallion. He set the horse lose in his parent's largest corral. Holy Terror snorted and kicked up dirt. The horse appeared to have an injured soul, but with nurturing he should come around.

Dinnertime. He came through the front door. The delicious

aroma of fried chicken made his stomach grumble. As he turned the corner to the dining room, he stopped.

What the heck? Lori relaxed in a chair next to Michael.

"Howdy," he said, trying to cover his annoyance through clenched teeth.

"Hey." Lori eyed him with a sultry gaze.

After supper, he'd cowboy up and again set her straight.

Michael wore a sober stare. "Didn't you get my text about Buttercup?"

"Left my phone in my bedroom. Something wrong with our mare?" Bottle-feeding her since she was a foal, Rhett's gut tied in knots.

"Hope not. This morning she pawed the ground." His brother said, "Her eyes seemed dull, listless. Thought it might be colic. Doc wasn't in, so I called Lori."

"Good thinking." Rhett would've done the same.

"I'm sure she's fine, but I took samples to be certain." Lori fiddled with the top button on her blouse. "We'll know by tomorrow if there's a problem."

"Lori wouldn't take a dime. Thought the least I could do was offer dinner," Michael said.

Rhett had come to an unfair conclusion about Lori, and he joked, "Should've taken the money."

Cami sauntered in carrying a platter of fried chicken in one hand, a bowl of green vegetables in the other, and placed the food on the table. Her sweater accented her tiny waist; her snug jeans stirred his desire.

Damn, she looked good.

"Be right back with the rest." Cami returned with mashed

potatoes and gravy. Dishes passed around. Rhett took generous portions of everything.

Michael chomped into a drumstick. "This is spicy. Love the extra kick."

Cami waited beside Michael and glanced at Rhett as he bit into a thigh. His eyes watered. He reached for a glass of milk and guzzled it. "What the hell did you put in this?"

"Just a pinch of cayenne pepper." Cami gave him an innocent look, acting like it was perfectly natural to make his fried chicken spicy. "Too hot for you?"

"Nope," Rhett said, resisting the urge to lay into the sassy woman.

"Join us." Michael tapped the chair to his right.

"Can't. Have to finish making a triple layer mousse."

"It sounds yummy." Lori smiled at Rhett. "My morning's free tomorrow. I'll check on the mare." Lori eased her thigh against his. "We could go riding after I'm done."

"Busy." He shoveled in mashed potatoes.

"Too bad." Her mouth quirked down for a fraction of a second.

Cami delivered fancy glass bowls, layered with pudding and whipped cream. Topped it with a cherry. "Enjoy." She raced back into the kitchen.

Rhett ate a spoonful and tasted brandy. Odd, Cami had never spiked their dessert with liquor before. What's up with her?

Michael's phone rang. "Gotta take this call." He picked up his dessert and headed towards his bedroom.

Lori savored her mousse and sighed. "This is delicious." Her left hand landed on his knee.

It'd be preferable to have a branding iron sear his butt. He grasped her hand. "Let's go outside and talk."

CAMI LISTENED from the other side of the kitchen door and pictured electricity charging between Rhett and Lori. Another arrow would make their attraction stronger. The front door banged.

Now's my chance.

She headed for the bathroom, stepped inside, and locked the door. The same bathroom where she'd seen Rhett naked. Remembering the man's muscular build, her pulse ticked faster.

She checked the vent above the toilet, the one she'd fallen through after the beer incident. Someone had secured the grill back in place. Edgy and frantic to get outside, she moved to the window and used the handle to roll it open. Thank the stars, it was screenless.

Taking the pouch from her pocket, she emptied the contents on the counter by the sink and held her five-inch bow and golden arrow in her left hand. Unscrewing the vial, she sprinkled half the magical dust over her head, recapped it, and set it inside the pouch. Sparkles swirled in a mini dust devil. Her body shrank, her clothing dropped under the towel rack, a glittering rose-colored gown swirled around her, wings grew from her shoulders.

It seemed odd to be fourteen-inches again. Her wings felt

awkward and oppressive. She adjusted her bow on her shoulder and held her arrow, flew out the window, and headed toward the porch. The light on the opposite end illuminated Rhett and Lori sitting on a bench. She fluttered directly above them.

"I like you," Rhett spoke in a quiet, romantic tone.

Why did his words bother Cami? *Quit being sensitive and do your job.*

She hovered, held her bow, and checked her aim.

"I like you, too." Lori scooted closer and gave him an adoring smile.

Take the shot. It'd better work this time. Cami released. The arrow hit Rhett's heart.

Yes! She'd done her duty.

Why did she feel empty inside?

Not caring to see the two kiss, she flew around the corner to the bathroom. Her hands shook as she held her human clothing, picked up the vial, and sprinkled the remaining dust over her. Her body grew. Her jean-clad legs were lean and muscular. Her pink cowgirl boots comfy.

A sense of belonging hit. Tears trailed down her cheeks. She wiped them away, thinking about how comfortable she'd become in her human body. Tiptoeing through the kitchen, she went out the door behind the laundry room, and trudged along the dirt path. Her boots stomped up the stairs.

Rhett and Lori belong together. This is a good thing. Her heart shouldn't be beating slower at the idea.

She should text the council of her success. They'd be relieved and send Cami home. Zander would pressure her to be his steady. The idea churned her stomach. Zander was like a cousin to her. After meeting Rhett, she wanted someone who could cause her body to tingle with a single glance.

Stronger and more independent now, she would explain to Zander that they were never destined to become soulmates. But that could wait. The council would contact her soon enough. No reason to expedite things yet.

Mindless entertainment was what she needed, and she clicked on the television. An old black-and-white movie played. A handsome actor kissed a beautiful woman.

Cupids assisted humans in finding love with their perfect soulmate. What about Cupids? Didn't they deserve true love?

CHAPTER 12

Rhett and Michael attended a rancher's meeting in town the following afternoon and would get dinner afterwards, leaving Cami with free time. Violet called, suggesting they shop. Cami could use a hiatus.

The council hadn't contacted her yet, but they'd most likely get ahold of her before the end of the day, thus, she left her communicator at her apartment on purpose. Why ruin her only chance to spend her salary? Instead, she shifted the strap of her pink leather purse and strutted next to her friend. Inside the Guilt City Boutique, music thumped a loud rhythmic beat.

"This store's badass," Violet said.

They passed a faceless mannequin donning a stretchy black mini-skirt. "You'd look good in that."

"Black's not my color." Cami preferred pink.

"Honestly, girl, your blonde hair goes with any color." She

fingered a crimson colored blouse on a circular clothing rack. "Everything I like clashes with auburn."

"Not green or royal blue." Cami eyed the colossal posters of voluptuous underwear models on the wall above the lingerie section. Interesting possibility.

"Michael's taking me to the movies tomorrow. Help me find a smokin' dress." Violet flipped through the size eight outfits and held up a peach colored gown with a modest neckline. "This would be cute on you." The back swooped open to the waist.

"I'm game." How would Rhett react if she wore that outfit to work? It was a moot issue since he only had eyes for Lori. Besides, Cami's job was done here. She'd be leaving soon.

Violet fished through the rack of clothes and draped a pink blouse on top of the collection on her arm. "Is it hard working for two bachelors?"

"I'm getting used to it. Michael treats me like his little sister. Did he tell you about the dishwasher fiasco?" Cami snagged a purple dress.

"No, what happened?

"I used regular dish soap." She rolled her eyes. "Pretty lame."

"I can see it now." Violet giggled. "Foot deep suds everywhere."

"And me falling on my rear." Cami had been embarrassed at the time, but now the error seemed trivial. "Michael came to my rescue, said he didn't want Rhett firing me on my first day."

"Rhett might have trust issues, but I'm sure he would've given you a chance." Violet held up a frilly white skirt. "What do you think 'bout this?"

"I like it."

Violet added the skirt to her growing stack.

"Tell me about Rhett's trust issues." Cami folded a couple blouses and several pairs of jeans over her arm to try on.

"I shouldn't."

"Come on." Cami's curiosity bloomed.

"Promise to never repeat any of this?" Worry washed through her friend's dark eyes.

"Never."

"Alright," Violet sighed. "Pinky swear."

"Sure." Whatever that meant.

Violet stuck out her little finger and looped it with Cami's.

"Rhett proposed to his girlfriend on Valentine's Day and got rejected."

"Why would she turn down a great guy like Rhett?" This amazed Cami.

"I'm not exactly sure, but I know it devastated him."

"How'd he meet her?" This might give her some insight to how his mind worked.

"At a rodeo. They dated while she stayed with her cousin. First time I saw them together was at the Boot Scoot. It's a great place to dance"

"We should go." She'd like to see where Rhett met his ex.

"You bet. We'll make it a girl's night out with Lori." Violet added another blouse to her stack. "Anyway, Rhett and Penny got serious quickly. It looked like she'd be making Cedar Springs her home." Violet's words spilled out faster than a chariot in hyper speed.

"Why'd they break up?"

"Rhett's proposal must've surprised her. In front of everyone at the dance, she said she wasn't cut out to be a rancher's wife."

"Holy Aphrodite. Didn't he see it coming?"

"Unfortunately, no. It explains why he's determined to remain a bachelor." Violet took in a deep breath. "Please don't say I told you."

"I won't. His broken heart will heal eventually."

"He seems happier since you arrive. These are getting heavy." Violet had at least a dozen outfits over her arm. "I'm going to the dressing rooms. You comin'."

"Of course." Cami followed her friend, took the second room, and secured the clothes on a hook. She stripped to her underwear and stepped into a slinky red dress. The hem barely covered her thighs, and she quickly removed it. Unzipping the back of a black dress, she slipped it on. The attached silver inlayed skirt billowed six inches above her knees.

"Tell me what you think," Violet called from outside.

Cami came out of her room.

Her friend modeled a knee-length hunter-green dress.

"That'll get Michael's attention."

"I hope so. He's taking things slow. Does he ever talk to you about his ex?"

"No." When Cami first arrived, she'd noted a fading love-light. "How long has it been since they divorced?"

"About a year. I hate being the rebound girl." Violet plunked onto a cushioned bench.

"He must like you, or he wouldn't have asked you out."

"Hope you're right. Let me see your dress." Her friend twirled her finger. "Turn around."

Cami pivoted. Her skirt belled.

"That's the one." Violet checked the price tag. "Forty dollars is a steal. You have to buy it. Wear it when we go dancing."

"Okay." She doubted that would happen. The arrow hit Rhett directly. He must be hopelessly in love with Lori by now.

And she could head back to her life in Cupid's Corner.

A MONTH INTO HER ASSIGNMENT, the council had sent a text saying Cami had only thirty days left to resolve her issue. She hadn't seen Lori and Rhett together but assumed they were head-over-heels-in-love.

Cami eased into the passenger seat of Violet's compact car. Her dress crept up, and she tugged at the bottom of her skirt to cover her knees. She looked behind her. No one sat in the back seat. "Where's Lori?" Rhett must've asked her out. Sadness pinged in Cami's heart,

"You heard Lori was accepted into vet school?"

"No, I didn't." Cami breathed in and out slowly. "Is her school nearby?"

"Colorado. She starts fall semester."

"At least she'll be here for the summer."

"That's what I thought. Then a ranch in Wyoming offered her a job. They needed her right away. Pay's too good to pass up."

Cami's pulse revved fast. *Please say Lori declined.*

"I helped Lori pack yesterday morning. She was on the road by noon."

"She's gone?" No, no, no! This couldn't be happening. She must have heard it wrong.

"Can't believe it myself. I already miss her," Violet choked out her words.

Lori must stay with Rhett and allow their romance to blossom. Panic surged through Cami's veins, her world spiraling into Hades. She had to do something to stop Lori. "What about her and Rhett?" Cami shot him with enough love potion to work on an elephant.

"They dated a few times. Nothing serious."

Holy Hogwash! Cami had to find him a different soulmate—if that were even possible.

"Let's get a drink at the Last Call Saloon. You've gotta experience the famous cowboy hangout."

Cami couldn't go to the same bar where she'd accidentally shot Rhett with her arrow. "What about dancing?" She glanced out the window and spotted the Ralphs' Shopping Center where Rhett bought her ice cream.

Violet stopped at a signal "The Boot Scoot's down the street. One or two drinks, and then we'll head there." She made a quick right into the parking lot. They pulled into the space next to a familiar truck. "Rhett's here. Wonder if Michael's with him?"

Cami pressed her lips together.

"Might as well find out." Violet held open the Last Chance Saloon's door. Cami's ears buzzed, and she struggled to breathe.

Violet uh-hummed and tapped her foot.

"Sure it's safe in there?"

"Yes."

The smoky room made Cami cough. Her friend approached a mahogany bar and slipped in between two cowboys. Men outnumbered women four to one. Wearing the stilettos she'd bought while shopping, Cami wobbled next to her friend.

Violet who leaned against the bar, asked, "White or red wine?"

"Red."

"Grab us an empty table. I'll wait for the bartender to get our drinks."

Cami spotted only one vacant table. The dreaded one where Mr. Smith sat when she made her fatal mistake. As a Cupid, the room had seemed gigantic. Now it felt cramped. She took a chair facing the bar and tapped her toes to a country western song about a spurned woman.

"I didn't expect to see you here." Rhett eased into the spot next to her, and she breathed in his musky cologne. He tipped the brim of his hat and smiled. Her heart loopty-looped. "Don't worry. I won't expect you to shag drinks for me."

"Whatever you say, boss." She saluted him.

Violet handed her a glass of wine and took the seat to her left.

"Thanks." Cami sipped her drink and checked the ceiling. Not a single Cupid in sight.

"What're you doing?" Rhett whispered. His warm breath tickled her ear.

"Seeing if the wagon wheel chandelier is secure." She crossed her legs.

"And why would you do that?"

"Why not?" She gazed into his eyes—dark, mysterious, and

focused on her. A buzz of attraction kept her from looking away.

Michael came up behind Violet. "Help me pick out songs." They went to the jukebox near the front door.

"You need to loosen up. How 'bout a game of pool—between friends?" Rhett said in a low tone.

Friends she could handle. "I'd rather play darts."

"Darts it is. Care to make a friendly wager?" His right brow rose.

Every instinct said to ignore him, but she couldn't ignore his challenge. "Ten dollars enough?"

"Winner decides." He shrugged, apparently unaware of how his nearness caused butterflies to quiver inside her stomach.

"You'll lose." Her competitive side kicked in. "Hope you're up to a week of laundry."

"Not gonna happen." He stood and offered his hand. "Best two out of three wins."

She steadied herself on her high heels, and they headed to the far corner of the poolroom.

Rhett nodded at the men playing pool. He led her to the back corner, pulled darts out of the target, handed them to her. "Ladies first." Their fingertips brushed, and a spark shot up her arm.

Not about to give him an advantage, she slipped off her shoes, set them on the floor, and eyed the target.

"You consider shoes a handicap?"

"You try wearing these stilts."

"Fair enough," he laughed. "Worried you'll lose?"

"No." She'd played darts in school. Her dad's voice echoed in her mind. "Do better than your best. Win."

"I'd ease up on my grip if I were you."

"Well, you're not me." She tuned out everything around her, kept her eye on the target, and hurled the dart. It hit dead center.

He gasped. "Beginner's luck."

"You wish. Watch and learn." She took another dart, threw it, and hit the bullseye again. One more and all three made their mark. A perfect game. "Beat that."

"You never mentioned you're a ringer?"

"And lose my edge, not on your life." She'd always competed as a champion.

He aimed and hit the red. Not in the middle.

"Is that all you've got?"

"Shh. I'm concentrating." His next shot marked the bullseye, and his lips quirked upward. "That's what I'm talking about."

"Let's see you do that again," Cami said as music crackled through the speakers. The balls on the table next to her clacked.

His dart swooshed into the white. "I'll get you next round."

The next game, she had another perfect score.

Rhett was up and shot his first dart in the yellow, two in the red. "Shit."

"You're just as competitive as I am."

"But not nearly as pretty."

"You vying for extra points?"

He put his hand on her right shoulder and winked. "Is it working?"

"Nope." She lied. Every touch he gave made her body tingle.

She took the darts from his hand and missed the center on her second shot. "You made me do that."

"Does it matter? You're way ahead of me." Rhett wore a devilish grin. "What do ya say we end this game now?"

"If you admit defeat. I won, so don't even think about getting out of doing laundry next week."

He laughed a full-on howl. "I've been underestimating you. You're a tigress when it comes to winning."

"Sweet talk won't change the terms." But his closeness made her pulse thump at warped speed.

He gave her a disarming smile. "If you hadn't distracted me, I would've won."

"You're delusional. At least you're not scowling at me."

"I don't scowl. I glower. Proves I'm in charge." He flexed his biceps.

She giggled. "You really believe that."

"I fooled you for a second." He laughed. "Where'd you learn to throw?"

"I'll never tell." She found herself flirting.

"We'll see about that."

"You done with the dart board?" A bald guy who'd been playing pool at the table next to them asked.

"Go ahead," Rhett turned to her. "The pool tables empty. Ever play before?"

"I haven't. It does look fun." She picked up her shoes and slipped them on.

He held a white ball. "I'll be happy to show you the basics."

Holy Zeus, his gaze intensified and zapped heat into her nether parts.

“Ready?” He arranged the balls inside a plastic form and lifted it off. The colorful balls stayed in a perfect triangle. “Grab a stick off the wall.”

She picked the lowest one. “This okay?”

“Yep.” He snagged his own stick from the top. “Here’s how you shoot. Hold the base with your right hand, rest the narrow end on top of your left. The object is to have the white ball hit another ball into one of the pockets.”

“It doesn’t seem hard.”

“Let me guess. You’re a pool shark, too?” His closeness made her insides quiver.

“Not even.”

Clack. He whacked the white ball. It scattered the other balls and three dropped in the holes. “If your first ball is solid, you’ll be hitting in all the solids. Your competitor has the stripes. Don’t sink the eight. That goes in last.”

She put the end of the stick behind the cue ball.

“Here, try doing it like this.” His arms went over hers. His contact created a delightful warmth as he nestled closer. She couldn’t help wiggling her bottom to see what he might do.

He groaned and took a step back.

She had his attention.

His hands guided her hand. The intimate closeness stopped her from focusing on the ball.

“Keep your head down when you take your shot.” Together they hit a ball into a side pocket.

“Go ahead. Give it a try.”

"Okay." Her hand shook as she hit the ball a bit too hard. It skipped off the table and banged into the calf of the bald guy playing darts.

"Ow!" The guy glared her way. "Who did that?"

She pointed to Rhett.

He shrugged, and said, "Sorry."

The man glared at Rhett.

A giggle slipped out.

"Pay back, huh?" Still standing behind her, he pressed his lips against her cheek. "I'm trying to resist you and failing."

"Really?" And to think he only wanted friendship.

"We've done enough damage here. Let's head to the bar." It surprised her when he took her hand and guided her into the other room. They joined Violet and Michael at the table. Rhett pulled out her chair, and she sat next to Violet.

A warm sense of belonging filled her heart.

"Rhett hustle you in pool?" Michael asked, giving her a hope-he-didn't-con-you grin.

"I beat him in darts. In fact, he's doing laundry for the next week."

"You picked the one chore Rhett despises." Michael punched Rhett's arm.

Cami sipped her wine, surprised at how much fun she was having.

"I promised Cami we'd go dancing at the Boot Scoot," Violet said.

"You still wanna go, Cami?" Michael's love-light seemed brighter than before.

"You bet."

"I'm in too, that is, if Cami promises to stay off my toes." Rhett's low timbre made her cheeks blaze.

"You're the one who left scuff marks on my new boots."

"Wasn't me." The side of his mouth quirked.

"Can I ride with you, Violet?" Michael said.

"All right."

"Then I'll take you, okay?" Rhett gazed at Cami with a lop-sided grin. The man oozed charisma.

"Fine."

"We'll meet you guys there after I finish my beer," Rhett said.

Michael and Violet strolled out the door.

"Want another drink before we go?"

Another drink and she'd float out of there. "No thanks. You trying to get out of going?"

Rhett set down his half-full beer and stood. "Not at all." He offered his hand, and they headed for his truck.

"Is the Boot Scoot where the band from your parent's party plays?"

"I think so." He opened her door.

A little buzzed from the wine, she almost looped her arms around his neck and brought her lips to his.

RHETT CLUTCHED Cami's hand as they entered the Boot Scoot and weaved her through the crowded aisle toward the dance floor. "Seems like the whole town's here tonight."

"You say something?" she shouted over the loud music.

"Said you're beautiful."

A subtle giggle escaped her lips.

At least twenty couples glided on the rectangular wooden floor. He navigated her into an empty spot. He'd been fighting his attraction to her. That wasn't working, so he decided to relax and enjoy the night. He slid his hand along her shoulder blade. When her fingers landed on his upper arm, his muscles tensed.

The fast tempo of the two-step tapped like his pulse. Her coy glances caused a jolt of desire to thrum through his veins. His large hand enveloped her smooth dainty one. "Suppose I'd better watch my toes around you."

"Not from me, boss?" she intentionally stomped on his right boot.

"You're sassy," he chuckled. For once, she'd let down her guard.

They danced forward. He spun her causing her dress to swirl and show off her shapely legs. She twirled back into his arms.

"You're a pretty good dancer."

"Why thank you, miss." They promenaded side by side and traveled counterclockwise back to their original spot. He turned her to face him and glimpsed cleavage. "Love the dress." He stepped on her toe.

"Watch where you're going."

He hauled her closer, no longer hearing the music with his heartbeat thudding in his ears. "This is more like it."

The song ended, and he released her.

"Thank you, sir," she said, slightly out of breath.

The band played "Achy Breaky Heart."

"I love this song."

"Do you now?"

They merged into the middle of the line next to Michael and Violet. Cami's short dress and high heels accentuated her toned calves. When she pivoted, wiggling her hips, her knees played peekaboo with the fabric, and he swallowed hard.

Michael nudged him. "You're in rare form."

"Suppose I am." He couldn't remember the last time he'd let loose.

Violet and Cami shouted the "Achy Breaky" lyrics along with the band's singer. Michael and Rhett burst out laughing.

The music ended.

Rhett slow danced with Cami and fought the desire swelling his jeans. He longed to taste her sweet lips on his and edged them towards the wall, stopped, and leaned down. His tongue ran along her lips, and he deepened the kiss. When she joined in, he felt like he'd found home.

The music switched to the "Electric Slide." Cami pulled away. Her moistened lips tempted him to yank her over for another kiss. "Come on. This song's calling us." She pulled him into a spot next to his brother.

His brother shouted from beside him, "You're crazy, happy today."

"Suppose I am. Feels good for a change."

An hour later, Rhett escorted Cami out to the truck. Instead of unlocking the door, he pressed her against the side and kissed her for the longest time. His heart thwacked against his chest, his pulse galloped. He didn't want to stop, but hell, they were in a parking lot. He whispered, "You are intoxicating."

IT WAS NEARLY TWO A.M., and Cami was wide awake when Rhett's truck slowed in front of her apartment.

"Had fun tonight." His sultry voice stoked embers that heated her soul.

Downplaying her attraction for him, she said, "It wasn't bad."

"You enjoyed every minute." He opened the door for her, and a blast of cool air made her shiver.

"I'll walk you to your apartment," his voice came out smooth.

They reached the stairs. "Careful." His hands gripped her shoulders as he helped her onto the veranda.

He pivoted her to face him and traced her bottom lip with his thumb. "Gorgeous."

She stood on her tiptoes and anchored her arms around his neck. A blissful sensation filled her body as he deepened the kiss. Intensity pooled in her core.

"Think we should call it a night," his tone sounded as disappointed as she felt. "Since it's late, feel free to sleep in. Get your beauty rest, not that you need it." He trailed his fingers along her arm.

Frazzled, she uttered, "Good night."

A smile quirked at the side of his mouth, and he strutted away.

She floated inside her apartment and settled on the couch. What had she been thinking? Thinking had nothing to do with what happened. She liked Rhett. She should go to bed, but her mind was amped up. A mindless TV show might cool her misguided thoughts, and she clicked on the boxy vintage set. The picture rolled and rolled and rolled. The image seemed as unbalanced as she felt, so she shut it off.

Grabbing a People Magazine from the coffee table, she flipped through the pages and tossed it aside. She thought of those sublime celebrities posing for pictures, smiling, feigning a phony, perfect life. Their free will often led them to choose the wrong person. When their relationship soured, Cupids like her assisted people with their love restorations.

Free will led Rhett to her.

She shook her head. Her *mistaken arrow* brought them together.

Five a.m., her wristband communicator flashed. So much for sleeping in.

Tapping the captain's icon, she read the message.

The council commands your presence. Immediately.

Had a Cupid on an Earthly assignment seen her kissing Rhett and reported it? She gasped. Don't be an idiot. It's unlikely the council knows anything. Take a deep breath and compose yourself. She ended up taking five before she tapped the button and ascended into the council's chambers.

Whoosh!

She landed on her feet. Her stature reduced to fourteen inches. Her nightie replaced with a glittery gown. Her wings furled back.

Since the council's table sat on an elevated platform, it forced her to look up at the members.

"Miss Calypso, thanks for arriving quickly. We believe an ingredient in the initial antidote may have been corrupted or compromised, and this is why your last arrow failed." Andre floated her a sparkling white arrow. "Use this the next time you see the two soulmates together."

"Of course, sir." She'd already hit Rhett with the extra arrow. It failed because he wasn't interested in Lori. Not that she'd tell this group.

Andre didn't dismiss her, he merely pushed a button, and she plummeted to Earth and landed in her apartment bed.

CHAPTER 13

Rhett couldn't sleep, so he shuffled into the kitchen, filled a glass with water, and guzzled it down. On the shopping list written on the whiteboard, Cami had dotted her i's with hearts.

Last night, she'd beat him at darts and teased him about losing. She danced with an abandon he hadn't seen before. Every touch inflamed his desire. Once they reached his truck in the parking lot, he'd kissed her. At her doorstep, he'd planned to make it quick, but when she'd placed her arms around his neck, he found her irresistible. If he were smart, he'd leave her alone.

Daybreak lit through the windowpane. A long ride in the fresh air should cleanse his mind. If he skipped breakfast, he could head to his favorite thinking spot. He snatched an apple, two granola bars, and a package of jerky from the counter.

Next, he filled a thermos with the coffee dregs from last night's pot. Cowboy coffee would spur his brain into a gallop.

As he headed for the stables, he refused to think about Cami, approached Starlight's stall, and stroked the star between his eyes. "Both of us could use a nice long ride, right boy?"

The stallion neighed.

Dawn's orange glow spread across the horizon. Cattle bellowed. His stallion galloped past the old barn, and he listened to horses nicker. He crossed the bridge over the Cedar Springs River and followed the shoreline as it snaked and wound through the land. He dismounted and allowed his horse to graze on a hill overlooking the valley and listened to a raven's caw.

He leaned against an old oak tree planted by his great-great-great-grandfather. The trunk's raw strength soothed his soul and made him appreciate living on the ranch. This very spot once brought him peace. He'd come here to heal after his dog was put down. He'd come here for the courage to tell his mom he'd broken her heirloom vase. He'd come here two years ago when he'd thought love between two people meant something. Penny ended that illusion.

A coyote howled to his mate. Nature did things right. Animals didn't worry about relationships. They took life as it came.

His dad's jet-black demon stallion would take patience, but once broken, he'd make a spirited ride.

Might as well head over there now.

His day was planned, organized, under control.

Cami began her day an hour later than usual. She expected to see Rhett drinking coffee on the front porch like he'd done for the past few mornings. His absence shouldn't bother her, but it caused a void in her heart. Was her own misguided attraction for Rhett blocking him from finding love?

How ridiculous. His human soulmate was out there somewhere. She pushed away the fluttering in her chest, determined to fix her mistake.

Stepping into the kitchen, she strategized as she added several ingredients into a bowl and stirred cinnamon muffins. What should she do to solve her dilemma?

She certainly wouldn't allow herself to think about last night.

The way his smile caused heartbumps all over.

The way his masculine scent made her snuggle closer.

The way his kiss heated her body.

Michael came through the door and picked up a dishtowel off the counter and swatted her.

"What's up?" She stopped mixing the batter.

"I saw you with Rhett last night." His voice a bit strained as he set the towel on the counter. "You're falling for my brother."

"No." She wiped her palms on her apron.

"If you can't be honest with me, at least be honest with yourself." His brows lifted.

"I like him as a friend." Her foot tapped.

"I've seen the way you gaze at him." He leaned back in his

chair. "Rhett's my brother. I shouldn't tell you this, but he's not up to anything serious."

"Neither am I. Don't make a big deal out of a night out dancing. You and Rhett are still my employers. I expect Rhett to continue yelling at me like he did the last time I burned toast."

"I'm not talking about him as a boss. He's gruff but fair." Michael let out a long breath. "With women, he's not so great. He'll end up hurting you like he did Lori. Like he's done to others who are looking for something serious."

"I'm stronger than you think."

"I don't doubt that. Date him. Just don't get your hopes up."

"I won't." Falling for a mortal would rip her life apart.

His phone buzzed. "Gotta run. Rhett and I will be at Dad's all day."

"What about dinner?"

"Don't' know what Rhett's planning, but I'm seeing Violet after we're done."

Cami smiled. Violet and Michael were growing closer.

The rest of the day dragged. Doing laundry, she picked up the flannel shirt Rhett wore the last night and sniffed his spicy, masculine scent. No way was she falling for him.

She slid a coffeecake into the oven, organized the pantry, rearranged the cabinets below the sink, vacuumed the living room twice, and made beef stew in a crock-pot. She glanced at her smartwatch communicator. Six p.m. Rhett's not coming. After setting the crock-pot on low, she texted Rhett about dinner and walked home.

Her communicator rang. Rhett's icon flashed, and her heart

jump-roped several turns as she swiped the green button. "If you're wondering about dinner," she spoke into the device.

"The stew was delicious. Thanks."

"What do you really want?"

"Honestly, I don't know." He hung up, leaving her more confused than ever.

A FEW DAYS LATER, Rhett sat at dinner next to Michael eating soup and charred bread.

"She's not working out," Michael said.

"What?"

"Cami."

That got Rhett's attention. "What do you mean?"

"The tension between you two is driving me crazy and affecting her work. Either ask her out or fire her." Michael shook his head.

"Nothing's going on." He'd been cordial to her.

"There lies the problem. You like her."

"I'm not ready for anything serious."

"Then don't make it that way. Take her out to dinner or go out riding. I can't take much more of your moping," Michael threw down his napkin, went to his room, and slammed the door.

Maybe he should ask her on a date. What would it hurt? The attraction was there, but that's how it started with Peggy.

Except Cami was nothing like her. He got up and entered

the kitchen. She was washing dishes with earbuds on and her ponytail bouncing.

"Hey," he tapped her on the shoulder.

"Wh-what?" She turned. "You need something, Rhett?"

"Well, it's more of a request. Would you like a riding lesson tomorrow?"

"With who?" She tilted her head and gazed at him with her gorgeous blue eyes.

"Me?"

"Why?" She her arms folded.

"Because you once said you'd like to go riding."

"I would." The corners of her mouth lifted.

"Then meet me outside the stables tomorrow at daybreak." He walked away smiling.

RHETT LOVED the solitude of early morning. He led his stallion and a mare out from the stable and tied the horses to a hitching post near the entrance.

Footsteps announced Cami's arrival, and he focused on her puffy pink coat. "Have I ever mentioned that jacket reminds me of the Michelin Man dipped in Pepto-Bismol?"

"It does not?" She giggled. "Pepto-Bismol's a darker pink."

"Always ready with a comeback, huh?"

"Pretty much." Her cheeks turned deep pink from the brisk morning. She stopped before the horse and looked into its eyes. "Hey, Buttercup, let's be friends."

The mare stood still, her ears relaxed. Cami presented her

hand, allowing the gentle animal to sniff before she scratched the horse between the ears.

"Thought you didn't know much about horses?" Greenhorns didn't know to present their scent.

"Had a pony, never a horse."

"I suppose you used an English saddle."

"Mostly rode bareback." She gazed directly at him as if expecting him to challenge her.

The word *bare* brought images of her riding naked, her long hair flowing and not braided. He snapped out of his fantasy and threaded his fingers together to boost her up. "Buttercup's a tad bigger than a pony."

As she put her foot in a stirrup and swung her right leg over, her tight jeans clung to her butt. He stifled a moan.

"Am I doing something wrong?" She smiled innocently.

"Nope." Shortening the length of her stirrups stirred him. He vaulted onto his saddle. "We'll take it slow."

They ambled along the dry wash's outer edge toward the hills. "Does this area ever fill with water?"

"Only when there's a bad storm."

"That happen often?"

"Maybe once or twice a season." The crisp air and Cami's company invigorated his soul. To the north, cows lowed in the distance. An eagle swooped toward the brush and soared off with a mouse in its talons.

"I'd hate to be that mouse."

"It's the natural order of things," he said. "Wanna go faster?"

"You bet." She kneed her mare and took off, her body attuned with the horse's gait.

He galloped to catch up to her, and they raced to the end of the wash. Strands of blonde hair escaped from her braid. He wouldn't mind unraveling the rest and running his fingers through her hair.

She slowed to a walk. "That was amazing."

"You sure are."

She blushed. "Where to?"

"Up this trail." He motioned to take the right fork.

Their horses climbed an embankment. Leaf dappled sunlight shimmered through a cluster of tall trees. A pair of ground squirrels scampered underneath a thorny bramble. The trail twisted and turned and meandered alongside the musky Cedar Springs River.

"It's awe-inspiring here," she sighed.

"My ancestors homesteaded this property. Couldn't imagine living anywhere else."

"You come to this spot often?"

"Whenever I need to think." Last night, he'd come here to ponder about Cami. "We may catch a raccoon dipping and rolling their food to wash their dinner or a goose preening himself on a flat rock close to the shore. We'll stop at that big tree to the left." He helped her down and tied the horses to a strong branch to graze.

"Was that a flying fish?" She pointed toward the water.

"Nope, probably a bass or carp." He reached for his backpack and got a blanket from his saddlebag. "As a kid, I used to count how many fish jumped out of the water. Once I got up to twenty."

"I used to count dragonflies or try to. Usually, I got

distracted and lost track."

"I can't imagine you distracted."

She winced, and he had no idea why.

Finally getting her to open up, he'd somehow blown it. "I mean that in a good way. You're efficient. And you make the best muffins in the entire state."

"That's sweet, crazy, but sweet." Her lips were mighty tempting.

Their boots crunched on gravel and twigs until they reached a grassy hill. They spread out a blanket together and sat several inches apart. From his backpack, he got out a box of Rice Krispies and a container of strawberries.

"Cereal for breakfast?" She eyed him as he filled two bowls and added milk from a water bottle.

"It's easy." He handed her a bowl and spoon.

"So I can quit making bacon and eggs?"

"No way, sugar." He fought the temptation to sample the upturned corners of her mouth.

"Look at the deer," she whispered and pointed to a mother and her two fawns drinking from the river's edge. "The fawns are precious."

He thought about saying they'd make delicious venison but nixed the idea and handed her a pink thermos from his backpack.

She unscrewed the top and poured tea into the lid cup. "You brought me tea? You're marvelous."

"What did you say?" He liked hearing admiration in her tone. Awareness zigzagged to his heart.

"Nothing."

"Stick with marvelous, and you can count on a good raise." The moment the words spilled out, he wanted to take them back.

She sipped her tea.

"What sports did you play growing up?"

"Archery."

"Just archery?" As agile as she was on a horse, he imagined her doing the splits in gymnastics class.

"Yes." She tilted her head.

"You any good?"

"Fair."

"Like you were fair at darts?" Her precision throwing impressed him. He took the bowl from her hand, placed it on the ground, pushed a wayward strand of hair behind her ear, and cupped her face. Her eyes darkened, as he pressed his mouth to hers. A shiver of need rocketed through him.

Her watch buzzed, and she pulled away. "Your brother's asking about breakfast. We'd better head back."

He flashed a grin. "Tell him he's on his own."

"I work for both of you." She didn't look at him as she packed the cereal and containers inside his backpack. He got the dishes.

Together, they folded up the blanket.

"Cami, what's bothering you?"

Her eyes teared. "There can be no us."

"Why the hell not? I feel a spark whenever you look at me." He walked her to the horses and pondered her abrupt change. He hadn't asked her out yet. He remembered the bow and arrows in the old barn. "You said you enjoy archery. Would you like to go shooting tomorrow?"

"I don't believe that's a good idea."

He moved inches from her face and breathed in her honey essence. "Please say you'll go."

"I'll think about it." At least, she hadn't flat turned him down.

CHAPTER 14

Cami glanced up at the white cumulous clouds, unable to see Cupid's Corner but knowing that was her home. Her lifestyle had been far different from this experience on Earth. On Earth, she could relax. She could make mistakes without worrying about the watchful community's eye. She didn't have to strive for perfection and tow the celestial line.

Doubts about going home lingered. Rhett and his scorching kisses jabbed at her conscience. Kissing a mortal—forbidden. She told her inner voice to shush. With only a few weeks left on Earth, there was no way she'd find Rhett another soulmate. She'd go home a failure. Well, she might as well enjoy her time here while it lasted. A spotted dove cooed as if agreeing with her.

Dressed in a sweater and Levis, she heard the gentle bubbling of the river as she walked to the house and went up the steps. Rhett waited in a wicker chair on the front porch. He tipped his Stetson and greeted her with an inviting grin. "Mornin'."

As usual, her pulse raced.

"You making muffins?" He asked, reminding her of a kitten mewing for a saucer of milk.

"We'll see."

"That blue sweater brings out your turquoise eyes."

She giggled. "Think flattery will get you extra portions?" It had, she just wouldn't tell him.

"Can't hurt to try." He whistled as he strolled toward the stables.

She focused on his derrière, and her insides quivered. She admired his broad shoulders. The man was hotter than a solar blast.

In the kitchen, she mixed pancake batter, ladled circles onto a hot griddle, and let them cook. As the strips of bacon sizzled, she scrambled eggs in a bowl, poured the liquid into a cast iron pan, and checked on her pancakes. The first batch of pancakes burned. She threw them into the trash and made more. Her concentration was in chaos.

Somehow, she managed to make breakfast.

Thirty minutes later, she brought out Rhett and Michael's food.

"Smells delicious." Rhett locked eyes with her.

Jittery, she looked away and sensed him watching. She stole a glance at him but resisted the desire to run her fingers along his arm.

"Sit with us, Cami." Michael motioned to a chair on the end.

She lowered herself into the seat.

"You've more than proved yourself for over a month now," Michael said.

"We'd like to keep you on permanently," Rhett tone crooned low and husky. "With a fifty dollar a week raise."

"Sounds great." The job would be perfect if she were human. Her moral compass wanted to tell them she'd leave soon, but her head said to keep quiet.

Michael jumped up. "Anyone else want milk?"

"No thanks." Rhett grasped her hand.

The heated room and his sweltering glances made it hard to concentrate. Her lips were dry, her breath caught, she swallowed.

"What do you think of our offer?" Rhett's smile could tempt a saint.

"It's good." If only she could stay.

"We'd offer double that if we could." He took her hand. "You're incredible, you know."

Money had never been the issue.

"Check out what I found." He slid out a long leather case from under his seat and handed it to her.

She placed the case across her lap and unzipped it. Four arrows secured with straps on one side and a bow on the other. Her heart expanded with happiness. She took out the bow and fingered the maple wood. "Exquisite. Is it handmade?"

"I believe my grandfather used his wood-working skills." His grin widened.

She strung it and pulled. “It’s in perfect shape.”

“You never gave me an answer yesterday. Would you like to go shooting?”

“And if I say, yes?” She couldn’t help smiling.

“Can’t promise I won’t kiss you again.”

Her lips tingled at the thought.

“You up for an official date?”

“Sure.” She practically skipped toward the kitchen door.

THAT AFTERNOON, Rhett glanced sideways at Cami seated next to him in his truck. Turning the key, the truck sputtered. “Come on, baby.” His nerves jangled like the keys on the chain.

“What’s the problem?”

“Old Red’s a being temperamental.” He tapped the gas pedal and jiggled the ignition. The engine chortled, grumbled, and vroomed. He accelerated forward onto the unpaved road.

“Quite a ritual you’ve got there.”

He couldn’t tell by her tone if she was impressed or appalled.

“You said your grandfather gave you the truck. I don't recall meeting him.”

“He passed away ’bout ten years ago.” His grandfather’s death left a void inside Rhett. “We were close. Granddad taught me to ride.”

“I bet he’d be pleased you’re still driving his truck.” Her eyes shimmered.

"Probably thinks I'm a fool for not borrowing Michael's to take you out."

He took the fork to the right, drove for a couple of miles past the old barn, and parked in the dirt. After snagging the archery bag from behind the seat, he met up with Cami by the front bumper and took her hand. "The range's this way."

They trekked to a field behind the barn. Earlier, right after breakfast, he'd stacked three bales of hay so the afternoon sunlight would be at their back. Empty beer bottles and a couple of tin cans lined the haystack's top. He'd found a leftover poster from the barn dance in his room and decided to tack the paper to the front of the stacked bales.

"You set this up for me?" Her eyes got soft and glittery.

"Yep." He wanted to impress her. "You're up first."

"Are we making this a competition?"

"Nope. Already know you'll win."

Her turquoise eyes sparkled brighter.

"Wanna try to nail the Cupid?" A solid black shape silhouetted against a red heart.

"Got something against Cupids?" Her tone sounded tense, and he wondered why.

"Not at all." He had nothing against Cupids specifically. He despised Valentine's Day and the whole lovey-dovey theme. "Best thing I could find on short notice."

"You don't believe in things you can't see?"

"Reckon I don't." Unlike his brother's fascination with UFO's, he'd wasn't into anything supernatural.

"You've never questioned what else might be in this universe?" Her hand went to her hip.

"Seems like a waste of good pondering. Don't tell me you're into that stuff?"

"As a matter of fact, yes." She eyed the poster, picked up the bag, and took out the bow and quiver. "How many points for hitting the tip of the Cupid's arrow?"

"A hundred. Five for anywhere on the poster."

Releasing her arrow, it sailed into its mark. "Got it."

His mouth fell open, and he snapped his jaw shut. "Wow, you're good."

"Thanks." She scrunched her brows together. "If I hit the next two, you'll have to promise to listen to me with an open mind."

"Thought I already was."

"Not exactly." Her lips pursed for some odd reason. "What's next?"

"The third bottle. The green one."

Her arrow hit the center and knocked the bottle over the back of the haystacks.

"Where'd you learn to shoot like this?" He'd never seen anything this remarkable.

"My father taught me." She flipped her braid behind her. "Do you believe in angels?"

"Hard to believe in something you can't see."

"What about Cupids?"

"Nope."

She looked up at the sky as if she'd find the words written up there. "What if I told you I am a Cupid?"

"Oh really." He stared at her stone-cold-serious expression. This was weird.

She turned her wrist up to him. "My heart emblem's proof."

"Lots of people have tattoos." He couldn't resist adding, "Bet you've got a butterfly on your butt."

"Rhett, you're not listening."

"Not a butterfly, then maybe a dragon." He teased, while he pictured her firm butt.

"I don't have a tattoo on my bottom." Unconsciously, she licked her top lip as she stood. Mighty enticing. "You don't believe me?"

"Be whatever makes you happy." He imagined her wearing a sexy Cupid costume. Cupid or not, he liked her.

"I give up." Her eyes miffed, her stance rigid, she secured the last arrow in place.

"Think you can hit the dot above the *i* in Valentine's?"

"Cherub's play." In seconds the arrow's tip wedged into the dot. She went to the target and removed the arrows, handed him the bow. "Let's see how you do?"

"As if I can match your flawless performance." Losing usually bugged him, but he didn't mind being bested by her. "What's my target?"

"I'll be generous and give you a hundred points for the Cupid's wing. Anywhere on the poster for five."

He aimed, released, and his arrow sailed over the top. "Shit. I could use a few pointers."

"Aim. Watch the arrow until it hits the target."

"Care to show me?" He anticipated her instructive arms around him.

"You're a big boy." Her slight pout made him think about kissing her enticing lips. "Figure it out for yourself."

"Where's the fun in that?"

"Take your turn or forfeit." She had that get-serious stance, the one where her hand cemented on her hip.

"Fine." He concentrated and hit the bottom of the poster.

"That's a little better."

He shot again, and his arrow hit a can that twirled behind the haystack. "That one's worthy of a kiss."

"You only hit one out of three."

He followed her to the target. They each removed an arrow. Reaching for the third arrow as she did, his hand covered hers. "You're quite a marksman." He admired her competitive spirit, turned to face her, and leaned in for a kiss, teasing her lips with his tongue. Temptation at its finest.

She splayed her hands against his chest and pushed back, her face flushed, her lips moist. "Are you going to take your turn?"

"I'd rather watch you shoot."

"If that's what you want."

He wanted her in his arms but kept the comment to himself and walked next to her at the shooting line. In seconds, all three arrows sailed inside different hearts on the poster.

"You're talented." He assisted her with retrieving the arrows. "Ever try out for the Olympics?"

Her smile waned. "I'm okay. I've competed against better archers."

"Are you kidding? You're phenomenal." He yanked her into his arms. Her body melted against his. When his lips grazed hers, she sighed his name, and he deepened their kiss. He got lost in the sheer pleasure as they kissed until she pulled back.

Her face flushed, her lips reddened. "Let's go back. I need to get started on dinner."

He couldn't fault her for being a competent housekeeper. Her tenacity was one of the reasons she drew him in, but her timing was plain awful.

CHAPTER 15

Dawn broke the darkness as it cast a rosy glow across the land. Rhett swigged coffee and listened for Cami's boot steps. He spotted her golden hair several yards away.

"Hello," she smiled with the kind of smile that made him happy deep inside his heart.

"I've got a surprise for you in the house."

"Really?" She raced inside.

"It's the package on the table."

She tore open the box like a kid on Christmas morning. Her eyes glimmered as she pressed the long-sleeved shirt against her chest. "A Silver Wings jersey. You're the best." She snaked her arms around his neck practically choking him.

"Glad you like it." He peeled off her hold on him. "Look at the back."

"Calypso! It has my name and number 39. I love it," she

squealed and slipped the jersey over her T-shirt. It fit loose. "You are the nicest human ever."

"Human? As opposed to what?" He couldn't resist teasing.

"Let me refrain. You're the best guy in the galaxy." She snuggled closer to him.

"I aim to please." He took out an envelope from his jeans' pocket and placed the two tickets in her palm.

"We're going to a hockey game tomorrow night! I can't believe it." She spoke unusually fast.

"You missed this." He reached inside the package, yanked out a cap, and placed it on her head.

"You went all out."

"I like making you happy." He surprised himself. With most women, he dreaded buying them gifts. Most women wanted expensive jewelry, not sports gear.

"Where's the Seismic Center?"

"Couple of hours drive depending on traffic. Since the game ends late, I've booked us a hotel room."

Her shoulders stiffened, and her eyes widened.

"You'll have your own room."

She looked toward the fireplace, not him.

He tugged on her hat's bill. "Might want to rethink the jersey. We're sitting on the home team's side. Everyone'll be wearing purple."

"Switching teams would be blasphemy. I've been a Silver Wings fan since I was ten." She kissed his cheek. "I'm wearing this shirt every day for the next week."

"Without washing it?"

"And take the newness out of the fabric?"

"Do what you want," he chuckled. "I'm rooting for the Seismics."

"You must love losing because the Silver Wings will win." She stood. "I'll make breakfast."

"Breakfast can wait." He seized her hand and brought her back on his lap, taking advantage that no one was around.

ABOUT FIVE THE NEXT EVENING, Cami and Rhett entered the Seismic's Center through one of the dozens of glass doors. She gripped Rhett's arm tightly, not about to be separated from him as the crowd's momentum pushed them forward.

"You all right," he asked, and led her to the left.

"I can't believe I'll see a Silver Wings game live." She gawked at a mural of a Seismic player slamming a goal into a net. Simply amazing.

"I forgot how awesome this place is." His arm went around her shoulders. The gesture gave her a sense of security and made her feel cherished.

"I'm starving. Pizza okay?" He took off his Seismic's cap and eyed her.

Without a doubt, she was falling for him. This was bad. Very bad. Forbidden. "Sure. Make mine half veggie."

Throngs of people paraded, fascinating her as she stood next to him in line. Families passed by in matching purple jerseys. An older man draped his arm around a much younger woman. Complexions varied from dark to light pink with freckles.

"Hey, pretty girl."

A chill crept up her spine. The man's voice sounded like her uncle speaking. She turned slowly and saw a man tugging on a three-year-old's pigtails.

Relieved, her pulse still ticked fast. She shouldn't be here with Rhett. Too late now.

"Here you go." He handed her a soda, held the box, and placed his beer on top. "

She glanced at the handsome man beside her. *Forget the mistaken voice and enjoy this marvelous night. Nothing bad will happen.*

"We're in the Terrace Center." They followed the arrow on the wall and stopped at the four-hundred section. The usher checked their tickets and pointed them to the front row.

Seeing the steep steps, she grasped the rail and clung on until they reached their row. Two women stood and let them pass by. One eyed Rhett's good looks, and Cami couldn't deny feeling proud to be his date.

She took her seat, sipped soda, licked her lips, and caught Rhett staring at her. His knee pushed against hers as he opened the pizza box. "Take a piece."

"I love it here. Thanks for the tickets." No one had ever done anything this thoughtful for her without another motive. As a little girl, her father took her out of town to watch an archery championship. At the time, she thought it was because she'd been really good. In actuality, he'd taken her to the meet to show her his future expectations. *This* trip was about her interests.

Rhett's free hand moved behind her chair.

The enormous screen zoomed in on a man smoothing out the ice with his machine. "I Want to Drive the Zamboni" drifted throughout the speakers. Folks sang along, herself and Rhett included. Rhett was a tinge off key, showing imperfection—her favorite new word.

The Silver Wings skated onto the rink. The announcer called out each player. His picture, number, and position flashed on the top of the screen. Then he called, "Playing center, number eighty-five, Vic Vanrazzo."

Excitement buzzed through her veins. "You're the best," she shouted at the player who'd been her crush for over a decade. When he skated, the dark-haired man owned the ice. His ability to maneuver around the opponent and steal the puck. Extraordinary.

The players placed their helmets over their hearts for the National Anthem. The singer blasted out the song, a little too operatic for Cami's taste.

The team captains shook hands signaling the game was about to begin. Cami held her breath and sent positive vibes to her team.

The referee dropped the puck, and the purple team snagged it.

"Don't let that idiot pass," she shouted, "take it back."

During an assist, Vanrazzo stole the puck. "That's it. Now go for the goal." Cami chewed her nails. Vanrazzo passed to Drayton. The Seismics kidnapped the puck.

"Good steal," Rhett said.

"Bite your tongue," she snapped and kept her eyes fixed on the game.

"The Silver Wings are down for the count." He put his arm around her shoulders, but she shook it off and stood.

"No, they're not. Bardoff will get the puck. See. He's close."

Smith passed the puck to his teammate. Rhett's laugh aggravated her. Then Bardoff stole it, preventing the Seismics from taking advantage of the play.

"Told you." She watched Bardoff bring the puck down the rink. "Yes," she yelled, "You're clear. Shoot!"

The puck crossed the goal line between the two posts.

Lights flashed. Many in the crowd moaned. She cheered, elated to see her team ahead.

"That's the last point the Silver Wings will get," Rhett snarled.

"You're deranged." She laughed, or more like hooted. "Now quiet down, I'm watching the game."

"Can't. The kiss cam's on us." Rhett leaned over. Their lips smacked as he heisted a kiss and savored her mouth. She forgot about the game until she heard the crowd's applause.

"Cami, look." He motioned to the monitor. The camera closed in on her and Rhett. A heart formed around the two of them. Their kiss replayed on every screen in the arena.

Her face heated, but she couldn't quit watching. The camera focused on Rhett as he glanced up. His smile broadened, and, my gosh, he was handsome. On the screen, she saw how he gently tapped her arm. His lips touched hers. It was as if she were watching a romantic movie, except it was one with her and Rhett. Her core tingled.

Wait, the video feed was public. Apprehension crept up her spine. Would the council see the video of Rhett kissing her? Not likely anyone in Cupid's Corner would be watching this hockey game. If they did, they'd assume she was a mortal. That didn't stop her stomach from twisting.

She concentrated on the game and found herself biting her lip as the opponent stole the puck.

"Go for a goal, Manny," Rhett screamed, "yes!"

"Accidental, if you ask me." She grumbled as the Seismics scored again.

"Now who's deranged." He leaned over and kissed her cheek.

"Hush. The Silver Wings will win." They had to win, but once again Rhett's team had possession, took the puck to the goal and shot.

The Silver Wings goalie blocked it. Cami gloated, "Thought your team would score, huh?"

"They will." He squeezed her hand.

"Hand holding won't save your sainted Seismics." She jerked away.

Darn Rhett for laughing. "Now about that wager?"

"Shh. Watch the game." She heard cheers, checked the screen. "Vanrazzo scored, and I missed it."

The game continued. Bardoff elbowed Smith and slammed him into the wall. Vanrazzo stole the puck. Smith and Bardoff swung fists. The referee blew his whistle. "Double-minor for unnecessary roughness. Seismics have possession."

"Unfair!" she shouted. "Smith elbowed first."

"Calm down," Rhett taunted in a slow drawl. "The referee's just doing his job."

"He's blind." She pinched her lips together, irritated he'd side with the idiotic official.

"No, he's not" Rhett chuckled, and she slapped his arm.

For the next hour, they bantered and watched the game until the end.

"Told you we'd win. I almost feel sorry for you." Cami had been on the losing end plenty of times.

"The Seismics will be the victor next time. I'll order tickets."

"You're not upset?" Most males hated losing.

"Maybe a little. Kiss me and make me feel better." His mouth pressed against hers. "Let's blow out of here." He offered his hand and helped her up, leaving her lips woefully disappointed.

CHAPTER 16

Well after eleven, Rhett guided Cami across the hotel lobby. She stopped in front of a three-tiered fountain and gazed into the water. "What's with all the coins?"

"People make wishes. Haven't you ever tossed a coin in one?"

"No." Curious she scooted closer. "What did they wish for?"

"Don't know? Money, health, love." He reached into his pocket and handed her a few quarters. "Have at it."

She held the coin, closed her eyes, and tossed a quarter toward the center. "Will my wish come true?"

"I'd like to think so."

"Then you must make your own." She gave him a coin.

"Not a bad idea." He flicked the quarter between his thumb and forefinger, and it sailed into the middle section.

"What'd you wish for?"

"If I tell, it won't be granted." Like he'd mention wishing they'd share a room. "You have any quarters left?"

"I'm done." She wore a satisfied smile.

"Check-ins over here." He put his hand on her shoulder and steered her several yards forward to the counter.

The desk clerk pushed up his thick black glasses and called Rhett.

"I have a reservation for two rooms," Rhett said, "would prefer connecting ones."

"We're pretty full. The best I can do is two floors apart." The young clerk typed on his keyboard. "Interesting." He clicked more keys and looked up grinning, "Since you're a premium member, for no extra charge we could upgrade you to a penthouse with two separate bedrooms. It's spacious, has a great view of the city."

"You game?" Rhett asked.

"Okay."

"The elevator's to your right." He handed Rhett two room keys.

As they walked, Rhett asked, "Ever stay in a suite before?"

"Can't say I have." The elevator dinged, and the door opened. She hesitated.

"You change your mind?"

"No." She stepped inside, and he pushed number twenty-four.

The compartment jerked upward, and she fell into him.

"Careful." Wrapping his arms around her waist, he appreciated how her body melded against his. The elevator climbed, stopped at the floor, and dinged open. Holding hands, they looked at the numbers on the wall.

"2415 is to the left," he said, and they roamed the long hallway to the far end.

"This is us." He put the key in the door. His wish came true. Figuratively, they'd share a room.

"Holy Aphrodite. This is fancy." She barreled inside and gazed out the floor length windows. "You've gotta see this view. We're practically up in the clouds."

He snagged his arms around her waist; his mouth teased her neck. A knock interrupted him.

"Room service," a voice called.

He snuggled before letting go and answered the door. A concierge rolled in a cart. "Compliments of the hotel. Where do you want this?"

"What do you think?" He asked Cami, now perched on the white leather couch.

She waved her slender fingers to the coffee table. "Here's fine."

"Would you like this bottle opened?" the man asked.

Rhett nodded, and the concierge poured two glasses. "Anything else I can get you?"

"No thanks." Rhett tipped the man ten dollars and the door shut. He handed her a fluted glass and took one for himself.

"Mine says, '*his*.'" She pointed to the flowery lettering a few inches from the rim.

"So it does." His fingers grazed hers as they switched glasses. "Must have gotten the honeymoon suite's set." He stared at her crossed legs and noticed her bare feet. He'd never thought feet were sexy, but by God, she wore pink toenail polish with red hearts. "To an enjoyable night, even if the Silver Wings won." He clicked her glass.

"You mean the right team." She sipped champagne.

"You aiming for a fight?"

"Maybe?" She giggled. "Try some strawberries." Two red slices dropped into his glass, berries the same color as her mouth.

He took a sip. "Delicious." Yearnings were strong as he delved his fingertips through her thick hair at the back of her neck. "You're gorgeous." He fluttered kisses along her neck, caressed his way to her chin, and flicked his tongue to indulge in her scrumptious lips. Angling his mouth over hers. Fire erupted through his body, fire that only she could quench. It took effort to pull back and not press her further. "You taste like champagne." He filled her glass and brought it to her lips.

A yawn followed, and she glanced at her watch. "It's midnight."

"Yep." He didn't want to end their night yet but let her make the call.

"Thanks for taking me to the game."

"Was my pleasure." His heart did a happy trot, and he pushed a wayward lock of her hair behind her ear. His fingertips traced her jawline, he softly kissed her.

She yawned, stretching her arms above her head. "I'm going to bed."

"Stay, please."

"And fall asleep on the rigid couch when a plush mattress

calls? Thanks for giving me my best day ever." She kissed his cheek and rose.

Arguments were pointless. "You're welcome. Sleep all morning if you want. Check-out is not 'till eleven."

"Sounds heavenly." She sauntered to her room, with every sway he prayed for an invitation to join her. She shut her door.

That was it.

No way could he sleep right now. He got his bag, went into the bathroom, and stepped into the shower. Imagining Cami with water cascading down her body, he switched the water to cold, rinsed off, dressed in a pair of flannel pants and a T-shirt.

Wide-awake, he went to the couch and clicked the remote to an old western. Gunfire ricocheted. A man tumbled from the top of the building. Bullets hit a water trough and streams jetted out. Gotta love a wild west shootout.

When the movie ended, he flipped to the sports channel. Highlights of the hockey game came on. He thought about Cami. She challenged him to enjoy little things.

He switched the channel, heard a woman's voice whimpering, and figured it came from the movie. The wall clock said it was one-fifteen. Might as well head for bed.

As he walked past her door, he found it ajar and heard her whimpering, "No, please." She must be having a bad dream.

He knocked, and she mumbled words he couldn't comprehend. Not sure what to do, he waited in her doorway.

"Don't make me go in there," she said as her arms thrashed.

At least it wasn't a bad dream about him. He sat on the bed next to her and said gently. "Cami, wake up."

"It's dark. So dark. I'm scared," she mumbled.

"Cami, it's alright. Wake up. You're dreaming."

"W-what?" Her eyes fluttered open. "Rhett, what are you doing in here?"

"You were talking in your sleep." To alleviate the darkness, he switched the light on the nightstand and gazed at her.

She grasped the white sheet covering her body "I was?"

"Wanna tell me your dream? It might help you settle down."

"It's silly." Her hands trembled slightly.

"Dreams rarely make sense. It's your brain trying to sift through your problems." He lowered into the edge and angled his body to face her "As a kid I dreamed I saw a kitten transform into a gargantuan tiger. For the next month, I freaked whenever I heard a meow."

"And what anxiety were you suffering from?"

"Too many Garfield cartoons," he said with a laugh. "Haven't had that dream since I was ten, but the thought of that terrifying cat's fangs still makes me shudder."

"You're funny." She sat up and fluffed the pillow behind her.

"So what frightened you?"

She let out a long sigh. "You sure you want to hear this?"

"Yes." He wanted her to open up to him.

"Well, I was being chased by a big guy who caught me and locked me in his dungeon?" She shivered.

"I once had a dream I was in a cellar full of rats."

"No rats, but it was cold and dark and scary. It seemed so real."

"Dreams usually do." He had his share of nightmares.

"You woke me before my dream got worse." Her fingers ran up his arm. Her touch kindled fire through his muscles.

"Thanks." She brought her mouth to his lips, still tasting like champagne.

It'd be easy to take advantage of the situation but being honorable, he said, "I better head for bed."

"I want you to stay." Her voice a velvet whisper as she eased down the sheet and motioned to the pillow. She wore a flannel nightgown, her breasts outlined by the light, and he stifled a groan.

"If you're sure." He lay next to her on his side.

"Kiss me, please?"

"Thought you'd never ask." He caressed the pulse spot on her neck, her chin, and nibbled on her lips. She opened her mouth, and he enjoyed deepening their kiss.

His hand stroked her arm, and he ran his fingertips along her covered breast and cupped them, while she slipped her hands underneath his T-shirt. Heated, he stopped kissing her and yanked his shirt off. Grateful the lights were on, he could see the passion in her eyes. "Now, where were we?" Instead of starting with her lips, he feathered kisses down her neck and unbuttoned the front of her nightgown to expose her breasts. He rubbed his finger and thumb over a pink nipple and watched it harden. "You like that?" He couldn't resist tonguing the areola and took it into his mouth.

She ran her nails across his back while emitting tiny, enticing sounds. He let go of her breast and brought his mouth to hers, savoring her sweet taste. Her fingertips tickled his upper back; his muscles twitched. She circled his nipple, copying the action of his thumb and forefinger.

He inched up her nightgown, his hand explored her flat

belly. His fingers massaged her outer thigh, and he traced her mound with his fingertips. Her pleased moan about undid him. He pressed her knees apart, tentatively dipped his finger inside her core and found her wet. He eased out and moved back in. She was tight. He continued toying with her core, while his thumb massaged her clit. Her eyes remained closed, as she whimpered, "Oh, Rhett."

"I like it when you say my name." He kept the motion, enjoying her response. Winding her tension tighter. He withdrew his fingers, bringing her to the brink of release.

"Please ... don't ... stop," she said, breathless.

He continued touching her. She spiraled higher and higher, until she climaxed, feeling her rippling tremors, and staying still while watching her body relax. He bunched up her nightgown. She raised it over her head, while he caressed her body with his eyes. They kissed, his fingers traced her waist and butt, and she lifted the elastic on his boxers. When her hand touched his manhood, a low growl erupted from him.

"I want you," she gave a desperate sigh.

He framed her face with his hands and kissed her cheek. "Be right back." He sprinted into the other bedroom, shaking as he grabbed a handful of condoms out of his bag, ran in panting, hoping, and praying in his absence that she wouldn't change her mind. Shedding his boxers, his hands shook as he rolled the latex over his erection. In the dimmed light, he saw her eyes glisten. "You sure?"

"Yes." Her voice low and breathy.

He parted her legs, positioned himself at her entrance, and looked at her face. Her eyes gazed at him with desire. His cock said to take her fast, but his mind told him to go slow, inching inside her womanly folds. He delighted in her tightness against his shaft … until he thrust through a slight resistance, and she whimpered.

"Why didn't you tell me?" He stilled. Rhett didn't do virgins. She hadn't seemed experienced or worldly, but dammit, she was over twenty. What woman her age hadn't slept with at least one boyfriend? He tried to pull out, but she wrapped her legs around his hips.

"It doesn't matter, not anymore," she spoke with a velvet whisper, "make love to me, cowboy."

He rolled her on top. "You set the pace."

She rode him tortuously slow. He pushed up with his hips, increasing their contact. It felt so damn perfect.

"My turn." He flipped her, entered her slowly, and gradually accelerated to a faster thrust.

Her insides bucked and buckled and quivered, "Rhett, yes, Rhett." Her exploding momentum caused his own climax.

When his breathing slowed, he rolled onto his side. "That was—"

"Wonderful," her voice like sugarcoated silk.

"I didn't hurt you, I mean, except at first?" He'd been rough. If he had known about her innocence, he would have been gentler. If he had known, he wouldn't have slept with her. There was no going back. If he were honest, he liked being her first lover.

"Hurt? What you did was extraordinary."

"I agree." He brought her hand to his mouth and kissed it.

Now that he had a taste of her, he wanted more.

CHAPTER 17

Cami woke to a heated grip surrounding her waist. Rhett held her in place, and she breathed in his manly scent. His length pressed along her backside sending a quiver of desire straight to her core.

What had she done?

Shooting stars, she'd slept with him. Her heart tripped. Cupids were not to become involved physically with humans. Still, she wondered why? She recalled hearing whispers about a Cupid who fell in love with a mortal and was banished to Earth for the remainder of her life. Could she handle that?

She wasn't sure.

She'd been taught to follow rules. Guilt had her mentally berating herself for sleeping with him. How had that happened?

Last night in her dream, she'd been thrown into a shadowy, blackened dungeon. The darkness scared her. Rhett came to her rescue. His eyes glimmered as he enfolded her into his arms, keeping her safe. It seemed natural for them to make love.

Except, he'd never been hers for the taking. She needed to get up, move, and wiggle out of his grasp.

He nuzzled her neck and emitted a pleasurable, "Mmm—"

How she longed to run her fingers through his tussled hair and pull his mouth to hers and make love with him all morning. That would be wrong, wrong, wrong. She unclasped his fingers and sat up.

"Mornin'," his voice came out smooth and enchanting. Everything about Rhett was smooth and enchanting.

"Hey. I'll be right back." She had to get away. Naked, she ran to the bathroom and leaned against the door. Her chest tightened, and her pulse sped. She'd had sex with Rhett and would forever savor the experience. She'd failed her job, failed to set him up with his soulmate. Instead, she'd slept with him.

What if the council finds out?

She slowed her breathing. Who would tell them? Certainly not her.

At the sink, she washed her face and stared at her reddened lips, the whisker burns on her body, a reminder of her night of passion. She'd given him her innocence.

The shower in front of her couldn't wash away her problems, but it might soothe her sore muscles. She stepped inside and allowed the warm water to flow over her. As she soaped her breasts, she imagined Rhett's calloused thumbs massaging her nipples. *Knock it off.* As much as she enjoyed being intimate with him, it had to be a one-time event.

Shame threaded through her worried mind. What would

happen when he saw the real her? She imagined the raw and vulnerable hurt on his face. She'd not only blown it for herself, she'd decimated his future.

Encased in a soft white towel, she went into her room. Rhett no longer slept in her bed although the rumpled bedsheets reminded her of their wondrous night. Deep in her heart, she wouldn't mind being his soulmate, but a massive obstacle stood between them—he was a mortal and she a Cupid.

Their love could not last an eternity.

RHETT STOOD in the doorway holding a cup of coffee in one hand and tea in the other. Cami perched on the edge of the bed combing out her wet hair. Wrapped only in a towel, her slender legs were in full view. He swallowed, and his cock stiffened against his boxer shorts. He wanted her.

She wasn't smiling, seemed pensive.

"Made you tea." He set both cups on the end table next to her and leaned over to kiss her cheek. "You okay."

"I'm fine." She wouldn't even look at him.

"You sorry about last night?" He sat on the bed and eased his arm around her.

She stiffened. "No. Yes. I don't know." Confusion showed in her wide eyes. She failed to give an inkling of a smile. Last night, she'd begged him to stay.

Sweet-talk didn't come naturally. With no idea what thoughts floated through her head, he remained motionless. What did she want to hear? Probably best to leave her alone.

"Think you could order breakfast for us while I shower? There's a menu by the phone."

"Sure," she said, her tone flat.

"Bacon and eggs for me. Thanks." He walked out baffled and somewhat dejected.

He stepped into the shower. What the hell just happened? Making love had been awesome, or at least it had been for him. But it'd been her first time, and he should have been gentler. Guilt coursed through his mind.

Dammit, he wanted to fix this thing. Not that he'd offer marriage. It was too soon to think about forever. But hell, he wouldn't mind making her his girlfriend and see where it went from there. Could be that's what bothered her. With women, it's hard to tell. Flowers might make her feel better. In this case, flowers would seem like an apology. He wasn't the least bit sorry they made love.

She'd been thrilled with the hat and jersey. That should've said he liked her plenty. He dressed, walked into the hotel's living room with hardly a clue what to expect, and took the barstool to her left.

She had changed into jeans and a black T-shirt and was reading the hotel magazine's featured article on the Disneyland Resort.

"I haven't been to Disneyland in years. Love Space Mountain."

"Never been," she said in a quiet mouse-like voice.

"Really? Then I'll have to take you. It's only a few hours south of here."

She shrugged and seemed distant.

"Come on, it's Disneyland. What if I promise to take you on *It's a Small World*?" He laughed. "The girly ride kinda blows my macho image, but for you, I'd be willing to sacrifice."

"Aren't you generous?" A slight giggle escaped. It was a start.

A knock rapped twice.

"I'll get it." Rhett opened the door.

The concierge pushed in a cart. He placed a cup in front of Cami. "Coffee, miss, or would you prefer tea?"

"Tea, please." He poured hot water into her porcelain cup, and she added a White Peony teabag.

He picked up the silver covering, handed her fruit and yogurt, and Rhett a plate with bacon and eggs.

"That will be all. Thanks." Rhett tipped the man. As Rhett walked back to his barstool, he ran his hand along her arm.

She dipped a strawberry in a dish of whipped cream without acknowledging him.

If only he had the words to break the coolness between them. Coolness? A freaking iceberg had developed. "Check-out's not for several hours. I know you didn't get much sleep last night so feel free to go back to bed." He'd leave it up to her. Maybe if she slept, her spunky attitude would return.

"I'd rather head home. Nap in your truck if that's okay."

"Fine." He didn't torment himself and watch, knowing her seductive hips would swing as she headed for her room. He finished eating, grabbed his things, and met her by the door.

"Ready?"

"Yes." She focused on her pink bag.

They stepped inside the elevator. "I don't want things to be awkward when we get back."

"Don't worry," she said, fidgeting with the strap on her bag.

"Dammit. That's not what I meant." He combed his fingers through his hair and cracked his knuckles. "I didn't plan on last night. But it happened."

Her complete silence had him on edge.

The elevator stopped.

"Cami, look at me," he said tenderly. "This was your first time."

The door opened and a family came inside.

Damn luck.

EXASPERATION FUELED Rhett's drive home. Cami slept for most of the way. When she finally stirred, he said, "What can I do to make things right?"

"I'm fine, really, just overly tired."

About noon, Rhett stopped in front of the ranch. "Come to the house tonight. I'll order dinner."

"It's my night off. How 'bout a raincheck?"

"If you change your mind, you know how to find me." He hated how she pulled away.

"See you soon." She bounded out of the truck and sprinted for her apartment.

Yesterday had been fantastic. Making love with her phenomenal. She had him wound up. Worn out mentally and physically, he headed straight for his room and slept. Didn't wake until about six hours later. He figured sleep would get him out of the funk he'd had earlier, but a restless unease about his future with Cami flustered his thoughts.

He walked into the kitchen, snagged a longneck from the fridge, and took a swig. The brew went down cold and refreshing.

The kitchen looked cleaner. The counter seemed whiter. The floor spotless. Cami had only been here nearly two months, and her imprints were everywhere.

He plunked into a spot on the couch.

"How was the game?" Michael came from his room.

"Cami's team won."

"Tell me you didn't get pissed off?"

"Of course not." The fact that he asked aggravated Rhett.

His brother stood. "I'm gonna get a beer. Want another?"

"Sure." Rhett figured he'd have several before the night ended.

Michael handed him a bottle. "Ain't none of my business, but … you don't seem happy? Wanna talk about it?"

"Hell, no." Rhett flipped on the TV and feigned interest in a cereal commercial.

"You and Cami fight?"

"Not really. She got quiet. Refused to talk." When women did that, it got his temper blistering.

"That's never good. What'd you do?"

"Slept with her."

"And that's a bad thing?"

"I didn't think so. This morning, well, she acted different." Guilt hit him smack in the middle of his chest.

"Women get funny after sex."

"You can say that again." Rhett refused to admit she was a … virgin. Hell, he still had trouble wrapping his brain around it. "I'm used to being a bachelor, but with Cami, I don't know what I want."

"I've learned to take each day as it comes." Michael grabbed the remote and switched to a basketball game.

Rhett's growling stomach reminded him he hadn't eaten since breakfast. "Got any ideas for supper?"

"Ordered Chinese. Violet's coming over."

"You two serious?"

"Just dating." A smile tugged at his brother's lips.

"In that case, I'll get something in town." He'd head over to the Last Call.

"You don't have to leave." The doorbell rang. "Must be dinner. I'll get it."

Violet came in with a six-pack of beer. "Hope you don't mind I brought a friend."

Cami cast Rhett a veiled glance. She walked toward the kitchen holding two bottles of champagne and swaying her hips. Her black sweater emphasized her tiny waist. Part of him thought to join her in the other room, but his pride said to wait. Let her make the first move.

Violet whispered to Michael, "Help Cami open the bottle," and he disappeared into the kitchen.

"I insisted she come." Violet lifted her shoulders, and her eyes narrowed as she stared at Rhett. Had Cami told her about sleeping with him?

They moved to the dining room. Rhett took his spot on the left side.

Violet plunked across from him and glared. "Had to practically drag Cami over here. What's wrong with her?"

"Nothing. I took her to the Seismics Center for a game. Think she's overly tired." He stretched his arms above his head and yawned.

"Promise me you won't hurt her. Lori's already moved to Wyoming, and I don't want Cami to leave, too."

"I'll try my best."

"You'd better." She hit his shoulder.

A champagne cork popped. Michael carried in a bottle and two fluted glasses and handed one to Violet. Cami did the same for Rhett.

"Here's to Cami." Michael held up his glass. "Look at how you've cleaned up our pigsty."

Glasses clinked.

Rhett cleared his throat and stared at her mouth. All he could think was how much he wanted to run his tongue along her lips.

"May we never have to live on canned soup and top Raman again." Michael toasted.

Glasses clicked again.

Someone knocked on the door.

Rhett brought the bags to the table and passed out the paper plates that came with the meal.

"Kung Pao chicken's my absolute favorite." Michael opened a container. "Be careful Rhett. It's so spicy it might burn a hole in your gut."

"I'll be fine." His brother made a reference to Cami's cayenne peppered chicken she served one evening.

Containers with sweet and sour pork, Egg Fu-yung, fried rice, chow mein, moo shoo vegetables, spring rolls, and broccoli with garlic sauce passed around the table. Rhett ladled a bowl of wonton soup and handed it to Cami. Their fingertips brushed, and chemistry sizzled between them.

Cami needed to loosen up. He filled her glass with champagne. She picked it up and downed the contents.

"Mighty thirsty, eh?" Michael laughed.

"I am." She hiccupped.

Drinking should lighten her mood. With one bottle empty, he grabbed another from the fridge and opened it. As he topped off her champagne, she nodded and lowered her eyes.

"You know, the Silver Wings victory last night was a fluke."

Her eyes flashed, and her mouth tipped up at the corners. "You wish."

"Care to make a wager?"

"My boss must like losing." She actually giggled. Might be the champagne. If that were true, he'd have to purchase this stuff by the case.

"Let's check our fortunes." Violet passed out the cellophane wrapped cookies. "I'll start. Mine says, "Drive like hell, and eventually you will get there."

"That's weird." Michael chuckled. "Mine must belong to Rhett because it says: A person who rests on laurels gets thorns in his backside."

"Not hardly." Rhett wasn't the least bit irritated as he cracked his cookie, his eyes riveted to Cami. "Listen to this. Don't be afraid to smile. You'll never know who will fall in love with it." He smiled at Cami. "Is it working?"

"Not in the least." She unconsciously licked her lips, and he wanted to pull her onto his lap and kiss her senseless.

"What'd you get?" Violet's dark eyes glittered.

"Your reality check is about to bounce." Cami gave a little laugh. "Happened the minute I stepped inside this ranch house."

Rhett had to know what was bugging her, and said, "Let's go outside and take a stroll."

"No thanks. I've got a headache." She turned to Michael and Violet. "Thanks for dinner."

"I'll walk you home." He thought she might fight him, but she allowed Rhett to take her hand and lead her. "I want things right with us."

"So do I." She sighed. "But everything's complicated."

"Can I take you to dinner tomorrow night? Give us time to sort this through."

"I guess."

They reached her door. He turned her to face him.

"I'm not inviting you in."

"Didn't expect you to." He leaned over and briefly touched his lips to hers. "See you in the morning."

CHAPTER 18

Rhett's measly peck on the lips had Cami longing for another night of lovemaking. He'd become a complication, one that couldn't last. She'd crossed the line and failed to find him a soulmate. How was she supposed to do her job when she wanted Rhett for herself? Conflicted, she walked toward the ranch house to make breakfast.

"Howdy, gorgeous." Rhett greeted her from the porch and flashed his mesmerizing grin.

"Hi." Instantly, she craved him. It'd be easy to slip her arms around his neck and kiss him. She knew where that would lead. Cami needed the diversion of the kitchen and dashed toward the front door.

"Don't rush off." He gripped her shoulders, pivoted her to face him, leaned down and savored her lips. He tasted like coffee.

"It's not even six, and you two are already kissing," Michael walked out chuckling.

Rhett dropped his hold on her, and said to his brother, "Anyone ever tell you you're a pain?"

"You do every morning." Michael smiled like a mischievous little boy. "You making breakfast, Cami, or am I on my own this morning?"

"You'll be fed."

"Good. See you in an hour." Michael headed towards the stables.

"Mind if I help in the kitchen?"

"Yes, I mind." Confusion whirled through her. "I'll never get anything done."

"Too bad. You're stuck with me. I'll start on the eggs." He placed his hand on her shoulders and pushed her forward into the kitchen. "This is how an expert works." Taking out a bowl, he tried to crack two eggs at once and ended up with mostly shell in the dish and egg dripping off the counter.

"Wipe that off." She laughed, snatched the bowl, and rinsed it out in the sink. "Think you'd better stick to ranching."

He stood behind her, wrapping his arms around her waist, he darted his tongue along her ear and bit her lobe. Her breathing came fast. He moved away and stretched out bacon strips into the frying pan.

His lips scorched her forehead. He ran his calloused fingers along her chin and up to her mouth. "I've got an appetite for you. Guess I'd better let you get back to work." He walked away.

Another few seconds, and she would have begged him to take her. She had no idea how long she stared at the door. She was falling hard for him. The compliant, obedient person who followed rules had changed. Rhett brought out her rebellious side.

The bacon crackled. She used prongs to take out extra crispy strips and set them on a paper towel. One at a time, she cracked a dozen eggs. Unlike Rhett, she found only a smidgen of shell in the bowl. While that cooked, she mixed batter for orange-cinnamon muffins. Holy Zeus. Her housekeeper's job would be over in five days. She dreaded living back in her hometown but couldn't fight the inevitable. What would happened to Rhett when she left? She was no better than his ex, wanting him when she knew she'd be leaving him, ultimately destroying the man she loves. Why hadn't she found him his soulmate? Because she had been selfish.

She kept busy.

What if she stayed? She doubted that would be a possibility.

Half-an-hour later, she brought out the food. Rhett polished off a muffin. "I taste orange and—?"

"Cinnamon."

"Add these muffins to my favorite's list."

"It's already too long." She laughed.

He grasped her hand and eased her onto his lap, smelling musky and mighty tempting. "Where should we go for dinner tonight?"

"I'd rather not go out."

"Dinner at your place?" He gave her a hasty kiss and helped her stand.

"I suppose."

"Pizza or Chinese?"

She chose pizza and watched Rhett walk out the door. My gosh, he was addicting.

Michael still sat at the table, and asked, "What's wrong?"

"Everything's moving so fast my head's spinning."

"Tell Rhett to slow down. He might not like it, but he'll understand."

"We're talking about Rhett." She rolled her eyes. "He works on two speeds, bucking bronco and runaway stallion." Stallion reminded her of riding him, and her face warmed a thousand degrees.

"Remember what I said, don't fall for him. He's not open to love."

Too late.

RHETT WALKED into Cami's studio apartment holding a box of pizza in one hand and a grocery bag in the other. "Hope this is okay." He swallowed hard as he stared at her. In a simple blouse and jeans, she stole his breath.

"Put everything on the counter."

"Couldn't find chocolate ice cream at the mini-mart. Hope vanilla and chocolate sauce will do." The idea that he worried about the flavor of ice cream was so beneath his macho image, but he didn't care. He'd do just about anything to break the tension between them.

"Anything chocolate is perfect."

He let out the breath he'd been holding. They unpacked the

bag together and filled the buzzing fridge. The fridge had to be older than his and Cami's ages combined.

He took out a champagne bottle and handed it to her. "Wanna open this?"

"Is this whole bottle for me?" She popped the cork over the sink.

"I was hoping you'd share."

She poured the drink into two empty jelly jars with Flintstone characters and handed him one. "Bet these glasses have been here since the Stone Age."

He shrugged. Many of the furnishings, in this apartment built over fifty years ago, were original. "Next time you're in town, buy yourself some glassware."

"Is that an order?" She grabbed two plates, flipped open the pizza box, and snatched a piece from the veggie side for herself.

"Not at all." If she wanted to role-play being the boss, he was all for it, later. Right now, his hunger for food won out.

He watched her as she took the far end on the quilt-covered couch, slid in next to her on the right with his plate in hand, and polished off two slices of pepperoni pizza.

"I'd turn on the TV to watch a game, but it barely works."

"You hinting for a new TV?" He'd add one to the list. "Anything else you want?"

"Maybe a diamond tiara." She grinned as she set down her empty glass.

He pictured her wearing a crown and using her scepter to lord over him as he stripped for his queen. "Are we okay now?"

"I think so. What happened between us is overwhelming."

"Appreciate your honesty." He saw her flinch but figured this discussion wasn't easy for her either. "You're really special."

She stayed quiet.

"I'm guessing you've heard about my track record." If Violet had warned him not to hurt Cami, chances were she'd been told him about his issues.

"You got your heart broken and now prefer playing the field." She said even-toned and matter-a-factly.

"Not anymore." He looped his arm around her shoulders. "I'd like you to be my girlfriend."

"We've only been out a couple of times."

It surprised him she wasn't pushing a relationship. "We've been working together for almost two months." He kissed her and tasted champagne and mozzarella. "You're delicious."

"Tell me about your ex."

"I'd rather keep kissing you."

"Please, Rhett." She stared at him, batting her eyelashes.

"Not now."

"Don't give me that macho attitude. I'm not asking you to hand me your man card." She kissed his cheek.

"Fine. I met Penny at a rodeo."

"And?" Cami wasn't letting him off easy.

"We dated for about six months while she stayed with her cousin in Mountain Meadows."

"Where's that?"

"About twenty-five minutes southwest of here." He couldn't resist pulling her in closer and kissing her neck.

"What went wrong?" She sat up straighter.

"Nothing really. She just didn't want to be a rancher's wife."

Funny how the pain that once shot through to his gut didn't happen. Since he found Cami, he realized his ex wasn't the one for him.

"Thanks for sharing. I know it must be hard." She grasped his hand and squeezed.

"Not since I met you." He leaned over, pressed his mouth to hers, breathed in her sweet scent, and kissed her. He expected her to hold back, not create such a heated response that he struggled to suck in air. It took fortitude to rein in his desire and pull away. "Ready for dessert, I mean, ice cream?" He struggled to talk right.

She sighed, her lips full, her face flushed. Beyond stunning. "I don't have a fancy scooper like in the shop."

"Any spoon will do just fine." He found one in the top drawer, made two bowls, and brought them and the chocolate sauce to the table.

"Help yourself."

She poured a generous helping and squirted a line of sauce in the middle of his shirt. "Sorry."

"If you wanted my shirt off, all you had to do was ask." He stripped, while her eyes glued to his.

"It was an accident."

"Sure it was." He leaned over and caressed her cheek.

"Quit distracting me. My ice cream's melting." She brought a spoonful to her mouth and dripped ice cream down the front of her light green top. "Oops." She gave him a sassy smile, lifted the garment over her head, and filled the sink to soak out the stain. Her lacy white bra made his cock harden.

He rose, turned her to face him, and brought his lips to hers.

The kiss they shared wasn't heated or wanton but felt natural and fitting. He wanted her, wanted the second time to be better than the first, wanted her to have no regrets. "If you want me to stop, say so."

"Don't stop."

He traced her lips with his thumb. Her pliable, oh-so-inviting lips. He kissed her slow and easy, leisurely enjoying the heat their tongues generated. "You're beautiful."

"So are you." Her words were as soft as a colt's mane. She tentatively flicked her tongue along his lower lip, unhinging a fever only she could cure.

He unhooked the bra, and her breast spilled out. Not overly large, the rosy tips stood out against her creamy white skin. He brought his mouth down to one, laved it with his tongue, and heard her sigh.

"My sweet Cami." He scooped her into his arms and dropped her onto the single bed. Her fingers caressed his chest, causing the muscles to tighten. His moan trapped in their kiss, his fingers trembling as he undid the top snap of her jeans, pulled the zipper down, and peeled off her lacy panties. He spread her legs apart, dipped his fingers inside her folds and found her wet. He fell to his knees, kissed a path from her inner thighs, brought his head down, and hooked a leg over his shoulder.

"What are you doing?" she said in a mere whisper.

"Loving you." His word choice surprised him. Once he tongued her clit, and she let out a little sigh, his mission became savoring, darting in and out, sucking, lapping, and enjoying her. Her body tightened and quivered and came in his mouth.

Smiling, he eased onto the edge of the bed. "What do you want now?" As hard as his cock was, it was important she had a choice.

"You."

He scrambled to get a condom from his wallet. She undid his belt buckle and buttons. His pants dropped. He kicked them off. Aroused and wanting to be inside her, he struggled to take things slow.

He glanced at the single bed. "This won't do." Wrapping her in the bedspread, he placed it on the floor, dropped next to her, his weight on his elbow allowed him to gaze at her soft eyes. They were welcoming pools. Her well-kissed mouth nibbled his chin and seared kisses down to his neck. He rolled her onto her back, kneed her thighs apart, and entered her at a slow pace.

She wiggled her hips. He slid in and out of her, his breathing shallow, the friction felt unreal. "How's that?"

"Faster."

Her little moans drove him to change the pace, he flexed his hips and thrust deeper.

Her body shook, her core squeezed his shaft, and her orgasm washed over her, wave after wave after wave. His own intense release racketed through him.

Happy and sated, he rolled to her side and drifted to sleep.

THE GRANDFATHER CLOCK chimed three times. Cami woke to a soft humming sound. Rhett snored. He lay on his back next to her, totally naked, stirring places she'd never knew existed. Still on the floor, she ran her hand over his massive chest. His muscles twitched, but he didn't open his eyes. If only he could be her *happily ever after* like Cupids provided to others. If only she could remain here forever. Maybe if she convinced him she was a Cupid, he'd accept her and ask her to stay.

Or not.

She turned to her back, to her side, and onto her stomach.

"What's wrong?" Rhett's voice startled her.

"Nothing." Except once he saw her in her natural form, his desire would die.

"Don't give me that. You're more fidgety than a rabbit caught in a snare." He held her captive in his arms, "You fretting about us."

"I like waking up in your arms," she whispered.

He outlined her wrist emblem with his finger. "Why'd you pick a heart tattoo?"

"It-it connects me to my home." She wished her voice hadn't come out choppy.

"Where's home?"

"Cupid's Corner. It's up north."

"Washington?" He played with a strand of her hair, curling it around his finger. "Canada?"

"Yeah, somewhere like that." Not ready to force the issue of her true identity, she caressed him on the cheek, the lips, and kept on kissing until her mind turned to mush. She climbed on top of him, deciding to convince him she's a Cupid another time.

Twenty minutes later, his phone's alarm went off. "You gave me quite a sendoff," he chuckled.

That's when she remembered he'd be out of town for an auction. "How long will you be gone?" She wrapped the comforter around her naked body.

"A long couple of days." He leaned down and kissed her. "I'll miss you."

"Me too." She traced his cheek with her hand, imprinting his face into her memory.

CHAPTER 19

For two days, Cami's life lost purpose. She had no reason to get up early, no reason to cook, no Rhett. Sitting on the sofa in her apartment, she flipped through a fashion magazine and admired a short, low-cut dress. She could imagine wearing this dress for Rhett, his whiskey-colored eyes darkening as he pulled her into his arms.

She heard two taps on her door. Excitement soared through her. Rhett must've finished his trip early. Wearing a T-shirt, she wished she had time to change into a sexier blouse. Why? She smiled. He'd probably strip all her clothes off in minutes anyway.

She swung open the door.

Instead of glancing up to meet Rhett's brown eyes, she stared straight into the artic blue eyes of Zander.

Holy Chaos. What was he doing here? She struggled to breathe.

"Cams." He adjusted his bow tie and shoved a bouquet of roses in her hand. "Bet you're surprised I'm here?"

Not happily surprised. "How'd you find me?"

"Uncle Andre gave me your Earth coordinates."

"And why would he do that?" That would be a breach of protocol. Unless … Andre suspected something with her and Rhett.

"He said you've been having a difficult time. Thought my visit might cheer you up."

She stopped holding her breath. His uncle would come himself and bring her before the council if he'd discovered she had unlawful interaction with a target, i.e.—sex with a mortal.

Crisis averted for the moment.

Now to get Zander to leave, but that could be problematic. The Cupid was like a cantankerous bull when he wanted something. If only she'd spoken her mind a long time ago. She should have stood up to her father, should have told Zander she'd never love him, should have been courageous. Well, she had changed. She refused to be a woman who wouldn't speak up for herself.

He eyed her jeans and T-shirt. "I've got reservations for dinner. Wear a fancy dress."

That's when she noticed his suit.

"What I'm wearing is just fine."

"Nonsense." He flicked ruby dust from his fingertips. Sparkles swirled around her body and replaced her outfit with a silky pink dress.

"I'm not going anywhere tonight." She stared down to pink leather flats. The darn Cupid had replaced her favorite boots.

"But you must, Cams."

"Says who?" For several weeks, she'd had the freedom to think for herself.

"I promise we'll have fun." His voice had the same demanding tone her father often used.

She thought back to when she was about five. Her father said he was grooming her to be the best archer in their world. He had mentioned fun. Fun to him meant precision shooting.

"Got us a Porsche convertible."

Us—he meant himself.

"It's quite fast." He spoke in a firm voice. "You've always loved speed, the faster the better."

Her friends, Belle and Serenity, adored racing and fast chariots. Cami preferred horseback riding.

He checked out her apartment and eyed the bed she'd shared with Rhett. "We could stay here if you'd prefer. It's cozy."

Her jaw dropped, and she snapped her mouth shut. No way would she spend an evening alone with Zander in the same room where she and Rhett made love.

"Let's go," she said sweetly and stepped outside, wanting him away from here and thankful that Rhett was out of town. The last thing she'd want would be for the two to meet, and for Zander to say Cami was dating him.

Zander walked her to a flashy sports car. She practically dropped into the low vehicle, deciding she preferred the higher view she had from the seat of Rhett's truck.

"Hold on." Zander hopped in and revved the engine. "Listen to this baby purr."

The car didn't purr, it gave a beastly roar and zoomed off, the noise most likely scared the livestock.

She coughed. "Please put up the top."

"Relax, babe. Once we get on the road, you'll love the feel of the wind on your face."

At the main drag, he turned right toward the neighboring Rolling Heights community. He floored the car. She closed her eyes and gripped the armrest.

"Isn't this great?"

"Not for me." She didn't bother to conceal her sarcastic tone.

Zander failed to listen as he careened around the curves of the winding road.

The tires scatter stones down a steep embankment, and she shuddered. "Slow down!"

"I'm only going seventy." He kept his foot pegged. "If I didn't have to be in human form to see you, we'd be traveling in a chariot at twice this speed."

"So, don't spend time with me," she whispered.

The car turned in front of the Log Cabin Resort. A dozen private cottages lined the curved sidewalks. He parked near the restaurant's entrance in the middle of two spaces.

He offered his arm. She didn't take it, walking beside him as he escorted her inside. A saxophone player began the medley for "In the Mood." The trumpet, trombone and piano player joined in.

"You look ravishing, Cams."

"It's Cami."

"Cams suits you better." He glided his fingers along her arm. "You're enchanting in that dress. Reminds me of

Aphrodite's Ball when you wore that sparkling rose-colored gown."

He may have noticed her clothing, but he failed in the listening department. Zander was attracted to the package, but not who she was as a person. Love went much deeper.

The hostess led them to a table with a view of the valley. She gazed out and squinted, trying to pick out the Double H Ranch but couldn't.

All the other tables were empty. Knowing Zander, he'd conjured up this place to impress her. A server brought out a chilled bottle of ambrosia, popped the cork, and poured them each a glass.

"To our future," he toasted.

Future, she didn't want a future with him. She ignored her drink.

"Are you ready to order?" The waitress eyed Zander like he were a dreamboat, and she his adoring admirer.

"Yes. My lady will have the pasta primavera," he ordered for her.

Cami would love to cram, *my lady,* down his throat and make him choke on it. Never once did he think to ask what she wanted.

"I've missed you. We should be celebrating our successes together." What he meant was he'd had successful missions, and she hadn't. He grasped her hand tightly. "How are you handling your dreadful ordeal?"

"It's not dreadful. In fact, I actually enjoy cooking without magic."

"Once you're back where you belong, I'll have you cook for

me." He wore a smug smirk, leaned over, and gave her a quick kiss on the lips. It was as enticing as kissing a turtle. No exploding fireworks like she had with Rhett.

Zander was part of her real life in Cupid's Corner, but the idea of him as a future lover had no appeal. She finished her drink. "Have you seen Belle or Serenity?"

"No time, babe. I've been blitzed with assignments." He said this to make himself feel important, but it seemed like a subconscious jab at Cami's mistake. He was a successful archer, whereas she failed on her first Earthly attempt.

"Uncle Andre discovered a loophole to resolve your issue."

"What do you mean?" She took a bite of pasta. The rich sauce clumped in her throat.

"One of our alchemists found a remarkable potion in an ancient book of spells. This potion erases a mortal's connection to a Cupid's arrow."

Did he mean the potion would erase Rhett's memory of her? Her stomach clenched. "How does it work?"

"All he has to do is drink an elixir." His exuberant tone was opposite to her utter despair. "For him, your mistake will be erased forever. You'll be forgotten."

Apprehension squeezed her heart. Rhett would have no memory of her and their relationship. No recollections of ever meeting her. No recollections of their shared kisses. No recollections of ever making love with her. Tears pooled and threatened to spill. She bit her bottom lip hard enough to make it bleed. She loved Rhett.

"I don't like this idea. You do know the original arrow antidote I used was corrupted. What's to stop something worse from happening with the elixir?"

The server brought dessert.

What if Rhett's desire for her had been due to the arrow? The thought was too painful. She quickly shook it away.

Not interested in food, she used her fork to make designs on the top.

"Babe, you tend to overthink things, but it's not necessary." He gave her an impish grin that looked idiotic. "Why aren't you eating? It's your favorite, cherry cheesecake."

"Cherry cheesecake is your favorite, not mine," she said.

He shoveled his last bite of cheesecake in his mouth and ignored her statement. "Just think, soon our childhood dreams will become a reality. Once the elixir is administered, everything will go back to normal."

Normal, as in her and both of their families expected them to start dating, and then marriage would follow.

"We should go." He stood and offered his arm, and again she refused it.

"Yes." Once she was alone in her ranch apartment, she'd be able to think clearly.

As they walked to the car, he secured his arm around her shoulder. His arm reminded her of a boa about to constrict. He opened her door, and she recalled Rhett leaning her against his truck and kissing her senseless. Her body tingled at the thought of Rhett's mouth on hers. Thank the stars Zander didn't try to kiss her. Getting in, she tugged on her gown's silky skirt. Jeans were much more practical.

The engine roared. A country song about a cheating heart

twanged on the radio as the sports car raced along. "How can anyone stand this drivel?" Zander grumbled.

"I like this song." The past month, she'd learned to appreciate country music.

"Let's see what else is on?" He swirled ruby dust from his fingertips, and "Stairway to Heaven" played. "Much Better."

It irked her that he didn't listen to anything she said. He drove straight instead of turning right.

"What are you doing?" She was supposed to go to her Earthly apartment.

"Taking you to the council for the elixir." He chuckled. Scratch that, it reminded her of a sinister snort.

"I'm exhausted. Take me there early tomorrow morning."

"Sorry, babe. The council expects to see you tonight."

Now she was his captive. She couldn't flee, couldn't run, couldn't get away.

His magical dust swirled around them. She shrunk to fourteen inches wearing a flowing gown. Zander shrunk, donning a silvery toga. The car shrunk proportionally to their new size.

"You're gonna love how fast this car goes now. Hold on." He pushed a button, they were in a chariot jetting upward. It landed in front of the Cupid Council Headquarters.

Not about to allow his assistance, she unfurled her wings and fluttered toward the building. He flew next to her up the steps, between two pillars, and inside the front door.

Flying used to give her the illusion of being free, but never as free as she'd been riding horses on Earth. She turned right, landed on the floor, and floated down to the mausoleum-like waiting area.

"Miss Cami Calypso has arrived," Zander informed the attendant guarding the council's chambers.

"The council is ready for you." A young intern parted the cloud-covered door.

Zander followed her, but she put her hand up to stop him. "I can handle this alone."

"If that's what you want, but I'll be out here if you need me." His hovering irritated her. She could take care of her own matters. At least he took a seat on the marble bench.

Trepidations clenched her stomach as she strutted inside the chambers. She did her best tall-and-confident stance, while five pairs of eyes stared.

"Good evening, Miss Calypso. The council is quite distressed the replacement antidote did not give you the desired results," Zander's uncle said.

"So am I." She had used the tainted arrows, not the newest one. "I hit Rhett directly in his heart. I can't understand why the male's not totally smitten with the woman."

"Neither can we, but all is not lost. The Annulment Elixir will remedy your predicament." Andre clasped his hands together and gave her a reassuring smile.

Did she wince? She hoped not.

His fingertips swirled magical dust and produced a small bottle glittering with red liquid. "The instructions are quite simple. Mix in a pinch of your own dust before you add the contents to the subject's drink. It is tasteless and colorless to humans."

"What should I expect to see?"

"Nothing until the final drop is drunk. Then the human goes

into a trance. You must place your hands on the side of his face and make sure he stares into your eyes. Then you say this incantation." He handed her a sheet of paper.

The binding of my arrow shall be set free.
All memory of my presence permanently erased.
My guardianship released for all eternity.

Permanently erased the memories. They might as well rip out her heart and feed it to a gryphon. She let out a long sigh.

She had to think about Rhett. Once he drank the elixir, he would be able to find his true love. As much as it hurt, she wanted him to be happy.

"Miss Calypso, you're rather pale. Is there a concern?" Andre's tone almost sounded empathetic.

"No, sir."

"Once you've completed the incantation, wait ten seconds and leave. The human shall wake fully within three minutes. Since he will no longer recognize you, your presence may confuse him." Andre continued by explaining that the elixir would erase all of her time on Earth with Rhett.

She thought about Michael, Violet, Heather, and the parents. "What about the others? Will they remember I worked at the ranch as a housekeeper?" She had to know.

"I'm not certain. Let me check." Andre floated the book in front of him and flipped pages. "It says here: This elixir voids the effects of the arrow, thus annulling the connection between the archer and recipient. Time itself shall not be altered, but any events that occurred with you will be forgotten by all mortal participants."

If she used the elixir, Rhett's life would go on as if she'd never existed, while her memories would live on.

Still, she must quit being selfish and do what was best for Rhett.

"The contents must be given within forty-eight hours of creation. After that time, the substance reverts to water. Do you have any more questions?" Andre asked.

"No, sir." Giving Rhett the elixir was the right thing to do—for him. For her, she'd give up the only male she'd ever truly loved.

"The clock's ticking. Once the task has been completed, we expect a full report."

"I have everything under control." Cami had nothing under control.

Andre pressed the button. Pop. She landed in her Earthly apartment wearing that ridiculous dress Zander created, collapsed on her bed, and cried.

CHAPTER 20

"Never figured we'd get back tonight," Rhett said to his brother as he fishtailed his truck through the Double H Ranch's gate. Adrenaline charged, he'd see Cami in a couple of minutes.

"Twelve-eleven is technically morning."

"Smart ass."

"Pitiful showing at that auction. Think I counted ten sway-backed old nags," Michael groaned.

"I should've stayed home."

"With Cami. You've got it bad, bro."

"Shut up." He wheeled around the corner and parked, anxious to see her sweet face, savor her sweet lips, enjoy her sweet body.

"She know you're coming?"

"I texted her before we headed home." He'd tried calling, too. Parking the truck, he got out, tucked his plaid shirt into his jeans, adjusted his Stetson, and told his brother, "See ya."

Outside her apartment, no lights were on. He knocked three times.

Nothing. He waited. "Cami, it's me."

"Oh, Rhett." The door clicked open, and she rubbed her eyes. "I missed you."

He stepped inside and wrapped her in his arms. "I thought about you. Couldn't wait to get back and do this." He kissed her, bold and demanding.

She matched him, tangling her tongue with his, her hands trembling as she unbuttoned his shirt. Her fingers stroked his chest and lowered, unbuckling his belt, unzipping his pants and allowing them to drop. She nipped his neck.

"Mmmm."

"You like that?" Her voice sang thick with built up desire.

"Hell, yes." Still in. his boxers, he ground his hips against hers making sure she felt his hard-on. He walked her toward the bed, inched her nightgown up to her waist, removing the flannel garment and tossing it on the floor. He skimmed his fingertips over her velvety skin.

With her arms around his neck, she feathered kisses along his jawline.

"I want you." He eased down her lacy panties, giving him a lovely view of her bare butt. She tugged on the elastic of his boxers, and he quickly removed them.

He pressed her against her twin bed and continued kissing her and touching her. When he slid his finger inside her, he found her folds slick. Her little moans drove him to continue as he rubbed his finger against her clit. He pleasured her, and she came quickly.

"Make love to me." Her hand grasped his member.

He grabbed a six-pack of condoms from his wallet. "Pick one."

She chose the leopard skin pattern, unwrapped the package with her teeth, rolled on the latex, and smiled.

He pushed her legs apart and filled her with one stroke. Being inside her made him growl.

"Oh, Rhett." She wrapped her legs around his waist.

Desperately needing her, he started out slow. It felt so freaking good to be inside her. He stopped to kiss her, pulled out. She thrust her hips up, and he kept up the game, bringing her to the edge of release. He withdrew and rolled her onto her hands and knees, positioned his cock and entered her from behind.

"Oh, my." Her squeal mixed with surprise.

His hand reached around her hip and his fingertip teased her clit, his tempo started slow and increased. Her body tightened around him, and he held her tight as she climaxed.

Still inside her, he tipped her sideways and waited for her breathing to become normal. She traced his cheek with her hand, her radiance beamed as she brought her mouth to his. Their tongues melded, savoring each other. Her hips rose to meet him, and he thrust deeper inside her. Excitement soared with each stroke. His pace picked up, building, and enjoying her body until her orgasm crested, and he had his own release.

His heartbeat raced and he breathed deeply, allowing his

pulse to slow. "Did I mention how I've missed you?" He rolled to the side and landed on the floor.

She giggled.

"Think this is funny." It really was. "Tomorrow, we're buying you a new bed."

"Whatever you say, boss."

He felt grungy after being on the road most the day and stood. "How 'bout a shower?"

"Okay."

He followed her to the bathroom, and she pushed back the shower curtain. Close behind her, he swatted her bottom as she reached inside for the faucet. He squirted honey scented shower gel on a netted bath sponge. "Turn around and face me."

She pivoted. As water cascaded down her body, he soaped her perky breasts. They hardened as the water rinsed the suds away. He engulfed her nipple in his mouth. Her fingernails dug into his back. He let go, nibbled her neck and up to her chin, and nipped her ear. His mouth met hers, sliding in with his tongue, teasing, and tasting. His hands roamed along her backside, and he kneaded her body.

She snatched the sponge, added more gel, and whispered, "Trade places." She squeezed past him.

He like this bossy side.

She lathered his chest, watched the water remove the suds, and flicked her tongue on his nipple and bit lightly.

A moan escaped. "You're killing me, sugar."

"That's my intention." She soaped his abs and moved down to his cock.

He closed his eyes as her fingers grasped him, and her hand

roved up and down, teasing him. "I need to be inside you." He lifted her, gazed into her eyes, and entered her slowly. Her pupils dilated with desire as she arched her hips against him.

He plunged in deeper, gave his all, reveling in the intimacy of their joined bodies. He gripped her bottom, pulling her closer, relishing every whimper she cried. Teasing her nipples, he pinched one. Her explosive climax came. His own detonated.

"Love you," the words slipped out on their own accord. Maybe she hadn't noticed.

LATER THAT DAY, Cami rode back from the Mattress Express in Rhett's truck.

"Did you have to tell the salesman we'd give the mattress a trial run this afternoon?" Her cheeks were blazing hot.

Rhett placed his hand on her knee. "Just being honest." He parked in front of her garage apartment with a new queen-sized bed in the back. Warmth settled around her, the giddy happiness was the love.

With the elixir tucked in her pocket, she pulled it out and stashed it inside the end table drawer. The hourglass icon on her communicator showed she had twenty-eight hours to complete the task. One more day before she erased all memory of her time with Rhett.

He brought in the mattress and box springs, set the bed up in what seemed like seconds, and assisted her with the sheets and comforter. "Now that's a bed." He held her from behind and pressed his bulge against her bottom.

"If you're hinting about messing up my perfectly made bed, the answer is, no." She turned.

"You think so, huh?" His tongue danced with her. When his kisses ceased, she had no recollection of being pressed against the roomy mattress where they lay side by side.

"Guess you showed me." She trailed her fingers through his thick hair.

"Shall we begin the christening ritual?" His sultry tone aroused her.

"Yes, please." For the next few hours, they made love countless times until they both collapsed and slept.

She woke up first. The sheets fell to Rhett's waist allowing her to enjoy his well-toned abs. His chest rose in a rhythmic pattern. A midnight shadow covered his strong chin, tempting her to kiss his jawline.

Outside an owl hooted. It wasn't yet dawn. 16:47:24 flashed below a sand-dial symbol on her communicator. Sixteen hours until she must administer the elixir.

It didn't seem right. He loved her—she loved him. Cupids believed in true love. Obliterating all memories of the love they shared tore at her heart.

"You're awake." He nuzzled her neck. They made love again and dozed off.

Her communicator flashed fifteen hours.

"Something wrong?" He noticed her staring at her watch.

"I need to make breakfast. Michael will be waiting."

"I can help if you'd like." He reached for her hand, but she slipped off the bed.

"You'll just distract me." She snatched his shirt from the floor instead of her own and buttoned it.

"You're smoking hot in that."

"Take care of your chores."

"Yes, ma'am. I'll meet you at the house in an hour." His eyes followed her as she hurried into the bathroom.

She closed the door, leaning against it and wishing the clock on her communicator would quit tick, tick, ticking. Her tangled hair took forever to brush and braid. Stalling didn't slow the clock. 14:30:29.

Each step to the house reminded her of the seconds passing. Inside the kitchen, Michael had left a full basket of eggs on the counter. Might as well make breakfast and decide what to do before the time runs out.

She mixed pancake batter, adding blueberries, Rhett's favorite. Had he really said he loved her? This meal with Rhett had to be perfect. He wouldn't remember. She dried her tears on a dishtowel, finished cooking eggs and bacon, and placed the food on two plates.

The front door banged. Boots clunked behind her. Rhett kissed her cheek. "I'm starving." He picked up both plates. "Let's eat."

After breakfast, Rhett would take care of his chores. She'd pretend that it was just another workday. They'd share dinner at his home, he'd come back to her apartment. She'd transform into her Cupid body. She couldn't recall if any other Cupid had done this or what the consequences might be if she were caught. She didn't care. At the moment, she had to be honest with Rhett and learn if he truly loved her.

There'd be no more secrets.

RHETT HAD a strange feeling in his gut during dinner. Cami kept checking her watch. He'd asked what bothered her, but she said everything was fine.

After a long day, he helped her clean up the dinner dishes, and they walked to her apartment. Her stance was rigid, her body tense. She didn't shift toward him as he strode with his arm around her shoulder.

"What's wrong?"

"I need to tell you something." She shrugged but wouldn't look at him.

They'd only known each other close to two months, but his heart was all in. He unlocked the apartment door. Seated at the edge of the couch, Cami put a distance between them and avoided eye contact.

"Go ahead." He stood by the kitchen table and waited for a response.

"We were never meant to be together," she said, still not looking his way.

His chest tightened. She was breaking up with him.

"I've got a secret. When I show you, I hope you'll still love me."

"Whatever you've done in the past doesn't matter. We'll get through it." He'd made his share of mistakes.

She extracted a glass vial from her pocket. It sparkled and shimmered. "It's not what I've done, it's what I am."

"What are you?" He didn't even see a flicker of a smile.

Her lips tightened into a grimace. "Please listen carefully to what I say."

"All right. Spill." He tapped the side of his pants.

She licked her lips and took a deep breath. "I told you I was a Cupid when you took me to the archery range."

"Okay."

She folded her arms. "I live in Zeus' Kingdom up in the clouds."

His teeth ground, as he sat next to her and said sarcastically, "Of course you do."

"You've seen my archery skills. Even said I was talented." She lifted her chin and blew out a breath. "I am a Cupid, a real live Cupid."

"That's crazy." Maybe she was crazy. His primal instinct told him to leave, but he couldn't move.

"My occupation is an archer." Tears pooled in her eyes. "I'm telling you the truth."

"If you're leaving me, say so, and quit making up this lame story."

"I don't want to go anywhere." She twirled a curl around her finger.

"You don't? And here I thought you were breaking up with me."

"If only things were different. I've got to return home." She looked at her watch.

"So, you are leaving me? Why?" He was confused.

"I don't want to. I'm happy here." Her body slumped, her chin dropped. "My whole life I've dreamed of being good enough."

"But you are good enough." She was the best thing to ever happen to him. "You're perfect for me."

"Don't make me cry, please let me finish." Her eyes softened. "I've dreamed of visiting Earth and infusing humans with arrows of love. When I got my first earthly assignment, I hit the wrong man, namely you."

Those blue eyes. "You shot me with your arrow of love?"

"It was a mistake. My assignment ducked, and I hit you instead. I was sent to rectify my mishap and set you up with your soulmate. We were never supposed to fall in love."

"You love me." His spirits soared.

"Yes."

"'Bout time you admitted it." He moved closer, but she backed up, out of his reach.

"Will you accept the real me?"

"What do you mean? The real Cami's right in front of me."

"Watch." Rocking back and forth on her heels, her cheeks flushed to a rosier red.

His eyes riveted to her hands.

She unscrewed the glass vial and poured out a glittery substance. Iridescent pink dust swirled and surrounded her. Her body shrunk to the size of a doll, dressed in a shimmering gown. Iridescent wings formed at her shoulders. She flew up midway between the floor and the ceiling.

"Holy shit!" He stared, not frightened, confused.

"I'm a C-Cupid." Her words came out broken.

He froze, became immobile. "This can't be happening."

"I love you, always will." She hovered close to him, and he felt her lips kiss his cheek.

"It's unreal."

"Tell me about it." Her eyes were wide. Wary.

"You really are a Cupid?"

"Yes. Do you still love me?"

He didn't know what to think. "It's too much." He turned his back to her, put his head in his hands.

His girlfriend—a ruler-sized pixie. It couldn't be true.

Except he'd seen her.

Could he live with her secret?

Love surged through his heart. He relaxed his shoulders and lifted his head. "Let's figure this out."

She was gone.

CHAPTER 21

Cami flew out the window and kept going until she reached the river. She perched on a branch and listened to a Whippoorwill calling its mate. The water lapped along the shoreline, reminding her of when Rhett took her riding by this river.

What had she done?

Cupids aren't supposed to reveal themselves to humans. What would it matter? Cami didn't care about rules anymore. She'd already broken a trillion.

She wrapped her arms around her legs and allowed the air to seep into her lungs. Clarity came. Her life on the ranch was over. It took little time to flutter back to her apartment and go in through the sliding glass door that had been left open. This place she had called home.

Devastation filled her brain. Rhett had never truly loved her.

His abject revulsion showed when he saw her as a Cupid. Since he didn't want her, he wouldn't need the elixir to push his thoughts of her from his mind, while Cami doubted she'd ever stop agonizing over him. She took out the glass bottle from the end table drawer, shook the bubbling red fluid, and hurled the elixir against the fireplace. The glass shattered. Splintered into fragments like her own heart.

She couldn't blame him for her misery. She knew better than to get involved with a mortal.

Tears clouded her vision. She no longer belonged at the ranch. She no longer fit in the Cupid society. Drinking herself into oblivion seemed to be her best option, but that would require more than the half-empty bottle of wine in the fridge.

Her communicator buzzed. She hoped to see Rhett's icon. Not Violet's picture.

She answered the call anyway. Her friend deserved to know she was leaving. "Hello."

"You up for a movie tonight?"

"Can't. My mom's in the hospital. Gotta fly home." Cami landed on top of the kitchen table.

"Sorry to hear that. Any idea how long you'll be gone?"

"No. I'll keep in touch." Cami doubted she'd ever talk to Violet again.

"You'd better." The call ended.

A sense of loneliness overwhelmed her. She'd never see her friend again, leaving her with a hollow hole inside.

A light on her communicator flashed, increasing her utter despair. A message from the captain appeared.

One hour left to give the elixir

She texted.

Mission completed

Her conscience should bother her about lying, but without Rhett nothing mattered. She'd face the council and returned to her life and responsibilities.

The button to the council's chamber lit. She pressed it and landed in front of the members on her butt. So much for arriving calm and collected. She rose with as much dignity as she could gather.

"The captain says you were successful, Miss Calypso, but I must ask if you followed the directions precisely as prescribed?"

"Of course, sir." Her heart thumped hard and fast.

"Very well." The corners of Andre's lips lifted for a brief second.

A lump formed in her throat. She should have given Rhett the elixir. His life would be better if he forgot her.

Andre nodded to the other council members. "Even though your mistake has been fixed, Miss Calypso, you are on probation until further notice. All archer privileges have been revoked."

"I understand, sir." She had no desire to shoot arrows.

"Earthly assignments shall henceforth be terminated. Your future has changed."

She bit her tongue to keep from crying. She had no future—not without Rhett.

Andre excused her. Thank the heavens, Zander wasn't waiting in the corridor. A third quarter moon shone as she flew to her apartment and entered the building.

"You're back" At the main entryway, Serenity's voice called from behind her. "You okay?"

"Not really. Do you have time to come to my place and talk?" Belle and Serenity were the only Cupids Cami trusted. If anyone could help her get over Rhett, it would be her friends.

"Sure."

Serenity and Cami fluttered upstairs to her apartment. Cami parted the cloud door, and both went inside. "Anybody here?"

Her auburn-haired roommate zipped out from the kitchen. "Cami."

Serenity furled her wings and headed for the couch. "After your ordeal, you want Ambrosia."

Cami had drunk Ambrosia since she turned thirteen. The mild drink was served at family dinners. "Make it a Cupid's Arrow." Cami needed a sweet drink with a spirited punch.

"You've got it." Serenity swirled coppery dust from her fingertips and three hurricane glasses filled with orange fluid floated to the coffee table.

Cami grabbed a glass, settled into a plush chair, and downed her cocktail. "Holy Aphrodite, this is heavenly."

"Another two or three and you'll forget all your troubles." Serenity sipped her drink. "But before you do, you might as well tell us what happened."

"I failed miserably."

"I'm sorry," Belle said.

"The initial antidote arrow never worked."

"Who do you think discovered that the solution wasn't right?" Serenity gave a Cheshire cat grin.

"When it comes to your talents, nothing surprises me." Cami motioned to Serenity for another drink.

"Slow down. Finish your story first."

"Are you dating Zander?" Belle gave her a questioning look.

"Holy Hades, no. I've always like Zander—as a friend. Did you know he visited me at the ranch?" Cami wished he hadn't.

"Really. Why?" Belle asked

"Because Zander believes they belong together—as the Golden Archers." Serenity flipped her strawberry blonde hair behind her shoulders.

"Zander made it clear he wants a relationship with me. I tried to tell him that we're better off friends. Guess I'll have to try harder." The idea made Cami's stomach twist. He could be a jerk, but she still thought of him as her sweet next-door neighbor. The little boy who used to chase dragonflies with her. As he got older, he bought into the idea that they should get married. He believed in the illusion of creating a family of excellent marksman. With her, he would have the perfect life. Now that she'd experienced how delicate love could be, she had to let him down easy. "He's not going to be happy."

"I have access to his calendar. You could avoid seeing him for the next few months." Her emerald eyes lit up with a mischievous gleam.

"Thanks, but that will only delay the inevitable. Zander deserves to hear the truth."

"If you change your mind, let me know." Serenity smirked. "Anyway, what made you realized you two won't work?"

"Because he has the listening skills of a flutterfish."

"And you just noticed that?" Belle sipped from her straw. "He's rather pretentious."

"I assumed you liked him. Why didn't you ever say anything?"

"We tried. Whenever we brought up his name, you changed the subject," Serenity laughed.

"You once thought you'd grow to love him." Belle said softly.

"I assumed love should grow like seeds do in a flower garden." Cami shook her head. "And my father's always expounding on Zander's virtues. He thinks Zander is practically on par with Zeus."

Serenity swirled her dust to refill everyone's glasses. "You don't have to please everyone. Please yourself first."

An image of Rhett wearing nothing but a sheet passed through her mind. Yep, the man sure knew how to please her.

"You're blushing. What aren't you telling us?" Serenity gave an exaggerated sigh.

"That I fell in love with a human." Cami's eyes misted. "I know it's wrong."

"This is unbelievable." Belle's eyes widened. "My goody-two-shoes friend did something forbidden. Tell us more."

"You're not upset? I'll understand if you never want to speak with me again."

"Of course not. You're my best friend." Belle hugged her.

"I'm fascinated." Serenity smiled. "Did you fall in love with the rancher? I saw his file. He's cute."

"I know. Couldn't resist him."

"Then what are you doing here?" Belle gazed at her with a dreamy expression. "I would've stayed."

"When I showed him my true form, he was afraid of me. Repulsed." What an idiot she'd been.

"If you never knew humans existed, you'd be in shock when you came face to face with one," Serenity said in a soft, soothing tone. "I'm betting he still loves you."

"Give him time," Belle said. "I mean, how could he not love you?"

"I wish that were true. There's more."

"Are you talking about the elixir?" Serenity shrugged. "I eavesdropped on the council's sessions."

"You did what?" Belle's eyes narrowed.

"Don't act shocked. You guys know how I am." Serenity swirled the liquid around her glass. "Now, Cami spill."

"I was supposed to give him a drink that would erase all memories of me. I couldn't do it. Not after he said he loved me. I didn't want him to forget what we had." Her tormented heart ached. "So I used a vial of dust to transform. It turns out seeing the real me was too much for him."

"I think your wrong." Belle's hand covered Cami's.

"A relationship with a mortal is wrong. If Rhett hadn't broken my heart, I'm pretty sure fate would've intervened and split us up."

"What if fate threw you two together?" Serenity created a milky white drink in a shot glass. "Drink this. It'll ward off a hangover."

Cami downed her shot.

"Things will work out. You'll see," Belle said, her smile sweet. "I'll take the day off work tomorrow. Let's pamper ourselves with a facial and have our wing feathers fluffed."

Cami hugged her friend. "Another time, I promise." She needed to be by herself.

The band on her communicator rubbed against her wrist. Why bother hoping Rhett might try to contact her. She tapped the button on the top to turn the device off, threw it on her dresser, got under her covers, and cried. Like Humpty-Dumpty when his shell cracked, no amount of glue could fix her shattered heart.

ROBINS CHIRPED OUTSIDE ANNOUNCING DAYBREAK, her favorite time at the ranch. She fingered silky sheets and reached for Rhett. His spot was empty. As she peeled her eyes open, she noticed a two-foot bed. A white comforter embroidered with red archers covered her. Gold and silver hearts glittered from the clouded wall covering. The bedroom's Cupid theme —overkill.

She headed into the kitchen to heat water. No kettle. No burner. No stove. Flicking her fingertips, fuchsia-colored dust swirled. A steaming cup of orange blossom tea floated to the table. Magic used to bring her joy. Now she prefered the mortal way.

Her wings unfurled causing a weird contracting sensation. She wore a glitzy gown that came to her knees. She missed wearing jeans and a T-shirt.

Her doorbell rang.

Peeking through her peephole, she spotted Zander. Cursed Cyclops. Why'd he have to come now? She opened the door.

"Since I have the day off, I'm taking you out." As usual, he ordered.

"Not today. I'm tired." She needed more time to prepare her speech. As a Cupid archer, she had people's fragile hearts at the tip of her arrow. She'd learned firsthand how much Rhett's rejection crushed her own spirit.

"Nonsense. I'll be back in an hour." He flew off without giving her a chance to speak.

She should wear an onyx colored gown and dye her hair black to match her bleak mood but opted for a navy dress. Somehow, she had to get Zander to realize they would never be a couple.

He arrived an hour later. "You'd look much prettier in magenta." His dust swirled and changed her gown's color.

What an ass!

Bestowing his smug signature smirk, he shoved a dozen red roses into her hand and a thorn stabbed into her palm. Not a good sign. She dropped the bouquet on the floor. Zander never noticed.

Inside his golden chariot, he said, "Got a pleasant surprise for you." He flicked the reins.

His surprises never turned out pleasant. He landed near the shore of Aphrodite's glassy crystal blue lake. His smooth hand clutched hers. He'd never done manual labor, never broken a sweat. Rhett's hands were strong. She missed him, missed how his eyes danced as he watched her, missed his passionate kisses. *Quit thinking about him. It's over.*

They stopped near a pond. A green dragonfly with periwinkle wings landed on her shoulder.

"Even as a little girl, creatures were drawn to you." He gazed at her with admiration.

"Things were simpler then." When they were friends without any romantic intentions.

"You know, I fell in love with you at this very spot."

No-no-no declaration of love! Holy Aphrodite, she didn't expect that.

"You flittered by a lily pad, snatched a surprised bullfrog, and kissed the warty croaker right on the mouth."

"I remember." She'd been young and naïve. "My mom read me *The Frog Prince*. Once I kissed the frog, I was certain I'd see my very own prince. We'd marry and live happily ever after."

"You can still have that with me."

"Honestly, Zander, I was a clueless five-year-old. I'm no longer that naïve Cupid."

He dropped to one knee. "I love you, Cams. Marry me." He opened a red velvet case. A diamond ring surrounded with rubies sparkled in the sunlight.

Zander was delusional.

Still, her pulse sped. "I can't." Not when Rhett would forever own her heart.

"Your mistake is fixed. Nothing hinders us from being together." He swirled glittery dust into two cushioned wicker chairs. "Please sit."

He actually said, "Please." Not a natural word in his vocabulary.

She plunked onto a chair and searched for the right words. Nothing came.

He dragged his seat closer to hers and gripped her hand. "I love you, Cams, and you love me."

"I don't love—"

He cut her off. "So, you'll marry me." Still holding her hand —despite her attempting to tug free—he got back on one knee. Extracting the ring from its case, he jammed it on her finger and tugged it over her knuckle. "See. It fits perfectly."

Typical Zander, he never listened for a reply. Assumed she'd accepted his offer.

"I can't do this." She tried to take off the band, but it wouldn't budge over her swollen knuckle.

"We're getting married!" He leaned to kiss her. She turned so his kiss landed on her cheek. "You'll make a stunning June bride."

"I'm not marrying you."

"Yes, you are. You're wearing my ring."

She twisted and tugged until her finger hurt. "I can't get your ring off. Did you put a binding spell on it?"

"No way. This is a sign we're meant to be together." He flicked his fingertips and his dust formed a bottle of ambrosia along with two crystal glasses. "To our own happily ever after," he toasted. oblivious to her protests.

"You're not listening. There will be no future for us."

"I've got it. Toasting in the New Year with our nuptials will give you plenty of time to plan your fairytale wedding." He reminded her of a pesky gnat, annoying her with his pointless chatter.

"We're never getting married." Why did she think she had to let this obstinate Cupid down easy? Zander wasn't her neighborly friend. He had changed and not in a good way. "I never said, yes!" she shouted. "I don't love you."

"Love you, too, Cams."

Why couldn't he get it through his obtuse head that she didn't love him?

CHAPTER 22

Five days. Five long, torturous days since Rhett had discovered the truth. The sexy blonde who rocked his world could transform into a pint-size pixie.

He grabbed the bottle of whiskey he'd left on his nightstand and took a swig. Empty. Empty like his life had become without Cami. Whiskey had become a poor substitute as a companion. His head pounded like a horse had trampled his brains. He went into the kitchen and downed a few aspirins, started a new pot of coffee, and watched the fluid as it dripped through the filter. The start of his day—pathetic.

He brought his coffee outside on the porch. Moths fluttering by the light were his only company. The darkness faded as dawn appeared. Daybreak used to set his thinking straight. His eyes drifted toward the dirt path to the apartment, half expecting to see Cami bounding toward the house and greeting him with her captivating smile. He had to forget her. Forget he'd ever sampled her lips. Forget about her hair in disarray after they made love. Forget how she left a hole the size of a horseshoe inside his heart.

Still, he waited until the sun shone through the clouds and took a sip of his stone-cold coffee. He stood, and liquid sloshed on the front of his denim shirt. A perfect welcome to another shitty day.

Inside the dining room, he found Michael eating a Pop Tart while scrolling his phone.

"Don't you ever put that damn thing down?"

"God, you're cantankerous. When's Cami coming back?"

Rhett groaned, went into the kitchen, poured himself a bowl of Corn Flakes, topped it with milk, and ate the cereal standing at the counter.

The kitchen had been Cami's domain. Reminders of her were everywhere. He needed to forget her. Figured his only option was to talk to his brother about his ex, not that it'd be easy. He slunk into his seat. "Mind if I ask you a question."

"You can ask. Not promising an answer."

"Fair enough." Rhett paused. "When you and your wife broke up, how'd you keep yourself sane?"

"Mucked out stalls, chopped plenty of firewood. Hell, I built a new corral in less than a week."

"And that worked?

"Not one bit."

Rhett laughed the first laugh he'd emitted in days. "Aren't you helpful?"

The corner of Michael's mouth turned up. "You and Cami break up?"

"Yep."

"So that's why she left?" His brother's brow furrowed.

Rhett shrugged.

"You're miserable, and I'm betting Cami's much the same. It wouldn't hurt to call her."

"Can't," Rhett said quickly. He'd tried to call her. After at least a dozen rings, he'd hung up. He'd texted her a few times. When she failed to respond, he assumed she didn't have reception in her Cupid realm. He racked his brain for other options to contact her. Nothing surfaced.

"Violet's worried about her. She's texted a few times. Cami hasn't responded."

He'd always love her, but she'd left and that hurt. "I'm going for a ride."

Snagging an apple from the basket on the sideboard, Rhett headed for the stables. Passing Buttercup, he recalled Cami riding the mare, her hips in sync with the horse's gait. She's gone. *I have to forget her.*

He grabbed his fishing pole and tackle box from the storage area, saddled Starlight, and headed for his favorite fishing hole. As he crossed the river and stopped near the shore, the crisp, cold air cleared his lungs. He took aim with a rock at a ground squirrel. It chittered and ducked under a bush. "Run you damn rodent."

A flat, round rock fit in his palm. It had a bump in the middle. With the flick of his wrist, he threw the rock underhand into the water. It spun and skipped four or five hops. That felt good. The next stone made it to the middle of the river. He continued, must've thrown a dozen more.

A pair of ravens scouted the area from above, screeched, and swooped at something a hundred yards further.

Emptiness settled in the pit of his stomach. Hard work would keep him from thinking.

He mounted Starlight and kept on riding. The position of the sun proved it was close to nine. The slanted roof of his parent's stable came into view. Might as well see how the demon stallion's fairing.

From the back of his mount, he could see the jet-black stallion standing in its coral. Holy Terror didn't snort, squeal, or run off. Quieter than usual, he reckoned the animal must be getting used to seeing him.

Rhett tied Starlight to a post, grabbed items from the tack room, and placed his saddle on the fence. Holding the halter, he waited outside the corral, pulled an apple from his coat pocket, unlatched the gate, and crooned, "Hey, big fella." He closed the latch behind him.

The stallion approached Rhett and took the apple from his hand. A first. "That's it," Rhett said gently. He walked to the animal's left side and slipped a bridle in place, secured the buckle, and attached the reins.

"Ready for a walk." He led the stallion around the corral without any trouble.

"Easy boy." He kept his voice soft as he grabbed a pad and placed it on the horses back. Waiting several seconds, he added the saddle and secured the cinch. Again, he used the lead rope to walk the stallion around.

"What'd ya say I take you to the ring like the other day? Maybe try to ride you?" Excitement thrilled through his veins, his pulse galloped, his adrenaline buzzed like a bee finding its first bit of nectar. Today, he'd ride Holy Terror.

The ring was about two hundred yards to the west. His Stetson kept the sun out of his eyes. A horsefly buzzed by his ear and landed on his neck, but he didn't dare swat at it. Any sudden action could spook the horse.

The foreman spotted him, tipped his hat, and opened the gate. "Think you'll ride him today?" He used a hushed voice and latched Rhett inside.

Rhett gave a lop-sided grin. "Hope so." He walked the horse around the ring, then ran alongside him and said, "Good boy."

Three ranch hands joined the foreman and watched from the railing.

If Rhett could gentle this horse, he might just find his purpose again. He slowed the animal to a stop, gradually pulled the lead rope, looped it around his arm and moved to the left side. Terror swished its tail and snorted.

"Promise I won't hurt you," Rhett held the reins and unbuckled the rope. The horse flicked its ears but didn't flare his nostrils. Normally, this stallion squealed and pawed the ground with its hoofs.

"Hey, fella. I'm gonna add my weight to your saddle." He placed his foot in the stirrup and mounted.

The stallion took two steps back, let out a loud neigh, kicked up his hind legs with a powerful force, and continued bucking. Rhett gripped the saddle horn and managed to hang on.

A car honked, and the stallion rose up on two legs. In slow motion, Rhett flew toward the railing, hit his head with a clunk, and his body dropped to the ground. His head ached, his muscles tensed, but he knew he had to get up and get away.

"Watch out!" The foreman yelled.

"Oh, shit." Rhett looked up at the stallion's front legs. It pummeled its hoofs down near his shin.

CRUNCH! His bones cracked. Unbearable pain shot through his body.

His vision faded as he heard the foreman shout, "Get Rhett, I'll go after Terror."

CHAPTER 23

The sun shone brightly in Cupid's Corner, but Cami refused to go outside. What difference did it make? Melancholy held her captive inside this apartment. She missed Rhett teasing her about hockey, missed how he helped her make breakfast, missed being held in his arms.

Her doorbell chimed.

She looked through the heart-shaped peephole. Her stomach clenched seeing the ratted blonde beehive hairdo. "Hello, Mother."

Cami escorted her mom inside and was enveloped in a lilac scented embrace. "I'm glad you're back home. Would you like me to make my specially blended tea?"

"That'd be heavenly." The tea had a calming agent, something Cami could use as she motioned for her to sit on the couch.

Her mother waved her fingertips. Pink sparkles swirled, and

two porcelain teacups of steaming brew floated to the coffee table.

Cami picked up the cup and sipped raspberry and persimmon tea. “Mmm … This is delicious.”

“If only I could have traded places with you,” her mother said with misty eyes. “It must’ve been dreadful living as a human. How did you ever survive?”

“You always told me when life gives you sugar, spin cotton candy.”

“It’s one of my favorite sayings.” Her mother’s turquoise eyes sparkled.

“You’ll be happy to know that your lessons in baking the old-fashioned way came in handy.” Cami thought back to mixing and stirring muffins with her sisters. Batter splattered on the marble countertops and the floor and all over them. They filled muffin tins and enjoyed the sweet scent baking. Cleanup done in seconds with the help of magical dust.

“Great Grandma started our baking tradition after she visited Earth. She had listened to a baker share his recipe with his granddaughter. Stole a muffin and ate it whole. To this day, she claims magic zaps out freshness.” Her mother winked. “As traditional as your father can be, he never turns down one of my muffins.” She took Cami’s hand and stared at her ruby and diamond ring. “Exquisite.” Like her father, her mother idolized Zander.

“I’m not marrying him.” The huge rock sparkled. “I never said, ‘Yes.’”

“Of course you did. You’re wearing his ring.”

“I can’t get it off. The dreadful thing’s stuck on my finger.”

"After your mishap, folks speculated Zander might choose another. I knew he wouldn't."

Cami wished he had. "We're not together."

"The boy loves you, always has. I know you're rattled by your experience, but once you're married, your world will be back in check."

Cami let out an agitated groan, and her right eye ticked.

"Something's wrong. I can tell by your twitching eye."

"I don't love Zander."

"After everything, you're just confused." Her mom's eyes glinted with concern.

"Oh, please." Why wouldn't she listen to her?

"After high school, I thought I'd never marry." Now Mom was humoring her.

Cami's teeth gnashed together.

"My friends and I became counselors at the Treasure Trove Camp near the bottom of Mount Olympus."

"I've had friends go there. Said they had a wing-ding of a time."

"Thinking back now, I regret we didn't send you." Mom's mouth pruned as she shook her head.

Cami had begged to go. Her dad adamantly refused. "I wish you had. Why didn't you?"

"You dad didn't want to chance an injury to your arm or fingers."

Sounds like dad. Always looking out for the budding archer.

"I met your father at the camp. He came in from his swim. Eyes the color of sapphires met mine and, my, I could barely breathe."

Her mother had fallen in love with her father. Unbelievable. With the way her mother seemed to pander to his every whim, Cami assumed their marriage was arranged.

"Your father smiled, and called, 'Hey, Cutie,' walked on, and put his arm around a female counselor." Her mom's voice became giddy.

She tried to imagine her mother at eighteen. "Why haven't I heard this story before?" Intrigued, she had to hear more.

"I doubt your father remembers. But I do." Her mother laughed. "I figured he was the worst kind of Cupid—a heartbreaker. Had a reputation for flirting with female counselors. So, I ignored him."

"Good for you, Mom."

"A day or two later, your father dumped the other female and zeroed in on me. Eventually, he won my heart." Her mother blushed, a full-on cherry red blush.

"Sorry Mom, but I just can't see father ever acting charming." Self-righteous would be Cami's word of choice.

"Oh, but he was." Her mother's eyes had a dreamy, faraway look. "He picked wildflowers, took me sailing, even sang me love songs."

"You are talking about Father, not a previous beau?" She couldn't picture him ever singing.

"Your dad is such a romantic. We married a month later," she tittered. "It shocked everyone. I fell for him. He's a perfectionist. I've learned long ago to walk away when he's in one of his moods. They don't last long. Once his temper cools, he's a softy."

Not the dad she knew.

"More tea, sweetie." Her mother picked up a pink and white teapot and poured liquid into Cami's cup.

"I'm not marrying Zander," Cami blurted again hoping her mother would listen.

"But you two are perfect for each other."

Cami had to get her mom to hear what she was saying. Talking about Rhett was out of the question. If her father found out, she envisioned him chaining her in a dungeon like the one she'd seen in her dream. "Zander's like an annoying cousin, not a boyfriend."

"I believe your stint on Earth deflated your confidence." Her mother cupped her hand and gave her a sympathetic smile. "You don't think you're good enough for him, but you are."

"It's nothing like that," Cami said.

"Then what is it?"

Cami let out a long breath. "Everyone loved the idea of a Golden Archers match—Cupid's Corner royalty fated to wed since we were cherubs. I kept quiet, assuming the love might come."

Her mother straightened and wrapped her arms around her. For the first time she could remember, Cami had her mother's complete attention.

"What's worse is that I never said anything because Father's eyes lit whenever I mentioned Zander. I thought if I got serious with him, I'd finally earn Dad's respect." Anything she did would never be up to her father's expectations, never be good enough. She'd spent her life trying to earn his approval—only to fail miserably.

"Don't you know your father loves you unconditionally?"

"No, he doesn't. He loved that I was a champion. I blew it when I messed up on my first assignment—no less. He's humiliated to have me as a daughter. The only way I could make amends would be to marry Zander." A tear slipped down her cheek. "But I choose my own happiness over father's."

"Sweetie, you're wrong. Your father doesn't expect you to wed Zander, not if you don't love him." Her mother pulled her tight. "When he gets back from his assignment you'll see."

When her mother left, Cami cried. She cried for her childhood lost to continual practice, she cried for a father who couldn't love her, she cried for Rhett—another man who didn't love her—but would forever hold her heart.

An hour later, Zander left a message saying he'd be gone the next two days. She silently thanked Serenity who'd probably hacked into his schedule.

Earth was a viable option for escape. If she stayed with Violet that might cause a rift with Violet and Michael. She had some money stashed in the apartment, but it would be too painful to go back to all those memories.

Her cloud covered door parted and in walked Belle and Serenity.

"We heard about the engagement at work." Serenity's tone was less than cheerful. "I thought you were going to tell him to fly away."

"He didn't listen."

"Let me see the ring." Belle took Cami's hand and whistled. "Wow. Okay, how'd he propose?"

Cami rolled her eyes.

"That bad, huh?" Serenity made a funny face.

"He took me on a chariot ride to Aphrodite's Lake, got down on one knee, and said, 'I've always loved you, Cams.'"

"You hate being called Cams." Belle whirled her silvery-purple dust and three wine glasses floated into the women's hands.

"I needed that, thanks. Anyway, Zander *said,* 'Marry me.' He didn't ask. Then he slipped on the ring. I tried to get it off. It wouldn't budge. He might have put a binding spell on it." Cami spoke fast, making it hard to breathe, and she gulped in air.

"See if this works." Serenity's sparkling dust surrounded the ring, and it dropped to the floor.

"You amaze me." Cami hugged her friend.

"I suggest wearing it on your right hand." Belle smiled. "That way you won't chance losing it when you give it back."

"No way will I wear this stupid thing ever again." Cami laughed. After her tense day, it felt wonderful to laugh.

"Makes sense. Anyway, gotta get ready for dinner with the family." Belle downed the rest of her wine. "Wynton's picking me up in thirty minutes."

"Sounds almost as fun as my day." Cami sipped her wine, glad at least she didn't have a weekly family ritual like Belle.

Belle scrunched her nose. "It'll be a barrel of flutterfish."

"Feel for you. Your grandmother scares me." Serenity giggled.

"That's why I'll have backup. Grand Dame adores my boyfriend." Belle rushed down the hall to her bedroom.

Cami still couldn't believe a grandmother would call herself Grand Dame, but after meeting her, the name suited the mean-spirited woman.

"I have an idea to get you away from this madness," Serenity spoke in a hushed voice.

"Really, do tell?"

"This morning, I contacted a friend who owns a cottage in the Forest of Enchantment. She'll be out of town for the next few months and offered the place to me. Once I told her your dilemma, she thought having you stay there was a great idea."

"What'd you tell her?"

"Just that you broke up with your boyfriend and needed to spend time in the forest to rejuvenate your psyche."

"You're a genius." Cami held up her glass to her friend.

"And don't you forget it." Serenity smirked as she handed her a note with glittery pink writing. "Here's the kicker. Since only you and I will know the location, no one else can pop in for a visit."

"When can I leave?"

"Whenever you want?" Serenity gave her a knowing smirk.

CHAPTER 24

Inside her bedroom, Cami set her streaming cloud to her favorite old movie, *Ghostbusters,* and packed her bag. The movie took her mind off Rhett. A woman became possessed, and acted alien. Was that how he saw her?

Desiring someone who'd never return your love, in that respect, she was no different than Zander. There was no talking to him, but maybe a note would get his attention. Moving to her desk in the corner of her bedroom, she took out pink paper and a fuchsia pen.

Dear Zander,

Wrong salutation. She waved her hand, and the words disappeared.

Zander,

I'm sorry to say I'll never marry you.

I'm not sorry. She erased the line.

I can't marry you because I'm not in love with you. Thus, I am returning your ring. You deserve better than me. You deserve a Cupid who loves you with her whole heart. Someday, I hope you will understand.

Sincerely,

Cami

She folded the ring inside the letter, sealed it inside an envelope, added his name on the front, and left the note on her desk. Her hand skimmed her dresser, and she picked up a stuffed flamingo she had since she was little. Something dropped onto the floor. Not something, her communicator. She'd forgotten she still had it.

She tapped the device to turn it on. A stream of messages popped up. The top message from Violet caught her eye.

Rhett's been in an accident. Rushed to Cedar Springs Hospital.

Oh no! Breathing fast, lightheaded, she held onto the dresser. This can't be happening to him. He had to be all right.

The message was sent at eight. Two hours ago.

She texted to check how he was doing.

Violet wrote.

He's been admitted

He wouldn't die—couldn't die.

Her mind blurred. *My sweet Rhett.* Even if he didn't want to see her, she had to go to him.

Thankfully, Serenity had come up with the forest cottage, but instead of going there she'd head to Earth. She used her wrist emblem and pulled up a virtual map of Cedar Springs. The hospital's five blocks north of the Last Chance Saloon.

She grabbed her backpack and sped down the stairs, past Serenity, out the door, and flew.

"Wait up, Cami." Serenity fluttered next to her along Bliss Avenue, breathing hard. "What's going on?

"Rhett's in the hospital. I have to see him." She slowed her speed.

"What can I do?"

"Cover for me. Tell my parents and Zander I left for the cottage."

"Sure."

They passed the street that led to her parent's residence and continued north.

"Thanks." She would have hugged her if there'd been time. At the corner of Bliss Avenue and Hearts Way, instead of turning left, she kept straight into the forest, slowed at the second sunbeam, and looked around. No guards posted. She wrapped her arms around the light and jumped.

Unlike her first experience that seemed to take seconds, this descent moved in slow motion. The golden rays seemed endless in the distance. As she got closer to Earth, doubt flittered through her mind. Would her presence upset Rhett?

She beamed through the bar's ceiling and landed on a pool table, finding the room dark except for the Budweiser sign flashing on the wall. A refrigerator buzzed. No voices. No music.

Beep-beep-beep. "You have ten seconds to enter the code," a voice blared.

Code? It must be an alarm.

Beep-beep-beep.

She swirled her magical dust. The lights came on, and the noise stopped.

I have to find the hospital, now. She checked her wrist emblem. Half pale pink. Half white. Her magic was disappearing rapidly. With no extra vial of magical dust, she'd better transform immediately. She quickly pulled out the human outfit she'd stashed in her backpack and held onto the items. Opening the vial, she poured out half the content. Dust swirled, enlarging the clothing as she grew to her five-foot-two size—dressed in a T-shirt, jeans, and pink boots.

She slipped out the back door. The bright sunlight blinded her. Blinking a couple of times, she hurried to the sidewalk.

An old man walked his dog and waved. She sprinted down the street, crossed the main highway, and kept running until she viewed the three-story white hospital building. She raced across the parking lot. Twenty to thirty vehicles filled the spaces, one with Michael's silver truck.

The main entrance door slid open. She approached a dark-haired woman behind a counter and learned Rhett was on the second floor in the surgery unit.

Surgery? Humans have been known to die on the operating table. *Please, please, please let Rhett survive.*

She pushed the elevator button, and the door opened. A month ago at the hotel, she rode in her first elevator. The hotel where she and Rhett first made love. Her eyes got teary.

The door closed, and she was jolted upward to the next floor. She stepped out and continued along a sterile hallway.

"You're here." Violet came running toward her and threw her arms around Cami.

"What happened?" Cami wiped away the tears streaming down her cheeks.

"Rhett tried to break Holy Terror."

"Holy Terror?" Rhett told Cami to stay away from that unpredictable and dangerous stallion.

"A car horn spooked the horse. Rhett got thrown into the railing, fell on the ground, and Terror stomped on his left leg. He's been in surgery for over an hour."

"That doesn't sound good."

"Rhett's strong. We're all praying for him. I'm sure you've been doing the same. The family's in the waiting room." Violet put her arm on her shoulder and walked her down the hall.

Inside a room, the chrome gray walls and pewter gray chairs and couches matched Cami's dismal spirit. Michael saw Cami and embraced her with a big bear hug. "Rhett's been miserable without you."

She figured the brother was being nice. "I've missed him, too."

"Glad you came." Rhett's mother hugged her. "I think your arrival may be the miracle we've been praying for."

Cami was no miracle. She found the space confining. Along the left side, the twins colored next to their mother on a couch.

"Cam-eee," Zoe shrieked and ran up to her.

Zia followed right behind her sister. "Uncle Rhett got hurted."

"I've heard."

"You gonna sprinkle fairy dust like Tinker Bell and make him better?" Zoe asked, her eyes twinkling.

"Yeah, sprinkle dust," Zia added as she latched onto Cami's hand and tried to drag her towards the door. "I wanna watch."

"I wish I had that kind of dust. Why don't you show me

what you're coloring?" She held each twin by a hand, walked the girls to their mother, and eased onto a chair closest to them.

"Rhett's hardheaded. He'll be fine." His sister joked, but her eyes showed worry.

A middle-aged man with thick spectacles and a white coat strolled in. "The surgery went well."

"Yes," Michael shouted and swung Violet around.

"Thank the Lord," Rhett's father said and embraced his wife.

The twins skipped around the room.

Rhett would live. She wanted to skip with the girls.

"He's not out of the woods yet. The fractures on his fibula required three pins, the tibia another two. The next twenty-four hours we'll watch for infection or other complications." He went on to explain about the cast and future physical therapy, but all Cami could think about was that he was alive.

She slipped out the door, needing air. Taking the elevator to the first floor, she found a grassy area outside to sit and reflect. Had the accident been a signal for her to come back—a sign that Rhett needed her—perhaps a second chance for them?

She could hope.

SALINE DRIPPED from an IV bag into a tube inserted in Rhett's left hand. His leg cast hung strapped to a preposterous contraption. A torture device disguised as a method to keep his leg elevated.

Doc said he'd been lucky. He'd cracked a few ribs, bruised

his tailbone, and broke his leg in several places. He'd eventually heal. Still, he never should've got on that horse.

A blonde woman's spiral curls bounced as she inched in. Her boots clicked. Groggy, he focused on the words across her T-shirt, *Cowgirls Make Better Lovers*. Must be an induced hallucination brought on by his pain meds.

"Is that you, Cami?" His throat felt drier than the Sahara Desert.

"Hi, Rhett," she said, stationary at the foot of his bed. Definitely Cami's voice.

"I had to see if you were okay. I'll leave if that's what you want."

"No. Please stay." He motioned to a chair next to the side railings.

She sat, her shoulders stiff, her lips pressed into a straight line. "You should be resting."

"I've been resting most of the damn day." As if he could nap between the hordes of doctors and nurses parading into the room to check on him along with his family smothering him with their concerned looks. "A little fall, suddenly I'm treated like an invalid."

"This was all my fault."

"You forced me to ride Terror?" He laughed, and his ribcage smarted.

"Well, no, but—" Her eyes were wide. "I've ruined everything."

"You're that powerful, huh?" He said, trying to get her to crack a smile.

Her mouth stayed somber. "You'd be better off if I wasn't so weak." She crossed her legs and jiggled her foot. "Before I left, I was supposed to give you an elixir, one that would erase all memory of me."

"Erasing my memory? I don't understand."

"I told you that my arrow never should've hit you, and I was supposed to find your soulmate."

"But you're my soulmate."

"Since the love potion in my arrows didn't work properly, I was given an elixir for you to drink. Once you drank it, you'd forget me and be a lot happier." Her shoulders drooped, her hand fell against her thigh. Very different from the sassy, confident woman he remembered.

"Yet, you didn't do it. What stopped you?"

"I fell in love with you. Instead of doing the right thing, I was selfish. I couldn't stand for your memories of me to be gone forever."

He allowed her words to settle in his mind and process what she said.

"I didn't mean to upset you." She stood.

He reached for her hand. "Don't go. We've got things to discuss." He gazed into her turquoise eyes and sensed her conflict. "Such as the fact that you still love me."

"How could I not? You're practically perfect."

Perfect, only Cami would see him in that light. "What aren't you telling me?"

Her eyes welled with tears. "I'm still a Cupid."

"I'll live with that. I can't live without you." Tubes kept him tied to the bed unable to take her into his arms. "Can you stay?"

"As in forever? No. I have to go back, but I'm here now."

"Then I'll take whatever time you can give me." He gripped her hands. The connection warmed his soul.

"Explain how it works, you know, becoming small. You poured glitter over yourself and shrunk." It stunned him at the time, now he'd like to understand the process.

"Magic comes from my heart-shaped emblem." She flipped over her wrist.

He ran his fingers over the heart. "Wasn't this white, not light pink?"

"My magic replenished in the Cupid realm but won't last long now that I'm in human form. Once it fades to white, the magic is gone."

"That's incredible." The fact that she came when he'd been hurt was fantastic.

"Does it matter than I'm different—a fourteen-inch Cupid?"

"Not really. Although I do prefer you like you are now." He threaded their fingers together. The simple touch jolted him wide-awake. "Cupids believe in love. Shouldn't we have a future together?"

"I've been wondering the same thing. My community says humans and Cupids should never have physical contact, but what we have is special."

"More than special, phenomenal."

She fiddled with a lock of her hair and wound it around her finger, an indication of her unease.

"I can tell something else is whirling through your mind."

"Are you psychic?" She bit her bottom lip.

"Just in-tuned to you." He felt closer to her than anyone.

"I kinda snuck away from Cupid's Corner when I heard you got hurt."

"Think someone will come after you?" His macho attitude kicked in. No one would hurt her. "I'll protect you."

"With your leg in the air, not hardly." She giggled.

That was his gal. "You're making fun of me?"

"A little bit." He expected a broad grin, not a tentative smile.

"Might as well tell me what else's troubling you."

Her eyes darted to his face. "I'm presumably engaged."

"What the hell?" Being kicked in the head by a mule would hurt a whole lot less than her marrying someone else. His heart monitor bleeped faster.

"I never said, 'Yes.'" She placed her hand on top of his. "How could I, when I'm in love with you?"

He let out a relieved breath. "Good answer, sugar." The bleeping slowed to normal.

"Visiting hours are over." The nurse came in and added a shot of something into his IV.

"Let my girlfriend stay, please." He couldn't chance her leaving and getting pulled back into her world.

"Not tonight." The nurse motioned to Cami. "He needs rest to heal."

Cami kissed his cheek. "I promise to be back early tomorrow." Her boots clicked away, leaving him alone and very sleepy.

CAMI WALKED into the waiting room. Earlier it had been packed with Rhett's friends and family. Violet left with Michael hours ago. His parents said that they'd be back in the morning. Exhausted, she thought about taking one of the benches and sleeping there until visiting hours.

A strawberry blonde reading a magazine across from her looked up. "Hey, Cami."

"Serenity, how'd you manage to find me?"

"Let's talk outside." Serenity stood wearing a short-pleated dress and four-inch heels. She seemed to maneuver the hallway with ease as they headed for the elevator.

"You walk better in heels than I do."

"Take's practice. I snuck these shoes from the clothing room in Cupid's Headquarters months ago." Serenity's smirk said there was more to the story

If Cami did something like that, she'd get caught. "You're nutty." She pushed the down button.

"How's Rhett?"

"Better than I thought." She let out a sigh. "He still loves me."

Serenity smiled. "That's wonderful."

The elevator door opened. They scrunched in between an older man and woman and descended to the first floor. Cami and Serenity let the others pass. They strolled through the lobby and walked to the side of the building where they sat on a bench under a weeping willow tree.

"There's so much to say, I don't know where to start." Serenity flipped her shoulder-length hair behind her shoulders.

"How'd you get here?"

"Same as you, but I caught the last sunbeam of the day. I

have until midnight to take a moonbeam back." She tightened her hands into fists then loosened them. "While I'm in Cupid's Corner, I'll cover for you and make sure you have a month or more to figure things out."

"Thanks." It sounded like an eternity to Cami. "Do me a favor and tell Belle about the letter I left for Zander on my desk. I put his ring inside. Think you could stash it in your safe for a while? He'll be livid I picked a mortal over him."

"Of course," Serenity said. "You know, mortals and Cupids have relationships quite frequently."

"After my time with Rhett, I can see why." The man had been legendary in her book.

"They keep these affairs secret." Serenity glanced around, most likely checking for a wayward Cupid who might be on assignment. "Most affairs occur with our male Cupids."

"Okay, so how'd you figure this out?"

"Does it really matter?"

"Yes, but you can tell me another time." Cami's tired mind wouldn't understand the techy explanation.

"Here's the interesting part. Over the centuries, there've been Cupids who became outcasts and remained on Earth. Never allowed to return to the Cupid realm."

"I've heard about this. It's better than banishment to a high cirrocumulus cloud."

"You wouldn't mind living here for the rest of your life?"

Cami imagined what her life would be like if she went back to Cupid's Corner. She'd be miserable without Rhett, inconsolable because she'd intentionally given him up. "I'd wither away if I returned."

"I thought you'd say something like that. I think if you marry a mortal, your fate is set. The council will probably banish you from returning, but who knows?"

"I can live with that." An image of her handsome cowboy and his adoring smile came to mind. Her love for him made her blissful.

"Isn't it about time you introduced me to Rhett?" Serenity's mouth quirked.

"Visiting hours are over."

"Like that would stop me. If we go in the back door and up the stairs, no one will see us. At nine, the floor desk nurse will be on break, so we'd better hurry." Serenity's intelligence was overwhelming.

A few minutes later, they were up the stairs, and inside Rhett's room.

He was sleeping when Cami kissed him on the cheek. He opened his eyes, rubbed them, and smiled. "You came back." His words were a little slurred.

"I did. I want to introduce you to my friend."

Serenity stepped up close to the side of the bed. "Hi."

"Are you a Cupid, too?" He squinted as if trying to picture a foot-tall person.

"I am."

"Pleased to meet you." He gave an endearing, lopsided grin. For a man on medication, he appeared rather alert. "Once I get back on my feet, you have an open invitation to stay at my ranch."

"What about Cami?"

He took her hand. "I'm hoping she'll be there for a long time, but she told me she may have to leave soon."

"I'll let you two deal with that. Just take good care of her, or you'll be answering to me." Serenity gave a tough-guy imitation.

"You have my word. I'll treat her well."

"I'd better go, but I'll try to come back in a week or two." Serenity hugged Cami. "I like him," she whispered and walked out the door.

He crooked his little finger. "Kiss me."

She brushed her hand along his chin and felt stubble. "You could use a shave."

"Later. Right now, let me feel your lips on mine."

"You heard what the nurse said. You need to rest."

"Your kisses are the only medicine I need." His voice came out low and seductive.

"You're incorrigible." Tentatively, she pressed her mouth to his.

He tugged her silky tresses and dragged her closer, deepening the caress and moaning into her mouth, "This is paradise."

She edged away.

He patted the bed. "I need you by my side. Scoot in next to me."

Her face heated as she skimmed her fingernails along his upper arm. "What if someone walks in? You just had surgery this morning."

"I wanna hold you."

"Did they put locoweed in your water bag?" She pointed to his IV.

"Might have." Admiration shone in his eyes. "The only way I'll relax is with you in my arms."

"You're impossible to resist." Clad in jeans, she hiked her leg onto the bed, wiggled next to him, and propped her head against his shoulder.

"I've missed you. Did Serenity say when you have to leave?"

"I have a month or maybe more."

"I vote for more." He ran his fingers through her hair.

"Me, too." She didn't want to get his hopes up.

"What is it, sugar?" He stroked her arm. "Are you worried your father will come after you or maybe the guy who thinks you two are engaged?"

She glanced at his monitor and focused on heartbeats that kept up at a steady sixty-five. It was easier than dealing with the truth. "They might, but I'll refuse to go." She got lost in his sparkling eyes. "I'm willing to fight for the benefits here—you know—like kissing a mortal."

"Any mortal in particular?"

"You'll do." She pressed her lips to his. "I love you."

"Marry me, Cami?" His love-light reflected his devotion to her.

"What if … I'm forced away?"

"Believe in us. Believe in our love. Say you'll be my wife, please?"

Life meant nothing without him. "Are you sure you want me?"

"Why wouldn't I? Besides, if you don't marry me, I might tell everyone your secret."

"Go ahead. Nobody would believe you." She kissed his cheek.

"Put me out of my misery and say, yes."

"Yes." She caressed her way to his mouth and kissed him, slow and deliberate. When she stopped, she said, "You understand we're not making love here."

"Not a problem, tonight, but tomorrow's a different story." He nuzzled her lips.

"I'll take my break after I check on Mr. Holloway," a male's voice carried from the doorway.

Cami ripped her lips from his. "I'm not supposed to be in your bed."

"It's fine especially now that we're engaged."

"If you say so." Cami stayed. The last few months proved rules could be broken.

A dark-haired male nurse changed out the IV. "How are you feeling, Mr. Holloway?"

"Not bad considering a horse trampled my leg."

Cami remained silent with her head against his shoulder.

"Let me introduce you to my fiancé, Cami Calypso." Rhett grinned.

The nurse held out his hand and gave her a firm handshake. "It's a pleasure to meet you."

"Same here." Cami smiled.

"Everything looks good. I'll let you rest." The nurse pointed to Rhett. "Nothing strenuous."

"She's already said the same."

"Then you'd best listen to her." The man winked and shuffled off.

"Thought he'd never leave. Now, about another kiss?" He grasped her hand. "You owe me one for thinking you couldn't stay next to me."

"If you insist." She moved onto her side, ran her hand across his chest, and brought her lips to his. When she pulled away, she accidentally tugged the strap on his elevated leg. He winced but didn't utter a sound. "You don't have to be a tough guy around me."

"I'm not tough. Not when you own my heart." He sure knew how to lay on the charm. "Let's get hitched tomorrow."

"I'd rather wait until you're back at home and able to stand on your own."

He groaned. "The minute I'm out of here, I'm making you my wife."

She laughed, and said, "We'll see." While on the inside, she worried her father or Zander would discover her here and wreck her life.

EPILOGUE

Seven weeks later, Cami peeked into Rhett's bedroom smiling. She'd asked to stay in the guest room and not make love until she became his wife. He had honored her wishes. His steady-tempoed snore meant he slumbered, and she slipped outside to watch the sunrise.

Tomorrow, she'd become Mrs. Rhett Holloway. The ranch would forever be her home.

Something fluttered above her. She glanced up figuring she'd see a moth or maybe a bat.

"Hello, Cams." Zander floated in front of her, his blue eyes glaring.

She gasped. Did he discover her wedding's tomorrow?

"You've had your fun. Now it's time to go home."

She remained calm on the outside when her visceral response said to run.

"Thought your little note would scare me away. You're

confused to think you don't love me. You've always loved me." He transformed into a human and took her hands in his.

"Zander, that's not true." Her heart pounded in her ears. Fearful Zander might use magic to force her to leave, she had to stay focused.

"Let me straighten out your thinking." His grip tightened as his eyes narrowed. "We belong together."

"You can't really believe that?"

He frowned for a moment and replaced it with his practiced smile. "I do."

Holy Zeus, the Cupid's unsound. "Zander. You deserve a Cupid who idolizes you, adores you, desires only you. That's not me. It'll never be me."

"You're wrong. You love me. I can see it in your eyes." If he squeezed her hands any harder, he'd break a bone.

"You're hurting me," she cried out.

He released his grasp. "Sorry." He blinked a few times. "I love you. Have since we were little."

"We're both different now."

"And you're more beautiful than ever." He smiled at her. "We're destined to be together. Once we're wed, our life will be perfect."

"No, it won't." She sucked in several deep breaths and counted silently to ten. Getting mad would fuel his desire for control.

"Everyone in Cupid's Corner has been waiting for the day we marry. Our children will have the blood of our powerful families. Think about how happy your father will be. He's always approved of us." His eyes shone when he mentioned her father's approval. Her father always treated Zander as the son he'd never had.

"You already know that ring didn't bind us," she said, since that had been one of the points he believed proved they belonged together.

"How'd you get it off?"

"Does it really matter?"

"I guess not." The misguided Cupid seemed uncertain. "You have to love me."

"I'm in love with someone else."

"Who?" Zander gawked at her.

"The rancher, Rhett." Now that she said it, there was no backing down.

He grimaced, and the veins in his necked stuck out. "The human. How could you?" His hands fisted.

"I couldn't help it. He's my destiny."

"Did you lie to the council about giving the elixir?" he chuffed.

"I tried to give it to him but couldn't. Rhett would forget our special times together, while I'd cherish our memories."

"Don't tell me that you've—"

"Slept with Rhett, many times." The words spilled out.

"What's wrong with you? We are supposed to be together." His face turned ashen, and he stared at her as if she had suddenly sprouted horns. "You've ruined everything, ruined our lives."

"No, I haven't. You'll know when you find your soulmate." Her heart ticked fast.

"You're crazier than Chaos," he shouted. "Wait 'till I tell your father what you've done. He'll disown you. You'll never be welcomed in Cupid's Corner again."

The thought of her father's disdain made her shudder. "I wouldn't be too hasty tattling to my dad. The fact that I don't love you will make you look weak."

"Go to Hades."

Her insides shook, but she wouldn't let him see fear. "Besides, my folks won't believe you. They think I'm in the Forest of Enchantment restoring my psyche."

"You fooled them for now, but you can't hide forever," he said through clenched teeth. "You would've fooled me too if I hadn't found your letter on your desk. The ring proved something was off, and I figured out you were here when I visited with Serenity and asked her a few questions."

He'd better not take revenge on her friend.

"I'll never forgive you." Zander used his magical dust to change back to a Cupid.

She watched him fly off to the north and almost felt sorry for him. He thought he loved her, thought she loved him, thought his life would be ideal once they married.

What if Zander wrecked her wedding? She tried to calm her runaway pulse. After she wed Rhett, no Cupid could break their bond, not even her father.

She went inside and sank into the couch.

Clunk. Clunk. Clunk. Rhett balanced on his crutches, his hair ruffled, his whiskey eyes teaming with love. "Hey, sugar."

"Ready to get your walking cast off?" They'd leave for the doctor in an hour.

“Sure am.” He dropped his crutches and hopped next to her. “What’s wrong? You change your mind about marrying me?”

“Never.” Still unsettled, she couldn’t look at him, but he gently took her hands in his.

“You’re trembling.”

“Zander just left a few minutes ago,” she said, her waning adrenaline making her weak.

“What’d he want?”

“To take me back to Cupid’s Corner and marry him.”

“Not happenin’.” Her macho cowboy tried to stand.

“Relax. He’s gone.” She proceeded to tell him about Zander’s visit

He hauled her onto his lap and kissed her.

“Save some for the wedding night.” Michael strolled in from his bedroom.

“No worries there.” The last time she had slept with Rhett had been the day she shattered the elixir bottle.

“I’m getting myself a bowl of cereal. You two are on your own.” Michael waved his hand and strode toward the kitchen.

“I’m starving for you,” Rhett whispered and nipped her ear.

She shivered.

“You’re blushing. Care to share what you’re thinking?” His deep voice stirred quivers through her core.

Holy Aphrodite, she couldn’t wait to share his bed again.

~

The Wedding Day

. . .

Rhett waved from the porch as Cami rode off in Violet's car. She was giving up her former life to be his wife. A tinge of guilt filled his mind, especially because she'd be severing family ties to stay with him.

A fluttering noise above him couldn't be moths, not at eight a.m.

A middle-aged male Cupid floated in front of Rhett and transposed into a human with Cami's eyes. "I'm looking for my daughter."

"Who's your daughter?" Playing dumb seemed his best option.

"Cami Calypso? Our neighbor, Zander, said she's staying here. Just go get her for me." For a short man, his wide stance made him look commanding. He cleared his throat. "Would you please get her for me?"

Yesterday when Zander showed up, Cami couldn't hide her agitation. If her father thought he'd bring her back to Cupid's Corner, he was wrong. "She's gone."

"Your soft blue aura reflects truthfulness. Mind telling me where she went?"

"Yes, I mind. If she wanted to see you, she would have mentioned it." Rhett fought the exasperation raging inside. Of all the days to show up, why'd it have to be on their wedding day?

"Are you her boyfriend?" Her father adjusted the vest of his silvery suit.

"Fiancé." The word tumbled from his mouth.

"It's quite a sacrifice for her to be with you. And given your injury, what makes you the right male for her?" Her father eyed him.

"The injury will heal." Since her father was a Cupid, and his community promoted love matches, what did he have to lose by telling the truth? "More importantly, I love your daughter, sir. I've never met anyone like her. She challenges me to be a better person. She's witty and fun—and gorgeous. Whenever I look into her eyes and see the love reflecting back at me, I know I'm a lucky guy."

"You have a strong love-light when you speak about my daughter."

"Cami says we're soulmates. I know she's giving up everything to be with me, but I promise to treat her well." Rhett could see the frustration on his future father-in-law's face. This was a man accustomed to calling the shots, to people catering to his wishes.

"You are aware that if she marries—a human—she'll lose the connection to the Cupid community, and the life she's always known?"

"That is her decision. As much as I love her, I'd never force her to wed. If she changed her mind to go back to Cupid's Corner today, I'd be heartbroken but wouldn't stand in her way."

"This isn't the future I saw for my daughter."

"True, but I'm the future she wants." Rhett saw the Cupid's eyes soften. The realization of Rhett's deep love for his daughter must have hit.

Her father stared at him for the longest time. His magic had the power to destroy his life with Cami.

"If my daughter really wants to marry you, you have my blessing." Her father reached out his hand, and they shook.

"That means a lot to me, sir. I promise to treat her well."

"All I've ever wanted was for her to be happy. When's the wedding?"

"This afternoon."

"That doesn't give me much time to gather the family and bring them here. I'd like to walk her down the aisle. Do you think she'll mind?"

"No, sir. I think she'll be happy to have her family's support, but the decision is up to her." He told her father the details about the ceremony. Rhett hoped he hadn't fallen into a trap. A trap where her father stopped their marriage.

"We have to go back. I forgot my shoes," Cami said as Violet reached the ranch's front entrance about to turn onto the street.

"I'll text Michael."

"He'll probably grab the wrong ones." Cami wanted this day to go by without a hitch.

Violet turned the car and drove. "You having doubts?"

"Never. I love Rhett." Within a few hours, she'd be his wife. Giddiness filled her heart.

They pulled up in front of the house. "Who's the guy in the silver suit?" Violet asked.

It was as if someone smothered the breath from her lungs. Chills crept up her spine. Her stomach twisted. She remained frozen, unable to move. "My father. This can't be good."

Violet opened her car door. “Come on. I won’t let him ruin your day.”

“You’re right.” If he thought he’d take her back to Cupid’s Corner, he’d have a fight on his hands.

They walked up the steps.

“Hello, father.” Cami sat next to Rhett and took his hand. “Why are you here?”

“To meet your fiancé.” His eyes narrowed as he looked at her. “I gave him my blessing to marry you.”

Cami looked at Rhett and noticed his smile didn’t reach his eyes. “I invited him to the wedding.”

“What?” She pictured her father using magic to wreck her plans.

“Can we talk alone? I have some things to say. I promise to be quick.” Her father’s brows drew together as he fidgeted with a button on his vest. Something was making him nervous.

“Not without Rhett.”

“I wouldn’t expect it any other way.”

“Michael’s in the stables.” Rhett said to Violet. “Why don’t you go see him while we settle a few things? We won’t be long.”

“Sure.” Violet rushed off.

“Okay, say your piece and leave.” Cami’s voice came out squeaky as she pointed at him. Defiance didn’t come naturally, and she cringed inside.

“When Zander visited me last night, I realized he didn’t really love you. He was in love with the idea of being the Golden Archers.”

“I said that to him. He didn’t take it well.” Cami couldn’t believe her father saw that Zander had flaws.

"Don't know why it took me so long." He sat in the chair next to her, his suit glimmering in the sunshine.

This didn't sound like her father. Could this be some kind of trick?

"You need a strong man who adores you, the way I adore your mother. I love you and want you to be happy."

"You do?" She eyed him and swallowed hard.

"Your mother mentioned you thought I was disappointed in you. That's not true. Do you know why I stopped going to your meets?" He tapped his hand against his leg.

"You didn't want to see me lose again. It is always about being the best with you."

"I couldn't take the pressure of watching. When you lost that first match, my heart tore in half seeing you cry." His eyes misted. "Guess I should've told you that at the time. You've always had my heart in your hands. I love you."

Her father loved her.

"I know you've got a big day ahead of you. This isn't the marriage I planned for you—it's better. It's the marriage you want, and that makes it perfect because you've found your soulmate. We can talk about building a relationship later."

"I…I'd like that."

"I'd better hurry home and get the family, otherwise we'll miss your wedding." He stood and held out his arms. "Nothing will keep us from sharing this day with you."

She got up and walked into his warm embrace, feeling his love wrap around her. He wanted to bring her family here, despite the fact that she was doing something forbidden—marrying a mortal.

"Think you'd allow this old Cupid to walk you down the aisle?"

"Of course, daddy." Tears streamed down her cheeks.

"See you at two." He kissed her forehead and brushed the tears from her cheeks. With that he transformed into his Cupid form and fluttered off.

She turned to Rhett. "After meeting my father, do you still want to marry me?"

"More than ever." He stood, wrapped his arms around her, and his fiery kiss proved he hadn't changed his mind.

RHETT ANXIOUSLY EYED the dirt road. He stood beneath the wooden arches adorned with blue Cupid Dart flowers and red roses. For the tenth time, he adjusted the cinch around his waist.

Michael and Jason escorted family, friends, and neighbors to seats lined up on both sides of the aisle. The guests' din became louder as they anxiously awaited the ceremony.

Rhett took off his white Stetson, put it back on, and played with his bowtie.

Michael stepped next to him wearing an identical black tuxedo. "You sure you want to go through with the wedding? It's not too late to back out."

"Not gonna happen." Rhett thought about his soon-to-be-bride. His little beauty brightened his days. Challenged him. Made him happy. He couldn't wait to wed Cami in the same location as generations of Holloways had said their vows. This spot had a spectacular view of the valley. The river meandered through their property and continued south. Horses and cattle grazed on the hillsides plush with grass and wildflowers. The ranch was rich with history. The weather cooperated with blue skies and only a scattering of thin, wispy clouds.

Cami's father arrived with three women in a glimmering horse-drawn carriage and dropped them off at the entrance. His brother escorted the women to the front row of the bride's side. He figured her mother was the one pressing a silky handkerchief to her eyes.

Her younger sister batted her eyelashes at Michael. Her older sister stared at Rhett. Obviously sizing up her future brother-in-law. He smiled at her. At the reception, he'd finally get to meet Cami's family.

The distant clippity-clop of the ranch's horse-drawn carriage indicated Rhett's dad would soon deliver his future wife. The carriage looped around the last corner and slowed to a stop in front of the white silk aisle.

"I'd better get Mom." Michael sprinted to the carriage and helped his mother out first, then Violet, Serenity, his sister, and the twins.

Leaning on a cane, at least he'd have a free hand to hold Cami's. A friend of the family sang, "When I Fall in Love." Recalling how hard he'd fallen for his very own Cupid, he blinked to stop his eyes from watering.

His brother-in-law, Jason, scooted in to his right. "Seems like only yesterday I married your sister. Best day of my life."

"Marrying Heather?" Rhett teased.

Jason shook his head.

The voices ceased.

The bridesmaids blocked his view of Cami, and he longed to see her.

The band performed, "Over the Rainbow." From now on, her home was with him.

His twin nieces strolled up the aisle throwing rose pedals, adorable in their tiny turquoise dresses. Serenity, Violet, and his sister followed in matching turquoise gowns.

Then he saw Cami, stunning in a long strapless dress. Her hair cascaded down past her shoulders to her waist in spiraling curls. His heart stopped.

She beamed as she took her father's arm.

"The Wedding March" played and everyone stood. His pulse quickened as he gazed at his radiant bride. Her eyes met Rhett's, and she gave him an impish grin.

Her father brought her under the arches and placed her hands in Rhett's. "Take care of my little girl."

"Always." Rhett drew her closer.

"You sure look handsome, cowboy," Cami faced him speaking in a whispery tone.

In a few minutes, this remarkable woman would be his wife. "Why thank you."

The pastor droned out words. Rhett struggled to listen. His eyes fixed on Cami. She'd always been beautiful, but today her cheeks rosy, her eyes sparkled, and she gazed at him with such warmth his heart melted.

A woodpecker tapped on a nearby eucalyptus tree. The preacher whispered, "Say I do."

"I do," his loud voice boomed.

When it was her turn, there was no hesitation in her melodic voice. Only Cami would think to curtsy.

“I now pronounce yo

u husband and wife,” the preacher said, “you may kiss the bride.”

She got up on her tiptoes and brought her lips to his. They kissed until the preacher cleared his throat.

“I'd like to introduce Mr. and Mrs. Rhett Holloway.

The crowd hooted and hollered.

“We did it,” she whispered, as they walked up the aisle. “I'm officially the cowboy's Cupid.”

He stopped at the carriage, his heart brimming with love. “Guess that makes me the Cupid's cowboy?”

THE END

If you enjoyed COWBOY'S CUPID, you might want to read Love's Magic Series Book 2, REBEL'S CUPID .

Rebel's Cupid

Love's Magic Series Book 2

Curiosity killed the Cupid?

Or just got her into a lot of trouble. Belle Brooks, a red-headed Cupid, ventures into the forbidden human world looking for her aunt. She finds a gorgeous hunk of a biker who's off-limits because he's mortal (gasp). She should stay away, except he's just the man to help her handle the shocking family secret her trip to earth has revealed.

Lucky O'Sullivan can't believe it. For once, he might be as fortunate as his name implies. A stunning red-head just walked into his bar. Turns out, she's just as handy with a wrench as she is hot, and that pushes all of his buttons. Small problem … he just got dumped and isn't sure his heart can handle Belle.

Enjoy this contemporary love story with a light paranormal twist.

If you enjoyed COWBOY'S CUPID, you might want to read TIME TO SAVE A COWBOY from my Western Time Travel Series.

The Cowboy Doesn't Deserve to HANG

Captivated by the story of a cowboy hanged as a horse thief in 1890, Mia Kellogg travels back in time with only thirty days to save an innocent man.

Dusty Mann is determined to buy his own ranch.

He doesn't need a modern, straightforward woman to barrel into his life or knock his plans off track.

But Mia steals his heart—and then says she's from the future.

Read an excerpt from TIME TO SAVE A COWBOY

In front of Mia, a gentleman in a dark suit and top hat assisted a lady into her carriage seat. The driver positioned himself to her left and picked up the reins. His horse neighed.

Mia shifted back a few steps, giving the horse plenty of room as she leaned her elbows against a railing behind her. The buggy took off leaving thin ruts in the powdery dirt.

Hot air raced down her neck. Something hit the back of her head, jerking her forward, pushing her, making her stumble into the street. She gained her footing. Spun around. Her arms pinwheeled. "Stop tha—"

Her words clogged her throat, cut off her breath.

A horse, oh no, a horse.

She stared at its large, triangular brown head inches from her face. No, not large. Gigantic. Her heart tripped in her chest; her legs became immovable.

Its nostrils flared, its obsidian-colored eyes widened.

She tried to move, but her limbs became rigid, her feet cemented in place. The horse stomped one hoof against the ground and swished its tail against its flank. A thousand pounds of imposing beast sniffed the air.

She stood frozen, watching its nostrils flair and flatten, flare and flatten. "Get, get back."

The horse's mouth opened, and it bared teeth the size of playing cards.

Move, she told herself. Move, before it stomps on you.

The horse let out a high-pitched snort and threw its head up.

She was gone, racing down the street, sprinting up the

hotel's wide wooden staircase, straight through an open door, running fast. Fear propelled her like a slingshot.

She charged inside and plowed into a solid object with an umph.

"Slow down." Large hands steadied her and released its hold. The man stepped away.

At only five-foot-two, she stared straight at his massive shoulders. This guy must spend hours at the gym. Okay, she had to quit gawking at his chest. She gazed up as he took off his worn-leather Stetson.

He gave her a lopsided grin. "Somethin' troubling you?"

"No." Not wanting to seem like an idiot, she stoned her expression, while her knees wobbled.

"You're kinda pale. Best you sit a spell." He placed his hands on her shoulders and guided her to an overstuffed couch near a brick fireplace. Heat sizzled through her gown's fabric, and her insides tingled.

"Excuse me." The cowboy flagged a waitress in a long black dress and white apron. "I'd be obliged if you brought this lady some water." He relaxed in an adjacent armchair and flashed her a brazen smile. "Never had a beautiful gal barrel into me. What's the hurry, miss?"

"Um, you see, this horse, it scared me. The horse, um, was huge, enormous." Sounding stupid, she concentrated on a multicolored glass-blown vase on the side table and rearranged the orange poppies to be in front of the violets and lupines.

"Must've been one of Ben's Belgian draft horses," he said, and she noticed his russet brown hair touched the top of his shirt collar.

The server handed her a glass of water. She took a sip. "It's warm."

"No surprise. This is the desert." The cowboy's drawl didn't seem practiced.

"I'm not as freaked as—" She looked at him, really looked at him, and recognized those wide-set gray eyes from somewhere. "You look familiar."

"I'd remember meeting a pretty gal like you." His smile lit up his handsome face, and her heart fluttered.

She focused on the people at the front desk. A clerk slid a key to a man, and he left with a lady in a long chiffon dress. Most likely people from the train.

A heavy-set woman approached her. "I'm Jenny Hayes. My husband, Bob, and I manage the hotel."

"Mia Kellogg." She held out her hand.

Jenny gave her a sideways glance.

Why wouldn't she shake her hand? Must be a germaphobe.

"Saw Dusty walk you in. Did the heat get to you?"

"Maybe a little. I'm fine now." Mia examined his features. His tan complexion set off his wolf gray eyes. He was a ringer to the cowboy from the picture in the antique shop. "Your name's Dusty?"

He straightened and rewarded her with a mischievous grin. "Yep."

"His given name's Harold Mann, but folks have been calling him Dusty since he was knee high to a grasshopper." Jenny butted in. She must be related to him somehow. "What brings you to our town?"

"A short vacation."

"Well, you certainly chose an ideal time for your stay. Tomorrow's our monthly ball." Jenny's cheeks reddened.

Now Mia was confused. She and Birdie had tickets for the Daggett dance. Maybe she got the name of the town wrong. Still, if her relatives were here, she should have seen them by now. "Could I borrow your phone and call my cousin?" Mia asked, anxious to talk with someone she knew.

"Golly, we don't have a telephone here. Our general store is the only business in town that has one. The shop's closed 'till morning," Jenny said.

Mia's throat got tight. Only one phone in town. This took the turn-of-the-last-century thing a bit far.

"I imagine you're famished, miss. May I find you a table in the dining room?"

"Please." Starved, at least her stomach didn't rumble.

Jenny turned to Dusty. "Will you be joining Miss Kellogg?"

Mia expected him to refuse politely. Not say, "I'd be honored." He stood and offered his arm. His scent of leather and masculinity made her lean closer. Wrong response for a guy she'd just met.

Jenny led the two of them through the spacious ballroom. Mia's right foot hit a slick, polished spot on the hardwood flooring. "Oh no."

Dusty tightened his grasp on her arm. "Careful, darlin'."

Was her lightheadedness from lack of food or … was it him? She took small mindful steps to their linen covered table. Mindful of the waxed floor. Mindful of clutching his muscular biceps.

"Here you go." He pulled out her chair. His gray eyes darkened when he looked at her. He appeared well-mannered, but she wondered if his kisses would hold a bad boy edge. She couldn't believe she thought about kissing him. Not exactly appropriate for a guy she barely knew—but he was cute.

Her eyes drifted to the five-o'clock shadow on his chin. Certain she'd been caught staring, she unfolded her napkin and placed it on her lap.

"Enjoy your meal," Jenny said and scurried off.

Mia should be looking for her phone, but hunger won out. She knifed jelly on a roll and bit into the warm orange-flavored dough. Wickedly scrumptious. She drank from a crystal glass. "The lemonade's sour." A pound of sugar wouldn't take away the tartness.

He held up a crystal bowl. "Want some sugar?"

"Please." She should use Sweet'N Low but being on vacation why not splurge a little? She added three generous teaspoons, deciding she'd make up for her indulgences at spin class on Monday. "What do you do?"

"Do?" His brow rose, and he looked at her like she asked him to explain the theory of relativity.

"Your job."

"Me? I'm a cowhand." His drawl came out a bit over exaggerated.

Her dad regularly watched old westerns. This guy had a casual Gary Cooper presence. She focused on the jagged scar on his chin. She liked the flaw, showed he wasn't plastic-perfect. "Where's your ranch?"

"It's not mine." He winced for a flash. "I'm the foreman of Los Flores Ranch."

The hot cowboy sitting across from her lived in the next town over. Moving back to her hometown suddenly had a big advantage, namely him. She could see him working on the ranch on the outskirts of Hesperia. Lifting bales of hay would explain his beefy arms.

She'd have to give him her number before she left.

TIME TO SAVE A COWBOY

FIREBRAND'S CUPID

If you enjoyed COWBOY'S CUPID, you might want to read Love's Magic Book 3, FIREBRAND'S CUPID.

A Contemporary Love Story with a Light Paranormal Twist

When a Cupid archer loses his magical ability while on Earth, he ends up falling for an athletic, alluring mortal.

Zander Eros has the perfect life—until his Cupid fiancé dumps him. He gets tossed in an Idaho jail, ending up with no magical powers and no way to get home. But when he meets a gorgeous, off-limits human, it turns out that she's a match made in heaven.

Ivy Venturi loves skateboarding down the streets in a beautiful resort town in Idaho.

She doesn't need to get sidetracked from her studies.

She doesn't need a handsome hunk to take her hiking and paddle boarding and ziplining.

But Zander steals her heart—and then he leaves town.

Firebrand's Cupid

Romance Novels by Niki Mitchell

COWBOY'S CUPID

TIME TO SAVE THE COWBOY

REBEL'S CUPID

TIME FOR LOVE

FIREBRAND'S CUPID

LOVE'S HIGH TIDE

Children's Books by Niki Mitchell

KURIOUS KATZ

KURIOUS KATZ AND THE BIG MOVE

KURIOUS KATZ AND THE PLAY DAY

KURIOUS KATZ AND THE NEW FRIEND

KURIOUS KATZ AND THE BIRTHDAY PARTY

KURIOUS KATZ AND THE HALLOWEEN COSTUMES

KURIOUS KATZ AND THE CHRISTMAS TREE

KURIOUS KATZ AND THE BEST CHRISTMAS EVER

FOSTER CATS: ARTEMIS AND HER SNEAKY BROTHER HERCULUES

KURIOUS KATZ AND THE FOURTH OF JULY

KURIOUS KATZ AND THE VALENTINE SURPRISE

KURIOUS KATZ AND THE SNICKERDOODLE STORY

COMING SOON

PRECIOUS PUPS: BREEZY, THE LABRADOR RETRIEVOR

ABOUT THE AUTHOR

Niki Mitchell writes children's books along with contemporary fantasy and historical time-travel romance. She was born in Chicago, Illinois, and moved to Whittier, California in first grade. With a houseful of books and a local library located a few short blocks, her love of reading began at a young age.

Married for over thirty years and a romantic at heart, she enjoys writing about strong female characters in unusual settings. When she isn't playing with her cats, she enjoys reading, taking walks, water aerobics, photography, and traveling.

CONTACT NIKI MITCHELL

Dear Readers,

Thank you for reading COWBOY'S CUPID.

I hope you enjoyed my story as much as I enjoyed writing it. Won't you please consider leaving a review? Even just a few works would help others decide if the book is right for them.

Best regards and thank you in advance.

Niki J. Mitchell

I look forward to forward to hearing from my readers.

Visit me at https://nikimitchell.weebly.com/

Follow me on FaceBook at author Niki J. Mitchell

Twitter Niki Mitchell@NikiMitchell7

Instagram NikiJMitchellAuthor

www.ingramcontent.com/pod-product-compliance
Lightning Source LLC
Chambersburg PA
CBHW030353310726
48979CB00001B/293

* 9 7 8 1 9 5 1 5 8 1 2 2 0 *